Behind Her Smile

Sandy Cove Series Book Six

Rosemary Hines

Formatting by 40 Day Publishing

www.40daypublishing.com

Cover design by Benjamin Hines

www.benjaminhines.com

Printed in the United States of America

To my sister, Julie

and

My Sisters in Christ
Who faithfully wield the Sword
of the Spirit

The steadfast love of the Lord never ceases; His mercies never come to an end; They are new every morning; Great is Your faithfulness.

Lamentations 3: 22-23

CHAPTER ONE

It seemed as though every bone of her body ached as Joan Walker rolled over in bed and pushed herself to a sitting position. She rested on the edge of the mattress and voiced the same simple prayer she prayed every morning, "Lord, thank You for another day. Make me a blessing to someone today, and help me to see the bounty of Your gifts in the simple things around me." She paused and then added, "And would You give my Phil a good morning hug for me, Father?" A lump formed in her throat as she thought about her husband and the sixty-five years they'd awoken together.

"That's enough, you silly old fool," she said aloud to herself. "You'll see him again before you know it."

Standing slowly and steadying herself before walking, she gradually eased her way into the bathroom. A glance in the mirror revealed she still inhabited the same eighty-nine year old body she'd gone to bed in the night before. Although a part of her heart never aged, there was no denying the years had taken a toll on the temporary tabernacle in which she moved and breathed.

A new body was sounding good right about now.

As she shuffled into her tiny kitchen a few minutes later, she saw a picture of her great granddaughter, Madison, appear on the screen of the newfangled photo frame she'd gotten for her birthday. Somehow her grandson had put a multitude of pictures into something on the back of the frame—he said he'd used his computer— and now it changed from one photo to the next in an unending slideshow.

Pausing to study sixteen-year-old Madison's face, the photo vanished and was replaced by another. "Just like my life these days," she said. "Seems to slip through my fingers faster and faster." It amazed her to think that she actually had a great granddaughter, who was about the same age she'd been when she met Phil. Was it possible Maddie might meet her life partner sometime in the next year or two? Joan shook her head in amazement.

Best step up my prayers for that one, she thought. The world had become such a complicated place, and she felt a special attachment to her precious Maddie. Tomorrow she'd be meeting with her prayer group—a cluster of five ladies who'd banded together to pray for each other and their loved ones. They fondly called themselves the Silver Sisters of the Sword, a name one of them had created for Shoreline Manor's newsletter. The retirement community liked to feature articles about its residents, and Joan's closest friend there, Margie, had written a short article about their group. "Prayer requests welcomed," she'd added at the end.

A knock at the door drew her attention. Her daughter was here, Johnny on the spot, to help her get started on her day. After a couple of incidents where Joan had left a burner on after removing her teakettle, Sheila had decided her mother needed some supervision and assistance. They were in the process of looking for a daytime caregiver to handle meals, laundry, and some of Joan's shopping. But in the meantime, Sheila was standing in the gap.

"Hi, Mom," her daughter said cheerfully as she entered the apartment. Pausing to pet little Josie, Joan's cat, she asked, "How's your back today?"

"My back?"

"Yes. Remember, last night you said it was bothering you all day?"

Joan drew a blank. That was happening more and more recently. "I guess," she stammered. "I have so many aches and pains these days, it's hard to keep track," she added with a grin. "But God is good. He keeps me going, and I can't ask for more than that."

Sheila returned her smile. "So what's for breakfast today? How about scrambled eggs?" she asked, heading into the kitchen.

Joan would have loved to have pancakes or waffles, but she knew that took more work. "Eggs sound good, honey." She rested her hands on the little dining room table and eased herself into her chair.

"I'll start the coffee and then get them going," Sheila replied.

Soon the aroma of freshly brewed coffee filled the air. *I am blessed*, Joan thought. *Thank you, Father, for my sweet daughter. How I wish I could do something for her. Seems I'm not good for much these days.* Sighing, she closed her eyes and rested back into her chair while she awaited breakfast.

As the two of them ate together, Sheila went over the schedule for the day. "I'll be taking you to your doctor this morning for a follow up on your blood work and that B12 shot. Then we'll stop by the pharmacy and pick up your refills."

Joan nodded. Sure took a lot of effort to keep up with things.

"I thought maybe we could have a bite to eat at the Coffee Stop before we head back here," Sheila said, and then added, "Do you need anything from the market?"

Joan considered the question for a moment, but before she could answer, her daughter had the refrigerator open and was surveying the contents. "Looks like you are low on milk. And you're almost out of fruit. How about if we stop and pick up a few things on the way home?" She paused and then suggested, "Or I could drop you back off here and then run over there myself."

"I hate for you to have to go to that trouble, Sheila. I'll be fine. I can even wait in the car if need be."

She saw the look of concern on her daughter's face. This was the hardest part of growing old. Depending on others to do what she'd always been able to do for herself. That and missing her Phil.

Give me a good attitude, Lord. Help me not be a burden to my daughter.

"I mean it, honey. I'll be fine," she said, mustering up her best motherly smile. Although their roles had reversed somewhat, Sheila would always be her daughter, and Joan yearned to keep that perspective, no matter how dependent she became.

Hopefully it would be easier when they found a caregiver to help out. Then Sheila could relax and go back to just visiting, not worrying about meeting all of her needs. Besides, Joan knew that Sheila should be focused on her new marriage and Rick. Although he was very understanding, the fact that Sheila was over here so much had to take a toll on their time alone together and the relationship they were building as newlyweds.

Joan had expressed her concerns about this more than once. Each time, Sheila tried to reassure her. "It's not like we are in our twenties, Mom. Even though we haven't been married that long, life is different for us than it would be for a couple just starting out to build a family together. Rick's busy with his teaching at the university, and I'm free all day."

But Joan knew Sheila's freedom could allow her to join Rick in his office for lunches on his busier days. Plus, with Rick's classes primarily scheduled on Tuesdays and Thursdays, there were probably multiple opportunities he and Sheila could have spent a morning or afternoon doing something together, if it weren't for Sheila's care for Joan.

It would be an adjustment getting used to a stranger helping out in her home, but Joan knew it wouldn't be for too very long. Each day required more energy than she seemed to have. Surely God would call her home soon.

Turning her attention back to the present, she asked, "How's Maddie these days?" The look of concern on her daughter's face told her she'd better step up her prayers for her great granddaughter. Although her tired body wasn't good for much these days, she could always pray, and pray she would, she and the Silver Sisters together.

The clock on her cell phone showed 5:00 PM as sixteen-year-old Madison Baron stood at the bathroom mirror examining her face. *Great. Another zit.* She pulled open the drawer and grabbed some concealer from her makeup bag. Dabbing it onto the offending red bump on her chin, she tried to blend the substance. Then stepping back, she surveyed the results. Not much different.

"Maddie!" her father called from downstairs. "Hurry up! We need to get going."

"Coming!" she called back as she dabbed once again at the zit. "Well that really helped," she sighed with a sarcastic tone. Shaking her head at her reflection, she dropped the tube of concealer back into the drawer and closed it, flipping off the light and heading into her room to grab her purse. She checked it for the essentials—lip-gloss, a brush, some gum, and a tampon, just in case. Then she bounded down the stairs to head to the Johnson's with her family for dinner. It was Luke's last night before leaving for college, and his parents Ben and Kelly had invited them over for a farewell get-together.

Madison's father, Steve, was standing at the open front door waiting for her. "Your mom and brother are already in the car," he said, his words laced with a twinge of impatience.

She nodded and mumbled under her breath, "Sorry." She could feel him on her heels as she hurried out to the van.

"What took you so long?" her brother Caleb asked exasperatedly.

"None of your business," she replied without even looking his way.

"Madison," her mother began.

"I know, I know. I'm sorry," Madison muttered, gazing out the window and near tears. The idea of Luke leaving had seemed so distant up to this point. Now it suddenly hit her. He'd be gone until at least Thanksgiving. That was nearly three months. Instead of bumping into him in the halls at school or hanging out with him on weekends, she'd be communicating with him through texts, emails, and maybe some phone calls now and then.

She flashed back to her first year at Magnolia Middle School. The year she and Luke had really clicked. First they were friends. Then it grew into something more. She'd felt her heart begin to race when he came into the room, and even the slightest touch of his arm against hers, when they sat side-by-side, had stirred something deep within.

Then he'd moved on to high school and had shifted his treatment of her to more of a brotherly friend than a romantic interest. After she'd graduated to high school herself, she'd run into him occasionally in the halls. But not like at Magnolia. Sandy Cove High was a much larger school and freshman classes were mostly clustered at the south end of the campus. Their lunch schedules were also different. Upper classmen ate after the freshmen and sophomores and had the privilege of leaving campus for lunch if they wanted.

Although they'd shifted to being friends, Madison still felt a spark when Luke would give her a big hug or drape his arm over her shoulder as they were walking together. Too bad he didn't feel the same.

She pulled herself back to the present as they drove into the familiar driveway that led to Ben and Kelly's home. The twins' bicycles were on the lawn near the front door, and a basketball sat on the porch. Madison loved the feeling of their place. It was homey and casual. Kelly had a more relaxed approach to housekeeping than her mother. Good thing since she was raising six kids. There were always toys and games scattered inside and out. But there was also a love that reached out to embrace all who entered.

"When I'm an adult, I want a house like this," Madison said aloud.

"What, honey?" Michelle asked.

"Nothing." She saw her mother's puzzled expression. "I like it here. It feels so homey," she explained.

Before Michelle could answer, the front door flew open, and the twins raced out. "They're here!" Lilly called over her shoulder, as she and Liam ran out to greet them.

Man those kids are getting big, Madison thought to herself, eyeing the two nine-year-olds. She'd been their babysitter at times since they were five. Pretty soon they wouldn't need a sitter. Except for baby Laney. She was only seven months old—the surprise baby they all adored.

She spotted Luke standing in the front doorway, leaning against the jamb and watching them as he munched on something. Taking his final bite, he straightened up and ambled toward their van.

"Hey," he greeted her, pulling her into a side hug. Then turning to Caleb, he asked, "What's up, Cale?"

"Hi, Luke," her eleven-year-old brother replied with a grin. "Where's Logan?" Madison shook her head. Caleb liked to hang out with Luke's brother, but at thirteen, Logan was moving into a new crowd and suddenly seemed much older than her brother.

13

"He's in his room," Luke replied.

Caleb nodded, tugged on the bill of his baseball cap the way he'd seen Luke do when he was on the pitcher's mound, and then took off to find his 'bro', a term Logan seemed to be resisting more and more.

"Hope he doesn't bug Logan too much," Madison said, as she looked up at Luke. He was nearly six feet tall now, and she'd never even made it to five feet four inches.

"Logan will be fine," Luke replied.

She could smell chocolate on his breath. "Were you eating a brownie?"

"How did you know?" he smiled. "Yeah, Mom made my favorites for tonight, and I snuck one before you guys drove in. Want one?" he asked with a mischievous glint in his eye.

She smiled and shook her head. "No thanks." *I already feel fat without stuffing my face with brownies,* she thought. The scales had read 118 that morning. Although her dad kept telling her she looked great, most of her friends weighed less than 110. She was planning to put herself on a strict diet before school began. Being thin was important. All the cute girls were.

"What are you thinking about?" he asked, as they walked up the stairs to the front porch.

"Nothing," she replied nonchalantly.

Luke's mom, Kelly, was in the living room with Laney in her arms. "Hi, Maddie," she said with a smile. Michelle stood beside her gazing at the baby's sweet face and talking baby talk to her. After handing her over to Michelle, Kelly gave Madison a hug. "You look more beautiful every time I see you," she said.

Madison forced a smile. *Yeah, right,* she thought as she fingered the new zit. But she remembered her manners and replied, "Thanks."

"When's dinner, Mom?" Luke asked. "I've still got a load of laundry to pull out of the dryer before I pack."

After learning that there would be at least a thirty-minute wait, he turned to Madison and said, "Wanna help?"

"Sure," she replied, following him to the laundry room off the kitchen. As Luke leaned down and reached into the dryer to pull out his clothes, she thought about how her mother still did her laundry. *Guess having six kids makes a difference,* she mused silently, making the decision to learn how to run their washer and dryer and start doing her own laundry. That would make her mom happy.

Luke slung the laundry basket up onto his one hip and used the other to close the dryer door. "Time to pack," he said with a grin.

And although Madison returned his smile, it never reached her eyes. Saying goodbye was going to be harder than she'd imagined.

As Luke dumped the clothes on his bed and they began to fold, Lucy popped her head into the room. "He's got you folding his laundry?" she asked.

"Hi, Luce," Madison replied, throwing a bundled pair of socks at her.

Laughing, Lucy plunked down on the bed beside the empty basket. Although a year younger than Madison, Luke's sister always seemed more confident and comfortable in her own skin. Madison admired that about her. She never seemed to get moody, or let other people determine how she felt about herself.

"So can you believe Luke's actually leaving Sandy Cove to go to college?" Lucy asked, as she picked up Luke's pillow and hugged it to her lap. "I asked Mom if I could have his room," she added.

Luke stopped folding and looked over at his sister.

"Don't worry. She said no. She wants it just like you left it, so you'll want to come home," she said. "Guess I'll be stuck with Lily for the rest of my life. Until *I* go off to college, too, that is."

Luke scoffed. "You'll need to spend more time studying and less time socializing if you want to get a scholarship and be able to go away for college. Otherwise, you'll end up living here and going to SCC."

Lucy looked at him with an air of dismissal. "I'm going to college in California. I've already decided." Then she turned her focus to Madison. "What about you, Maddie? Where do you want to go?"

Shrugging, Madison replied, "I'm not sure."

"You better start thinking about it," Lucy warned. "You only have one more year before you have to start sending in applications."

Luke glanced at Madison and seemed to be reading her mind. "Lay off, Lucy. Madison knows that."

"Just trying to help," she said as she stood and dropped the pillow back against the headboard. "Want to go shopping with us tomorrow afternoon?" she asked Madison. "Mom's taking me to the mall in Portland after we drop Luke off at the airport."

"Maybe. I'll talk to my mom."

"Catch you two lovebirds downstairs," Lucy said with a smile as she left the room.

Madison felt her face turn crimson, but Luke just laughed. "Crazy kid," he muttered, picking up a stack of tee shirts and placing them into his suitcase.

As the two families gathered around the table to say grace before helping themselves to the various dishes on the buffet, Lily slipped in next to Madison and took her hand, gazing up at her with a sweet smile of admiration. "I wish you were my sister," she said softly. Although Lily could hold her own with her twin brother, Liam, she was much quieter than her sister, Lucy. She sometimes reminded Madison of herself.

16

Giving her a squeeze, Madison replied, "Me, too."

Luke stood across from her on the other side of the table, holding his baby sister up to his shoulder as they bowed their heads and prayed. When Madison looked back up at him, he winked, and she felt herself blush again. *He sure looks natural holding little Laney like that. He'll be a great dad someday,* she thought.

The dinner conversation centered mostly on Luke's plans.

"So tell us more about your school," Steve asked, leaning forward and making eye contact with Luke.

"Well, it's a four-year college with a work-study program," he explained.

"No tuition or payments for room and board," Ben added. "It's all student work based."

"Which is why we can afford for him to go," Kelly said. "Otherwise, he'd have to have a scholarship, and he'd probably still need to take out loans." She looked around the table at their brood of six. "It's a good thing his counselor told him about this school."

"And that they accepted him," Ben added, looking proudly at their son.

"Didn't you have to go for some interviews a couple of years ago?" Michelle asked.

Madison was paying close attention to everything. Lucy was right. She needed to start thinking about all of this. And maybe, just maybe, she should consider this same school.

Luke jumped back into the conversation. "So the thing is, this school is really small and they only accept a couple hundred freshman each year. The counselor told me that most students begin visiting the campus during ninth or tenth grade. You can actually start meeting with the Dean on your first visit."

"What's the campus like?" Madison heard herself ask.

"It's nice. They have lots of acreage with trees, grassy areas—stuff like that. The buildings are older style. Kind of east coast looking," he replied.

"Sounds pretty," she said, trying to picture herself that far away from home. "Maybe I'll come out and visit." She looked up to see all the adults looking at her. She blushed and glanced over at Luke. He was smiling.

"Good idea," he said. "I'll show you around."

As the conversation continued, Madison learned that Luke would not be home for Thanksgiving. "It's too expensive to fly home for every break," he explained.

"My brother and his family live a few hours away in St. Louis. He might rent a car and drive up there for the holiday," Kelly explained, sounding like she was trying to be cheerful and upbeat about it.

Luke looked at Madison again. "I'll be home for Christmas for sure."

She nodded and smiled.

After dinner, Luke surprised her by asking if she wanted to go for a walk. "Sure," she replied.

"Don't be gone long," Kelly said. "We've got dessert, and then you've got to finish packing."

Luke flashed a smile at his mother. "Don't worry. It'll all get done."

The long summer evening provided daylight for their walk. They strolled side-by-side, but not touching. "So are you ready for junior year?" he asked.

"I guess." She paused and then added, "I'll miss seeing you at school."

"Nah," he replied, giving her a playful shove. "The guys will be swarming around you. You won't even notice I'm gone."

She felt a stab to her heart, but shoved him back with the best smile she could muster. "Yeah. Like they always swarm around me," she added with a twinge of sarcasm.

They walked on in silence for a few minutes, down the familiar streets they'd known their whole lives. "Hey, remember when your dad took the training wheels off your bike and helped you ride it on the sidewalk here?" he asked.

She smiled and rolled her eyes. "Yeah. Remember the gash in my knee when I fell on that driveway," she replied, pointing to the offending concrete.

"But you got right back up. I was really proud of you."

"You were?" Her heart felt lighter.

"Yeah."

"So do you know who you'll be rooming with in the dorm?" she asked.

"Some guy from Texas. He's into music."

"Oh. Like worship?" she asked.

"Like band. He'll be playing the trumpet in the school band."

She looked up at him. This time it was her turn to shove. "So I guess you'll be listening to a lot of practicing. Hope he doesn't keep you up all night," she added with a glint in her eye.

Nodding and laughing, he replied, "Better get some earplugs, I guess."

As they rounded the corner and headed back, he asked casually, "So will you write me while I'm gone?"

"Uh, sure. If you want."

"I want. Not just emails either. Send me some real letters."

She noticed the change in the tone of his voice. His playfulness was pushed aside by earnestness.

"I will. Promise," she replied. "And you'll write back. Deal?"

"Deal." He lifted his hand, and they high-fived each other. Then for just a brief moment, he looked almost like

19

he would kiss her. But he seemed to catch himself, and turning away, he just draped his arm over her shoulder, gave her a squeeze, and then let go.

"Did Maddie seem quiet to you tonight, honey?" Michelle asked Steve, as they got ready for bed.

He shrugged. "I don't know. Maybe a little. Why?"

"I think Luke's leaving is harder on her than she expected."

Steve nodded. He sat on the side of the bed and pulled her down next to him. "Our little girl sure has grown up," he replied, taking Michelle's hand and lifting it to his lips for a gentle kiss.

Affection swept over Michelle. It seemed like her love for Steve grew deeper every year.

"She'll be fine, honey. Once school starts, and she gets involved in things with her friends."

"Yeah," Michelle replied, with a smile. "You realize she'll probably start dating pretty soon, too, right? I mean we did say sixteen."

He nodded. "But group dating only. And I need to meet the boys first."

She sighed. "I'd really hoped she and Luke would one day..." Her voice drifted off, leaving the rest unsaid.

Steve squeezed her hand. "Yeah. Remember what little love birds they seemed to be when she was in middle school?"

Michelle laughed as she remembered them sharing the earpieces of his iPod as they listened to music together. "They were a cute couple, weren't they?"

"Yep." He took a deep breath and let it out. Then he turned to look at her, putting his finger on her chin and moving his face toward hers. "We're a cute couple, too, you know," he said slyly.

"Are you going somewhere with this?" she asked, pretending to be clueless.

"Maybe," he replied, pulling her into a kiss that began playfully and then deepened. Soon they were dissolving into each other's arms.

Later, as Michelle drifted off to sleep, she voiced a silent prayer. *Jesus, please watch over Maddie. Keep her close and help her through the letting go process with Luke. And, if it's Your will, would You bring them back together in Your perfect time?*

Peace replaced the concern that had gripped her heart, and she sank into a restful, uninterrupted night's sleep.

CHAPTER TWO

Madison watched Luke sling his backpack onto the conveyor belt at the security checkpoint at the airport. He turned and gave her one final smile before walking through the metal detector and disappearing into the sea of people on the other side. "Bye," she whispered to herself, and then turning and giving her mother, Lucy, and Kelly her best fake smile, she said aloud, "Time to shop!"

"Yep!" Lucy exclaimed in reply, taking Madison's arm in hers and leading them toward the exit.

They headed out to the parking structure, piled into Kelly's SUV, and drove off toward the mall. As Michelle and Kelly chatted in the front seat, Madison gazed out the car window, watching an airplane taking off and wondering if it was Luke's.

"Did you hear me?" Lucy asked.

Maddie turned to her friend. "What?"

"I was asking if you'd seen the latest issue of *Sixteen* magazine. They have a big fashion section. Lots of cute dresses."

"No. I haven't seen it," she replied.

"Well, lucky for you I brought it along." Lucy reached down, retrieved her backpack from the floor, and unzipped it, pulling out the large, glossy publication. A cute blonde on the cover wore a turquoise tee shirt with a sterling silver heart necklace dangling in its v-neck. Lucy quickly paged through to the fashion article and then handed it to

Madison. "See what I mean? I hope we can find some like these." She pointed to a few of the pictures.

"Yeah, those are cute," Madison agreed. *I wonder how they'd look on me,* she thought. *These girls are all so thin.*

When they arrived at the mall, Kelly and Michelle suggested the girls do a little looking at their favorite shops while they grabbed a cup of coffee. "If you see something you like, just ask them to hold it," Michelle told Madison.

"We'll meet back at the food court at noon, get some lunch, and then we can go see your finds," Kelly added.

Turning to Madison, Michelle added, "Remember your budget, honey."

"You, too, Luce," Kelly said.

"Okay, okay. Let's go," Lucy said, grabbing Maddie's hand and dragging her in the direction of one of the teen clothing shops.

As they walked through the first store, Lucy pulled multiple dresses from the racks, throwing them over her arm in wild abandon. "Everything's so cute!" she said blissfully.

Madison found five dresses that appealed to her, and they headed for the dressing rooms.

"How many?" the attendant asked.

Lucy began counting her hangers. "Fourteen."

"You can only take six in at a time," the woman replied.

Sighing, Lucy replied, "Okay." She began weeding through the pile, choosing her favorite six. Reluctantly, she handed the others over.

"They'll be right here," the attendant promised, gesturing to a rack nearby. Handing them each a number, she led them to their dressing rooms.

"Let's come out and show each other each dress," Lucy suggested as they walked into the adjoining cubicles.

Madison nodded. "Okay."

A couple of minutes later, Lucy said, "I'm ready!" Madison could hear her unlatch and open the dressing room door next to hers.

"Just a minute," she replied, perusing herself in the mirror. The dress was cute, but her hips looked fat in it. "I'm not sure I like this one," she called out.

"Let me see," Lucy said.

As Madison tentatively opened the door, she spotted Lucy admiring herself in the three-way mirror across from the dressing rooms. She looked really cute, and her dress fit perfectly. Seeing her in the reflection, Lucy asked, "What do you think?" as she twirled around to face her.

Madison smiled. "It looks really good on you," she replied.

Lucy turned back to the mirror, gave herself another once over, and nodded. "Yeah. I really like this one." Then, almost as if it was an oversight, she turned back to look at Madison's dress. "That one's cute, too," she said, sounding like she was trying to convince herself as much as Maddie.

"It's not for me," Madison replied. "Maybe you should try it on."

Lucy smiled. "Okay. Do you want to try this one on?" she asked.

Madison knew it wouldn't look the same on her as it did on her friend. "No. That's okay. I'll just try on one of the others I've got in there."

Lucy looked almost relieved. *Probably didn't want me to buy the same dress as her,* Madison thought.

They both disappeared into their dressing rooms again, repeating their showing and sharing until all the dresses had been tried. Madison spent the last twenty minutes retrieving Lucy's other dresses from the rack, a few at a time, as Lucy rejected the ones she didn't like.

By the time they left the shop over an hour later, Lucy had five dresses on hold and Madison had two. They spent the next hour moving from store to store, trying on more clothes and then shoes before stopping at a kiosk and checking out jewelry and scarf accessories. Then it was time to meet up with their moms at the food court.

"How was the shopping?" Michelle asked the girls as they plunked down at a table together.

"Great!" Lucy exclaimed. "I found five dresses at one shop, some jeans and sweaters at another, and a great pair of boots."

Michelle turned to Madison. "How about you?" she asked hopefully.

Madison tried to act enthusiastic. "I found a couple of dresses, a skirt, and a sweatshirt." None of them were great, but she didn't want to go home empty-handed. She knew they wouldn't be back out to Portland before school started, and the shops in Sandy Cove were expensive. Besides, they didn't usually have that much that she liked. Seeing her mother's surprised expression, she added, "I'll probably order some stuff online, too."

Nodding, Michelle replied, "Okay. After lunch, we'll go see what you found."

The food court had a variety of cuisines. Michelle and Kelly both wanted French bread soup bowls. Lucy suggested pizza, but Madison opted for salad. "Is that all you're having?" Lucy asked when she saw Maddie's tray.

"Yeah. I'm not that hungry," Madison replied, hoping she sounded convincing while her stomach churned. If she wanted to look good in her new clothes, she really needed to lose a few pounds.

After they ate, the girls led their mothers back through the mall to the shops where they had items on hold. After several negotiations with Kelly, Lucy was able to purchase most of the clothes she wanted. Madison was under budget, so Michelle encouraged her to look at a few more items. They found several sweaters and a pair of jeans that Madison agreed upon.

"I wish *my* mom was trying to convince *me* to get more stuff," Lucy said wistfully.

"You got plenty," Kelly replied with a laugh.

Bags in hand, they headed back to find the car and make the long drive back to Sandy Cove. As they wove through the countryside, Madison found herself thinking about Luke again. He'd be landing in Missouri soon and starting a whole new life at college. And although her friend was sitting beside her, Maddie suddenly felt very much alone.

Later that afternoon, Madison was sitting on her bed gazing at pictures of young models on her laptop, when her mother walked in.

"Almost time for dinner, honey," she said, glancing down at the screen. "What are you looking at?"

Madison flipped the cover of the computer closed. "Nothing."

Her mother just stood there for a moment and then asked, "Is something bothering you?"

The concern and compassion in her voice pierced Madison's defenses. She looked up, and trying not to cry replied, "Guess you could say that."

Michelle sat down beside her and rested her hand on Madison's leg. "Is it about Luke?"

Madison hesitated. "Yeah. But it's also this," she added, pushing the laptop off to the side, her voice bitter.

Her mother picked it up and flipped it open. Faces of beautiful teens flashed on the screen. Super slim bodies with cutting edge fashions hanging on their skinny frames.

Madison could feel her mom's eyes studying her. "See what I mean? I'll never look like them. Not in a million years. Even if I go on a massive diet and dye my hair, I'll still be too short."

"Why would you want to look like them? You're beautiful just the way you are."

Maddie shook her head. "You're just saying that because you're my mother. If anyone's the beauty in this family, it's you, not me." As soon as the words were out of her mouth, she wished she could take them back. Her mother's face looked stunned and even a little hurt.

"Madison, listen to me. When I was your age, I felt the same way you do. Really. And even if I weren't your mother, I'd be looking at a beautiful young lady right now."

She's just saying that to make me feel better. What's she supposed to do? Agree with me? she thought. "Okay. Whatever," Madison replied. "I'll come down and set the table," she added, hoping to change the subject.

Michelle reached over and gently tipped Maddie's head so they were looking eye-to-eye. "Luke won't be gone forever. And believe me, he thinks you are beautiful, too."

Tears threatened again as Madison felt her chest tighten at the mention of Luke's name. Afraid her emotions would come tumbling out if she said anything, she simply nodded, forced a smile, and gave her mom a hug. Then they both stood and headed downstairs.

As Michelle followed Madison down to the dining room, her heart felt heavy. Why did teenage girls have to be under such pressure to live up to the world's perception of beauty? And where on earth did Maddie get the idea that Michelle was so much more attractive than her?

Later that night, as Michelle was washing her face before bed, she noticed more clearly than ever the toll of aging. She plucked a gray hair, and studied the weathered skin on her neck and smile lines radiating from her eyes.

The beauty she'd once been told she possessed was clearly fading. So fleeting was youth, and yet at the peak of its radiance, insecurity often robbed young girls of the perception and confidence one would expect it to inspire.

"What are you thinking about, my brooding bride?" Steve asked, coming up behind her and nuzzling into her neck.

Michelle sighed. "Our daughter."

"Something wrong?"

"She thinks she's not attractive. I caught her perusing models on her laptop. You know, those hyper skinny girls with the gaunt faces that give them the big-eyed look." Michelle paused and shook her head as if to shake off the images. "It concerns me, Steve. I've seen a few girls at school fall into eating disorders because of their determination to obtain that look."

Steve sank down on the bed, clasping his hands between his knees. As he leaned forward and rested his forearms on his legs, he stared down at the floor and shook his head. Then, glancing up at her, he asked, "Want me to talk to her?"

"Maybe. She needs to hear from you just how attractive she really is. You've been her prince charming growing up. Now she needs that more than ever." Michelle sat down beside him, and pulled one of his hands into hers. "It boggles my mind that she can't see how beautiful she is. She actually told me that if there's any beauty in the house it's me. Can you imagine that, honey? To think your mother is more attractive than you are?" Michelle gazed into space and rolled her eyes.

"Don't undersell yourself, gorgeous," Steve replied with a grin.

"I'm serious, Steve. Lately I've noticed that when she and I are at the Coffee Stop or the Igloo together, the guys working the counter have their eyes on her. When she was young, like around six or seven, I remember waiters sometimes acting flirtatious with me. It was flattering, even though they were obviously too young for someone my age. But that's definitely flipped. Now they all have eyes for Maddie. And she doesn't even realize it."

"Well, maybe that's a good thing. I like her sweet innocence about it, and hopefully it will keep some of those boys at bay." Steve stood and began unbuttoning his shirt. "I'm sure this whole insecurity about her appearance is normal for a teenage girl. She'll get over it."

"I hope so. But I do think it's a good idea for you to beef up your compliments and attention. Maybe you could take her out on a couple of father-daughter dates or something," she suggested.

"Sure. As soon as this merger case is over, I'll have some time," he replied. Turning and looking at her still sitting on the bed, he added, "Anything else?"

She shook her head. "No, I guess not." Then she followed him into their walk-in closet and began getting ready for bed.

Madison leaned up against her pillow and flipped open the novel she was reading. It was a love story of two teens, who met at a summer camp. As she dove into the tale of their secret rendezvous under the stars, she imagined what it would be like to have someone really love her like that. She pictured the heroine with the same slender body as the models in her magazines. Oh, to look like that! And to find a handsome guy who pursued her with the same tenacity and passion of the hero.

Sinking further into her bed, she closed her eyes and let her imagination go. She was walking on the beach, hand-in-hand with a tall, gorgeous guy. The waves were crashing, the sun was warm, and her heart soared. Her partner squeezed her hand gently, and looking up she found herself gazing into Luke's eyes.

Then her heart returned to earth. Luke was gone. He didn't love her. He probably never did and never would.

She stood and walked over to close the closet door, a habit from when she was little and feared a monster would come out during the night. As the mirrored door slid shut, she stared at her body in its pajama shorts and tank top. Her hips looked big and her legs stubby. Turning to the side, she pushed her hand against the soft pooch of her stomach.

Walking over to her desk, she picked up the magazine on top of the stack. Flipping to the article in the back about modeling classes, she sat down and reread it, soaking in its promises of beauty and glamour. She flipped open her laptop and did an Internet search for classes in their area, spotting one near her father's law firm. *Perfect*, she thought. *I'll talk to Mom about this tomorrow.*

Then, before climbing back into bed, she looked at the mirror again. "You are going to start dieting, exercising, and learning how to do your makeup, hair, and clothing," she instructed herself. "It's time for a new and improved Madison." She set her alarm clock to get up early and go jogging, then made a list of everything she would eat the next day.

When morning came, she hopped out of bed, threw on some shorts and a tee shirt, pulled her tennis shoes out from under the bed, and bolted down the stairs.

"You're up early," her father said, as she passed him in the kitchen.

"Yep. I'm going for a run."

"Really?" He looked surprised.

I'm going to show all of them how beautiful I can be if I try, she thought happily before answering. "Yeah, really. It's time to get rid of this," she said as she patted her stomach.

He laughed. "I don't see anything to get rid of, princess."

Princess? He still saw her as a little girl. "Well, I do," she replied, adding, "I just want to get in shape."

"Okay. Nothing wrong with that," he replied as he filled his coffee cup. "Maybe we could run together sometime."

"Sure. That would be great, Dad. See you later. Gotta go." She grabbed a water bottle and headed out the door.

With her iPod earphones in place and her favorite music filling her head, she began jogging down the street. *I'll try to do at least a mile today,* she thought. Then maybe tomorrow she'd do a mile and a half. *When I get home, I'm going on the website for that modeling course.*

Within a few blocks, she was winded. A side cramp slowed her to a walk. She took a swig of water, bent at the waist, and rested her hands on her knees for a moment. Then she walked a short distance and started jogging again, this time at a slower pace. The toot of a horn caught her attention, and she glanced over to see her father driving by. He smiled and waved, and she nodded, returning his smile.

This was going to work. It had to.

By the time she got home, she was hot and tired. Her mother was in the kitchen sitting at the table with her breakfast. "Your dad said you went running."

"Yeah. I've decided to get in shape."

Her mom looked a little concerned.

"What? Why are you looking at me like that?"

"Is this about what you said the other day, honey? About not feeling attractive? Because I'm all for being in shape, but I don't want you obsessing about being thin. You've got a cute figure."

She doesn't get it, Madison thought. *No one thinks my figure is cute except her.* Not wanting to get into a big discussion, she just said, "Don't worry, Mom. I'm not obsessing." *Should I mention the modeling class?* She wondered to herself.

No. Better wait until I have more details. Maybe I can even get Lucy to go with me. Then she'll say yes for sure.

"Want some pancakes?" Michelle asked, gesturing to a stack by the stove.

"No thanks. I'm not that hungry. I'll probably just have an apple for breakfast," Maddie replied as she headed out of the kitchen. *Good girl,* she thought to herself. Pancakes were her favorite breakfast. But not anymore.

CHAPTER THREE

Madison began weighing herself in the morning and evening each day. Within a week, she'd lost five pounds, and she was feeling pretty proud of herself. School would be starting in another week. Maybe she'd be down ten pounds by then! She threw on her shorts and tee shirt and headed out the door for a morning run. Her mother had promised to look into the modeling course as a Christmas gift, so she had until then to get in shape.

"Don't you think you should eat something before you exercise?" her mother asked.

"No. I'll have something when I get back," she promised. "Eating first just slows me down." She bolted out the door before her mom could reply. As she ran, she thought about Luke. *I wonder how he's doing? Probably loving being off at college.*

She tried to picture his dorm room and what the campus was like. *Maybe I will go visit sometime. Might be a place I'd like to consider for myself.* Her thoughts drifted to images of walking the campus with Luke by her side. They'd be talking about their classes, and what they were going to do over the weekend.

Jogging out into the crosswalk, a car turned left onto the street she was crossing and came close to hitting her. "Watch where you're going!" she called out to the unseen driver.

When she got home, she grabbed a banana from the fruit bowl on the counter and nearly collided with Caleb as she headed out of the kitchen. "What's with everyone today?" she asked under her breath. "It's like I'm invisible," she added.

"Hey, do you want to go with me and Mom to the Igloo this afternoon?" her brother asked.

Madison pictured the ice cream parlor with its delectable flavors. *Maybe a non-fat frozen yogurt without a cone,* she thought. Then she changed her mind. *Better not. I'll see the almond mocha fudge and want that.* "No thanks," she said. "I'm on a diet."

"Why?"

"Why do you think, dummy? So I can lose weight before school starts."

"Whatever," her brother mumbled. Grabbing his baseball mitt and ball, he headed out to practice throwing pitches through a tire hanging from the tree out back.

After Madison's shower, she plunked down on her bed and flipped open her laptop. *Think I'll email Luke and see how he's doing.* She glanced at the inbox of her gmail account and noticed his name. "Cool!" she exclaimed, quickly clicking to open his message.

Hi Maddie,

I was thinking about you this morning, and I thought I'd send you an email. How's life? Are you and Lucy ready for school to start? She told me about your shopping trip. Sounds like she bought the stores out.

Did you get your class schedule yet? Hope you have Barnes for history. You'd love him. He's always got some interesting back story to tell about people who seem so boring in the textbooks. If you get Fry, try to switch. He'll put you to sleep in a minute with his boring lectures. And for English, you should be good with Harper since you're honors. She's tough, but you're up to it. And she's pretty funny sometimes.

If you want any other advice or input, just send me a photo of your schedule. It's really weird to be here instead of getting ready to go back to Sandy Cove High.

But the campus is great and I've got a decent roommate, so I'm getting pretty excited. Classes start Monday. I've already checked out reviews on my professors, and so far most of them look pretty reasonable. One is new here, so we'll see how that goes. It's just a general ed writing class, so I'm not too worried.

I'll text you some pictures of the campus and my dorm later today. Mom's been bugging me to send her some, so I'll just do a group text. Tell Caleb hi, and keep an eye on Lucy, okay? She can be pretty out there sometimes, and I won't be around to make sure she stays out of trouble. She can be fun, but sometimes she goes overboard. I'm sure you get what I'm saying.

That's all for now. Stay cool.

Luke

Madison smiled. She could almost hear his voice with the familiar "stay cool" phrase he used in place of goodbye. It sounded like he was having a good time, and she appreciated his input on teachers.

"Hey, Mom?" she called out.

"I'm downstairs," came the reply.

Walking to the top of the stairway, Madison spotted her in the living room. "Has the mail come today?"

"I think I saw the truck, but I haven't been out to the mailbox yet," her mother answered.

Madison bounded down the stairs and out the front door.

"Expecting something?" her mother's voice followed her.

"My class schedule," she threw back over her shoulder.

Pulling open the mailbox, she lifted out the contents and flipped through the envelopes. Halfway down the pile, she found it. Return address: Sandy Cove High School. As she walked back into the house, she deposited the other mail on the coffee table in front of her mother.

"Did you get it?" Michelle asked.

"Yep." Madison sank into the rocking chair and tore open the envelope. "PE first period?" she asked with a groan. "That mean's I'll be a mess all day." Her frustration rose when she scanned the rest of the periods. "Great. Just great. I got Fry for history. Luke said he's a loser. And right after lunch, too."

"Maybe you can talk to your counselor and get some things shifted around. Mr. Woodruff seems to really like you, Maddie. He'd probably do whatever he could."

"Yeah, maybe." Madison shrugged. "Think I'll call the school, and see if he's working this week. It's probably better to talk to him now than after classes start."

"I agree," her mother replied.

Returning to her room, Madison grabbed her cell phone from the nightstand and scanned her contacts for the school's number. When the office manager answered, she asked for Mr. Woodruff. "I'll transfer your call," the woman said. "He should be in his office."

"Woodruff here."

"Hi, Mr. Woodruff. It's Madison Baron."

"Madison! How's your summer been?" The warmth in his voice helped calm her agitation.

"Pretty good. How about yours?" she asked, trying to be polite with the hopes of gaining favor before her request.

"Too short as always. But I'm eager to get back into the swing of things here. How 'bout you? Ready for classes to start up again?"

"Well, actually, I wanted to talk to you about that," she began. "Is there any chance I could come in and see you today or tomorrow?"

"Sure. Let me look at my schedule." He paused for a moment, and Madison could hear the shuffling of papers.

"How about three o'clock this afternoon? I have a staff meeting at one-thirty, but it's only supposed to last an hour. So that would give me plenty of time to be back here in my office."

"Three sounds great. Thanks!" she replied.

"You got it, kid. See you then."

Madison flipped open her computer and replied to Luke's email.

Hi Luke,

So I just got my schedule. UGH! PE first period, and Fry after lunch. Can you believe it? I'm going to meet with Woodruff this afternoon and see if he can change things around. Maybe I can switch PE and history if Barnes has a first period class. If you get this before three o'clock our time, please pray that it works out.

I'm really happy that things are going well for you. Sounds like college will be a great change. I'll keep an eye on Lucy. I know exactly what you mean.

Looking forward to the pics this afternoon. If I don't answer right away, I'm with Woodruff.

Miss you. Stay cool yourself. ☺

Maddie

Closing the laptop, she walked over to her closet and rummaged through her clothes, looking for just the right outfit for her afternoon appointment with the counselor. A skirt. Perfect. She'll look studious. She pulled it out and found a top. Standing in front of the full-length mirror, she held the hangers up to her body and approved the outfit. *Good thing I lost five pounds. This skirt was getting tight last spring.* She laid the clothes across the bed and headed downstairs to tell her mother about the appointment with Mr. Woodruff.

"Mom, are you guys ready?" Madison asked as she paced by the front door. Michelle was going to drop her off at school for her appointment and then take Caleb over to the Igloo.

"Coming," her mother called from upstairs.

Just as Michelle came down into the living room, Caleb appeared from the kitchen. "Let's go! I'm ready for my double-decker fudge brownie cone."

"That's disgusting," Madison remarked, trying to convince herself she was glad she was passing on their outing.

"Got your schedule?" her mother asked.

She held it up. "Right here. It's ten 'til three. We'd better hurry."

When they pulled up in front of the high school a few minutes later, Madison threw open her door and hopped out of the van. "I'll text you when I'm finished," she called over her shoulder, hurrying toward the main office.

She found Mr. Woodruff standing at the counter talking to a parent. He glanced her way and smiled. "I'll be right with you." Then he finished his conversation and led her down the hall to his private office. "Have a seat," he said, lifting a stack of student files off the chair facing his desk. "Sorry about the mess. I always think I'll be more organized for start up, but it never seems to happen."

She smiled. "No worries." Sitting down across from him, she pulled her class schedule out of her purse.

"So tell me what brings you here during one of your last days of freedom," the counselor asked.

"It's about this," she replied, handing him the piece of paper. Her heart picked up its pace, and her fingers were feeling a little clammy. "I was really hoping for Barnes for history, and PE first period is…well…you know, not exactly every girl's dream."

He studied the schedule and then placed it on his desk. Leaning forward he made eye contact with her and smiled, nodding his understanding. "Normally I'd say just give it a try. But since you went to the trouble of coming in, let me see if there's anything I can do."

"I was thinking maybe we could switch PE and history periods. If Mr. Barnes has a first period class, that is," she suggested.

Mr. Woodruff jiggled the mouse for his computer and then clicked on a link. He scrutinized the screen silently, while Maddie held her breath, praying for a miracle.

"Hmmm…" he murmured. "Let's see, here." He clicked a few more times, typed in something, and then leaned closer to the screen. After a moment, he said, "Okay, it looks like Mr. Barnes has a fifth period class, too. But it's pretty full," he said, leaning back in his chair and directing his attention back to her.

"What about changing PE?" she asked.

"All the PE classes are impacted this year. And the PE teachers just spoke at the staff meeting about how they are unhappy about being the class everyone thinks of as flexible or disposable. So, you're probably stuck with first period on that one."

"Oh."

"But here's the good news. First period is homeroom, so you have ten extra minutes. They usually give half of that to the students on the back end so they get more time to get ready for the rest of the day. You can just wear your PE clothes to school and then change into your regular clothes after class is over." He paused. "Let's give the fifth period class a try on the computer and see if it will take another student."

Madison smiled, shooting up a silent prayer as she watched Mr. Woodruff click on something on the screen again, type, and then sit back in his chair. "Okay. You're on his roster. Want to walk over and meet him? He's in his classroom working right now. Good way to get in his graces," he added with a wink.

"Sure," she replied, her nervousness returning. As she stood, she rubbed her palms against her skirt, wiping off the perspiration. *Breathe*, she told herself silently, following her counselor out of the office.

In contrast to Mr. Woodruff's room, the history class was neatly organized. Textbooks were stacked in even rows on the back counter; a smart board and computer were in place in front. Mr. Barnes was seated at his desk, a dozen sharpened pencils in a cup next to the lesson plan book spread out before him. As they entered, he stood to greet them. "Hi, Chuck. Do you have a new student for me?" he asked the counselor.

"This is Madison Baron. She came to see me today to request your class," he replied.

Mr. Barnes extended his hand to her. "Nice to meet you, Madison."

"You, too," she said, shaking his hand. "Luke Johnson told me you're a great teacher."

He smiled. "Luke's going to be missed around here."

Madison nodded in agreement.

"We're looking at putting Madison into your fifth period," Mr. Woodruff said. "I know that's your largest class but according to the computer, you have one opening left."

"Okay," he replied. "Sounds like you're in, Madison."

"Thanks," she replied. "I'm looking forward to it."

Mr. Barnes smiled. "I hope your enthusiasm is contagious, young lady. You may be aware that many students aren't too fond of history."

"Luke said you make it really interesting," she replied.

"Well, you tell Luke I appreciate his endorsement," he said.

"We'd better let Mr. Barnes get back to his work," Mr. Woodruff commented to Madison. "Let's go back to my office and get your new schedule printed out."

That night as they sat around the dinner table, Madison's father brought up her appointment with Mr. Woodruff. "So I heard you went to see the school counselor today, and he changed your schedule for you."

"Yeah. Sort of. He changed my history teacher, but I'm still stuck with first period PE," she replied.

"Seems like you are into running in the mornings these days," he said. "Maybe that will turn out to be a good fit."

"Yeah," Caleb piped up. "You could just run in your PE clothes and then go straight to school."

Madison nodded. "I guess."

"Want a potato, honey?" her mother asked. "You don't have much on that plate of yours."

"No thanks. I'm good." Madison kept her eye on her plate, but she could feel both of her parents studying her. Trying to change the subject, she turned to Caleb. "How was your double-decker fudge brownie cone?"

"Delish! You missed out," he replied. "When's your stupid diet going to be over?"

She glared at him.

"Diet? You don't need to be on a diet, Madison," her father said. "You look great just the way you are."

"Your father's right, honey," her mother added.

"She thinks she's fat," Caleb replied.

"I do not!" Madison pushed her chair away from the table and stormed out of the kitchen.

Her mother was on her heels as Madison headed for the stairs. "Wait, Maddie. Can we talk?" Michelle asked.

"There's nothing to talk about. Caleb's a jerk. He needs to mind his own business." She turned from her mother and bolted up the stairs to her bedroom.

After both kids were in their rooms for the night, Michelle approached Steve. "We need to talk. I'm really worried about Madison."

"Is it the diet thing?" he asked.

"Yeah. She's eating less and less, and I can tell she's losing weight."

"Seems like every one of her magazines has something on the cover about weight loss."

"Yeah," she replied. "I've seen some pretty scary anorexia cases at Magnolia," she added, thinking about one girl in particular who'd been in her eighth grade English class the prior year until she ended up in a treatment center for eating disorders.

"You're thinking about your student from last year, aren't you?" he said, as if reading her mind.

"Mmm hmm. It was really sad to see how far she took the thinness thing."

"So what do you think we should do?" her husband asked.

"I'm not sure. I'll talk to the counselor at my school and see what she suggests. But I really think we should do something."

"You've got my cooperation, honey. I've already mentioned to her how great she looks, but I'll be happy to do whatever you want."

"Maybe I'll try making some dinners that are higher in calories too, like that lasagna she loves. You know, my mom's recipe?"

"Oh yeah," he replied with a grin as he patted his stomach. "Good idea, honey."

Madison had her earphones in her ears, as she listened to some music and paged through a fashion magazine. Suddenly she remembered that Luke was going to send her pictures of his school. She picked up her phone and tapped the text icon. Nothing. He must have forgotten or gotten busy with something else.

Returning to her magazine, her eyes fell on a model about her age. The girl was wearing an off-the-shoulder shirt and very short cut-off jeans shorts. With one hand on her hip and her head cocked to the side, she had a smile on her face and a glint in her eye like she knew someone's secret. Her long, dark hair was almost to her waist and her makeup was a little heavy but so cute.

"That's the look I want," Maddie said softly.

She studied the size of the girl's arms and legs, and then stood and looked at hers in the mirror. She had a long way to go before she'd be that thin. But each time she turned away food, like the ice cream and potato today, she felt stronger and more successful. She'd just have to press on and ignore her parents and little brother. What did they know anyway?

She carefully pulled the picture out of the magazine and placed it on her bulletin board. Tomorrow she'd try to apply her make up like that. And maybe her mother would take her shopping again. She needed more sophisticated tops, and her shorts were all way too long.

CHAPTER FOUR

When Michelle looked up at her daughter the next morning, she had to do a double take. A thick swash of black eyeliner on each lid, along with shorts that had been rolled up to her rear end, gave Madison a completely different appearance.

"What?" Madison asked innocently, clearly aware of Michelle's stare.

"You look…different," Michelle replied tentatively, not wanting to put her on the defensive.

"Oh, that. Yeah, it's time your little girl grew up, don't you think?"

Before Michelle could answer, Caleb walked into the room. "Hey Mom, can I have a ride to the park this afternoon? Some friends are meeting for kickball."

"Will there be any adults there?" she asked.

"Buzz's big brother and his friends are going to be playing basketball on the courts near us."

Since Michelle knew the older boys from church and deemed them responsible enough to keep an eye on Caleb and his friends, she agreed. "But it'll have to be after two-thirty. I'm working in my classroom until then."

"Sure. No problem." Caleb grabbed a muffin from the counter and sat down with them. "What happened to your eyes?" he asked Madison.

"It's called make-up, dummy."

Michelle gave her a warning look.

"Well it looks weird if you ask me," Caleb replied.

"No one's asking you."

"That's enough, you two," Michelle cut in. Then turning to Madison, she asked, "What are your plans for the day?"

"I was hoping you could drop me off at Fashion Depot on your way to school. Lucy said she'd meet me there."

"It's not exactly 'on the way,' honey. What are you planning to shop for?"

"School clothes. I didn't get that much in Portland."

Michelle nodded. "Okay, I can give you a ride and a little cash, but you'll need to be ready to go in about fifteen minutes. I have a department meeting at ten."

"No problem," Madison replied, standing and grabbing a cup of coffee.

"Coffee?" Michelle asked, trying to contain the shock in her voice.

"Yeah. I'm skipping breakfast to finish getting ready," she replied as she walked away.

"Madison is really getting weird, Mom," Caleb observed.

Michelle smiled. "Part of being a teenager, buddy." But inside she felt as baffled as Caleb. *Should I make Maddie remove that thick eye makeup before we leave? And what about those shorts?* she thought. *Should I have her roll them back down?*

All of this was new territory, and Michelle wasn't sure she was completely ready for it. Glancing over at Caleb, she also began questioning their decision to leave him home alone while she worked on her classroom for a few hours. Steve had promised to drop by during his lunch break, and her mother was nearby, but was eleven really old enough?

"Don't forget what we discussed with your father last night," she said to him.

"Yeah, yeah. Don't answer the door for anyone, don't play in the front yard, stay off the computer. I got it, Mom.

Besides, Dad gave me that list of chores to do so I can earn money toward my new skateboard. I'll be busy weeding out back and straightening up the garage."

"Okay. But you know you can call your grandmother anytime. She's home all day, and your dad will be here for lunch."

"Got it, Mom," he replied, giving her one of his adorable grins as he signaled a thumbs-up.

She reached over and ruffled his hair. "When did you get to be such a big boy?"

He rolled his eyes playfully and pushed away from the table. "Have fun at school," he said as he walked out the back door.

Michelle went upstairs to finish getting ready. Popping her head into Madison's room, she saw her daughter studying a picture on the bulletin board over her desk. "What's this?" Michelle asked, hoping her voice sounded casual.

"My new look." Madison spun and gave her a smile. "It's cute, isn't it?" she asked.

How do I answer this one? Michelle wondered. "Well, yes, she's a cute girl."

"I mean the clothes."

"Oh." Michelle leaned in to look closer. The outfit was definitely suggestive. "It looks like an outfit for someone who's trying to get attention."

"What do you mean?" Madison's voice had an edge to it.

Michelle turned and placed a hand gently on her daughter's shoulder. "I just mean, it looks a little suggestive. Like she's trying to advertise that she's available."

"It's the fashion, Mom. All the models in these magazines are wearing stuff like this."

Michelle nodded. "I get that, honey. But you've been brought up to be more modest than this. Besides, what about the school dress code? I don't think that top or those short shorts would pass inspection."

"No one cares about dress codes anymore, Mom. I see girls like this all the time at school. No one does anything about it."

"Oh, really?"

"Really. And it's not like anything is really showing."

Michelle could sense this would take more time than she had this morning. "Let's talk about it more later. I know you want to feel stylish for school. I get that. But I think this," she gestured toward the picture, "is pushing it a little."

"Whatever," Madison replied, clearly disappointed in her mother's reaction. "But I need new tops and shorts for school," she added.

"That's fine. But the shorts need to be a little longer than those, and no off the shoulder tops."

Madison took a deep breath, and Michelle could see her trying to control her emotions. "Fine. But I'm getting some open necklines. I'll just keep them on my shoulders."

"Whatever you purchase will have to be run by me and your father before you keep it for school," Michelle said.

Madison was silent.

"Agreed?"

"Fine. Agreed."

Madison studied the picture on her bulletin board one more time before heading downstairs. Her stomach was growling, but she didn't want to eat anything before trying on her new clothes. After all, she planned to lose at least five more pounds in the next week. And she always looked so bloated after she ate anything. She'd have to run tonight since she slacked off this morning. *I'll add another mile when I go after dinner. Maybe I'll just have vegetables, too. Meat is so fattening.*

As they pulled up to the shop entrance, Madison waved to Lucy, who was waiting for her by the door.

"Have fun, honey," her mother said.

"I will. And good luck getting your classroom all set up." Madison hurried off before her mom could say anymore. Surely Lucy would understand and help her find some cute outfits.

After she got home from school that afternoon, Michelle went upstairs looking for Madison. She found her in her bedroom on her laptop. "So how did the shopping go?" she asked.

"Fine. I got a few tops, two pairs of shorts and a couple of skirts. They were having a big sale at Jessie's next door."

Jessie's was a boutique geared toward teens. Michelle had seen some pretty edgy looks in the windows. It was popular with the kids from Magnolia Middle School where Michelle taught, as well as with the high school crowd. "Can I have a look?" she asked.

"Sure," Madison replied, closing her computer and walking over to her closet. She pulled out her finds, already on hangers as if at home with her other clothes. She held them up, one at a time, for Michelle to see. "This one's my favorite," she said, showing off a soft blue cropped tee shirt with a torn neckline.

"I like the color," Michelle said, trying to sound positive. "How does it fit?"

"Fine. I really like the neckline because it can be worn either on or off the shoulder. So you don't have to worry about me and the dress code at school."

Michelle nodded warily. "Let me see the shorts and skirts."

Madison began holding them up, and Michelle could tell right away that they were all shorter than anything her daughter had owned up to this point. "They seem a little short," she said, working to keep a casual tone.

"That's the style, Mom." Madison put the clothes on her bed and picked up one of her magazines. "Just flip through here and you'll see. It's what everyone's wearing now."

"I think I'd like to see them on you before you take the tags off," Michelle said. "They are returnable, right?"

"The skirts are, but the shorts were on final clearance for the end of summer. Those can't be returned." Madison paused and then added, "They're really cute. I promise you'll like them." She picked up one of the hangers and held the shorts up to herself. "See, Mom. They're not bad."

But Michelle noticed that the top of the hanger was held pretty low on Madison's torso to give the illusion of more length. "Just let me see them on you before you think about wearing them to school."

"Fine. But everyone will be wearing them. You'll see. I'm sure it'll be the same at Magnolia." Placing the clothes back in the closet, Madison said, "I think I'll go for a run before dinner."

Michelle nodded. "Okay. Guess I'd better get dinner started. Your dad said he'd be home early tonight."

"Oh, and Mom?"

"Yeah?"

"Thanks for the money to buy the clothes," Madison said with a smile. "You're the best."

Michelle gave her a hug and then headed downstairs, a mixture of emotions churning inside. Madison was changing, but the sweet girl she'd always been was still in there, too.

"Can we go for a walk?" Michelle asked Steve as they cleared the dinner dishes together.

"Sure. I just need to make a quick call, and then I'm all yours," he replied, placing the plates he was carrying onto the counter by the sink.

Michelle loaded the dishwasher and went to find Madison. Her daughter was stretched out on the floor doing sit ups. "Should you be doing that right after you ate?" Michelle asked.

"Forty-seven, forty-eight, forty-nine, fifty." Madison let out a breath and glanced up at her. "Did you need something?"

"Dad and I are going for a walk in a few minutes. Caleb's playing his motor cross video game, but I just wanted to make sure you weren't planning on going anywhere while we're gone."

"I'll be here," she replied, hopping up and heading for the stairs. "I'll be in my room if he needs me." She turned and added, "But make sure you remind him to knock. Last time he just barged in."

"Will do," Michelle promised. "And thanks, honey."

Madison waved without looking back.

Michelle peeked into Steve's study and saw him on the phone. He held up one finger and mouthed, "Be right there."

She smiled and nodded, then went over and sat beside Caleb on the couch. "Dad and I are going for a walk, but Maddie will be upstairs in her room if you need her."

He continued to stare at the screen and manipulate the buttons on the controller he gripped in both hands.

"Did you hear me?" Michelle asked, a little louder this time.

Caleb nodded without looking over. "Got it, Mom."

"If you go up to get your sister for any reason, be sure you remember to knock."

"Yeah." Caleb twisted his wrist and stood in excitement as he watched a racecar flip on the screen. "Got you!" he called out to the game.

Michelle shook her head and stood. As she turned to go find her tennis shoes, she almost collided with Steve. Steadying her by placing his hands on her shoulders, he said, "Hey, there, gorgeous. I'm ready for our walk."

She smiled. "Give me a minute to find my shoes."

As she pulled away, she noticed him turning his attention to the video game. "Nice one, sport!" he exclaimed as Caleb's car crossed the finish line. Their son turned and grinned, holding up his hand for a high five.

Michelle spotted her shoes under the dining room table, and soon she and Steve were headed out the front door.

"So is there any ulterior motive for this walk tonight?" Steve asked. "Or are we just getting some exercise and time alone?"

"You really can read me like a book, can't you?" she replied.

He grinned, draping his arm over her shoulder and pulling her close. "Is that a bad thing?"

"No," she admitted. "But it would be nice to have some element of mystery remaining."

"There is," he replied.

"Really?"

"Yeah. I don't know what the ulterior motive is yet, do I?"

She nodded. "You're right. You don't."

"Okay. So spill." Steve released her and ambled by her side.

"It's about Maddie," Michelle began.

"The terrible teen?" he asked with a wink.

Michelle gave him a playful shove. "Yes. That's the one."

"So what's up? Are we back to what we talked about last time, or is this something new?"

"It's a little of both," she replied, searching for the words to explain her concern. "I feel like Maddie is trying to transform herself into someone else. Like she isn't happy with the way she is. Do you know what I mean?"

He seemed to be pondering the question.

"I think Madison doesn't realize how beautiful she is, Steve. All this dieting and exercising. And now she's got a whole new look she's trying to create."

"Like the eye makeup?" he asked.

"Yeah. And the kinds of clothes she wants to wear." Michelle knew Steve wouldn't be happy with Madison's purchases that day, but she also knew if they came down too hard on their daughter, it could easily spark a rebellion. "She went shopping today while I was working in my classroom. The stuff she bought was pretty revealing."

Steve stopped and looked her in the eye. "Seriously? Madison?" He seemed surprised. "She's always been pretty modest, and I thought the dieting and exercise meant she wasn't all that hot about her body right now. I'm surprised she'd go for more revealing clothes."

Michelle sighed and nodded. "I know. But again, I think it's her way of trying to be something that she's not."

"So what do we do? You're the female here. Plus you've got the experience with adolescents. What do you suggest?"

"I'm thinking maybe you could be the key to helping her realize how beautiful and valuable she is…and that she doesn't need to change."

"Me? I mean, I know we've talked about this a few times already. I'm trying to give her more compliments, honey. But, hey, I'll do whatever else you say."

"I'm thinking maybe you could take her out. On a date, I mean. Just the two of you. Remember, I mentioned that before?"

"Okay. Where should I take her?"

"I don't know. Maybe out to the Cliffhanger for dinner and then to see a play at the theater or something like that." Michelle searched her mind for ideas. "I think the main thing is to make it a really special evening. One where both of you get dressed up."

Steve nodded. "Like the time I gave her that purity ring?"

"Exactly. Like that."

"You think she'll go for it?" he asked.

"I think so. And it'll give you a chance to make her feel like a princess again."

"Okay. See if you can get some tickets for the theater, and let me know when to make the dinner reservation."

Michelle felt a surge of hope. "Great! I'll get on it tomorrow morning." She wrapped her arm around his waist. "Thanks, honey."

He gave her a side hug and kissed the top of her head. "You bet, babe."

The following evening, Steve knocked tentatively on Madison's bedroom door. *Why am I feeling nervous about asking my own daughter out on a date?* He wondered.

"Come in," Maddie's voice called to him.

Walking into her room, he noticed the clutter on the floor and desk. Not Madison's usual way. She tended to be neat and tidy.

"What's up, Dad?" she asked, flipping her laptop closed and leaning back against the headboard of her bed.

"Mind if I sit?"

Madison pulled her legs up toward her and gestured to the edge of the bed. "Be my guest."

Steve moved a sweatshirt and sat down. "How's life?" he asked.

She looked a little puzzled. "Fine, I guess. Why?"

"Oh, I don't know. Just seems like we don't get much chance to talk anymore," he said.

Madison nodded. "How's your life?" she asked.

"Well...I guess pretty busy. Work's been a little hectic lately." He paused and then added, "But hey, I'm never too busy for you, princess." He noticed her roll her eyes slightly at the nickname and decided to quickly plow ahead with his request. "So, anyway, I was wondering if you'd be willing to go on a little date with your old dad."

"A date?"

"You know, just an evening out. The two of us. We could go to dinner and the theater." He reached into his pocket and pulled out two tickets. "They're pretty good seats. *The Wizard of Oz*. It sounded like fun."

She hesitated.

"I'll take you to the Cliffhanger for dinner, first," he quickly added. "We could share a piece of that mud pie you love for dessert."

"I'm trying to watch my calories, Dad," she replied. "But the play sounds good. And I'm sure I could find a salad or something on the menu."

"So you'll go?"

"Sure. When are the tickets for?"

"Friday night. Eight o'clock show. So we should do dinner around six-thirty."

"Sounds good," she replied. "I should probably dress up a little, right?"

"Yep. I will, too." Steve reached over and squeezed her knee. "I'm really looking forward to this," he added, before standing up. "I'll let you get back to whatever you were doing on the computer."

She nodded. "Okay."

Steve found Michelle in the kitchen with her lesson plan book spread open on the table in front of her. "So how did it go?" she asked.

"Good. At least I think so. She said yes, so that's the most important thing. But she did roll her eyes when I called her *princess*."

Michelle laughed. "She's trying to grow up, honey. Someday she'll treasure that nickname again. Trust me." She reached out and squeezed his hand then pulled him down for a kiss. "Whether she admits it or not, I'm sure she was happy to have your attention and be invited out for a special evening."

"Hope you're right, babe. We'll see how it goes on Friday."

CHAPTER FIVE

"Maddie? Are you ready?" Michelle called from the bottom of the stairs. No answer. She glanced over at Steve and smiled. "I'll go up and check on her."

Steve checked his watch. It was already 6:40, and they needed to get going. Otherwise their dinner would be rushed or they'd miss the beginning of the play.

A moment later, Michelle appeared at the top of the stairs with Madison following behind. Steve could tell from Michelle's expression that she wasn't happy. When he saw their daughter, he knew why.

Madison had on a skirt that would have fit her when she was seven years old. It barely covered her rear end as she carefully walked down the stairs, keeping her legs together and trying hard to navigate the descent gracefully in shoes that looked to have five-inch heels. Her sweater was off one shoulder with a bra strap clearly displayed across her bare skin.

She looked at him guardedly. Her face clearly poised to defend the outfit.

Michelle's eyes met his. She looked tired and disappointed. Steve knew he had two choices. Confront the outfit and risk an outburst that would ruin the evening before it got started, or choose to ignore it and hope for a chance to breech the subject later that night. He chose the latter.

Glancing over at his wife, he gave her a reassuring smile. "All set?" he asked Madison.

She looked a little startled. "Yeah."

Steve held out his arm. "Then let's go."

Madison reached for it and wobbled a bit on her heels. Steve just held firm, and she was able to regain her balance. "See you around eleven," he said to Michelle, who nodded, her eyebrows raised in a skeptical expression.

As Steve glanced over at their daughter, he saw a smug smile on her face. *Triumph over Mom,* he thought. *This should be an interesting evening.*

After Steve and Madison had left, Michelle picked up the phone and called Kelly. "Can you talk?" she asked, when her friend picked up.

"Sure. Just give me a minute."

Michelle heard muffled voices in the background. With Kelly's large brood, there was always someone needing something.

"Okay, I'm back," her friend said. "What's up?"

"Remember I told you about Steve and Madison's date night?" Michelle began.

"Yeah. It's tonight, right?"

"Mmm hmmm. They just left."

"You don't sound happy," Kelly observed.

"You should have seen what Maddie was wearing, Kelly. She had on the shortest mini skirt and off-the-shoulder sweater along with a pair of spike heels that were at least four inches, if not more."

"I take it you've never seen the outfit before?"

"Never," Michelle replied. "She's been doing some shopping for school recently, but this was not from any of the purchases I knew about. I asked her where she got the things, and she said, 'What does it matter? I used my own money.' She's really changing. I'm worried."

"What did Steve say?"

"He played it cool and gave me the 'I'll handle this' look."

"I think that was smart. Madison knows how to push your buttons, Michelle. She's a teenager. She's going to try stuff like this. It's part of figuring out who she is and how she wants to live her life."

"Yeah. I guess it's just a combination of everything—the dieting and the clothes—that have me worried. She's such a beautiful girl. Why can't she see that?"

"Could you, at her age?" Kelly asked.

Michelle paused. She thought about how many people had complimented her on her appearance over the years. She still had a hard time believing them. Had she passed along the same doubts to her own daughter?

"Are you still there?"

"Yeah. You're right. Why is it always so hard for us to see ourselves as others do?"

Kelly laughed. "I don't know. I guess maybe it's society and the push for a certain look that is plastered on every beauty magazine on the newsstands. Or the enemy's attempt to derail us from viewing ourselves the way God does."

"What about Lucy? Does she wrestle with this, too?" Michelle hoped to find some affirmation that every teen had the same struggle.

"My Lucy? She's a different breed. You know that. Ever since she was a toddler, she's been storming ahead, grabbing life by the reins, and plowing forward with zeal. So it's not as easy to see it in her as in your sweet, sensitive Madison. But I'm sure there are times Lucy faces her own internal struggles. She's just not one to let on. She'd rather have everyone think she's got it all figured out."

Michelle sighed. "I sure hope this date night goes well. She was mad at me when they left, but hopefully Steve will be able to reach her."

"I'll pray. Let me know how it goes." A shouting match could be heard in the background. "I'd better go. The boys are at it again."

"Okay. Thanks, friend."

"You're welcome," Kelly replied. "Talk to you tomorrow."

Michelle set the phone down and sunk into Steve's chair. Folding her hands in her lap, she closed her eyes and began to pray that God would use this evening to make an impact on their daughter's life. An image of her grandmother flashed across her mind. Picking up the phone, she called her.

"It's so good to hear from you, sweetheart," Grandma Joan said.

After exchanging pleasantries, Michelle pressed on with her request, carefully choosing her words. "Would you pray for Madison, Grandma?"

"Of course, dear. Is something wrong?" Joan sounded worried.

"Just teenage girl stuff. I think it's a combination of Luke leaving for college and some normal insecurities at her age. But we're trying to nip it in the bud. I'd really appreciate your prayers."

"I'll pray. And I'll get the Silver Sisters on it, too," she replied.

Her grandmother's prayer group had made such a difference in her life. Michelle smiled as she pictured them huddled together, interceding for her daughter. So many spiritual mountains had been moved by God through her grandparents' prayers. Now that Grandpa Phil was gone, she was glad her grandmother had such close friends to link with in prayer.

"Thanks, Grandma. I feel better already," Michelle replied with a smile.

Steve could see eyebrows raised as the restaurant hostess led him and Madison to their table at the window, overlooking the surf.

I can just imagine what some of these people are thinking, he mused. Madison looked to be about eighteen or nineteen in her makeup and outfit. And there was no denying that Steve was in his early forties.

He was actually relieved when Maddie said, "Look, Dad. What a great sunset."

Hope everyone heard that, he thought.

They took their seats and accepted menus from the hostess. "Our special tonight is the salmon," she said, pointing to a parchment page inserted into the menus. "It's marinated and grilled over an open flame, then served with wild rice and asparagus."

Madison didn't look impressed.

"She's not a fish lover," he explained.

"Can I get you a drink to start with? Your server will be with you in a minute," she added.

"I'll have an iced tea," Steve replied. "How about you, honey?" he asked Madison.

"Just water." She gave the hostess a smile. "With lemon."

"You've got it." She replied, disappearing in the direction of the kitchen.

They studied their menus for a minute. "The pork chops sound good," Steve offered.

Madison nodded, but didn't say anything. She fingered her exposed bra strap as she continued perusing the menu.

Since when did it become fashionable to have your bra showing? Steve wondered. Then images of pop stars flashed across his mind—performers who were continuously pushing the envelope for shock value and attention. He shook his head, and then caught himself. Turning his attention back to Madison, he asked, "Did you find something you'd like. It's my treat," he added with a wink.

She closed her menu. "I think I'll just have a salad."

"That's not much for dinner. How about a side of stuffed potato skins? You used to love those."

She shook her head. "No thanks. Salad will be fine."

Steve winced inside. As Madison gazed out the window, he noticed how her bones were beginning to show on that exposed shoulder. "Well, I think I'll order a starter of artichoke dip," he said, hoping another of her favorites might tempt her.

Madison just nodded. "Okay."

A busboy delivered their drinks, followed by the waitress. "Can I get you an appetizer before you order?" she asked.

"I'll take the artichoke dip," Steve replied. "Do you want anything else?" he asked Madison.

"No thanks."

The waitress nodded and said, "I'll be right back with that."

Steve followed Madison's gaze out to the ocean. The sun was perched on the horizon, and pink and purple clouds contrasted with the iridescence of the water. "Beautiful evening," he said.

She nodded again. "Yeah."

Grasping for a conversation starter, Steve said, "So tell me more about your classes. Were you able to straighten out that history teacher thing?" He already knew the answer, but hoped it would help her open up to him.

A beep caught Madison's attention before she could answer, and she dug into her purse, pulling out her cell phone. Staring at it for a minute, she began typing. Then she stopped and set the phone on the table. "Sorry, Dad. What were you saying?"

"I was asking about your history teacher this year."

"What about him?"

"Did you get it changed? I think you said Luke recommended someone else."

"Oh. Yeah. It's taken care of," she replied. The phone beeped again, and she picked it up and began reading the message.

Steve could feel himself getting impatient. He was about to say something when the waitress approached the table. "Here you go," she said, placing the dip and chips in the center of the table. Are you ready to order, or should I come back in a few minutes?" she asked.

Steve glanced at his watch—7:00. "We'd better order. We have a date at the theater at eight."

She whipped open her pad and stood poised to write. Looking at Madison, she asked, "What can I get for you tonight?"

"I'll have the spinach salad, please. With dressing on the side and no bacon."

The waitress nodded as she wrote. Then she glanced over to Steve.

"I'll have the pork chops," he said.

"Great. I'll get those orders in right away." Leaning over, she took their menus. "Enjoy your dip."

Steve dug in. "Try some, Maddie. It's really good."

She hesitated and then picked up a chip, scooping a tiny bit of the dip before popping it in her mouth.

Steve smiled. "Good, huh?"

She nodded. "I'm going to the ladies' room," she said, pushing back her chair. "Be right back." She stood to her feet and walked carefully on her stilts in the direction of the restrooms.

Steve took a deep breath and sighed. He looked down at the dip. *Someone might as well enjoy this,* he said to himself silently. By the time Madison returned five minutes later, he'd eaten most of it. As she took her seat again, he pushed it slightly in her direction. "The rest is yours," he said.

She shook her head. "No thanks. I'll just wait for my salad."

Once the dinner arrived, Steve knew they'd need to hurry. They ate mostly in silence as the sun disappeared and the sky darkened.

"Any dessert tonight?" their waitress asked when they were finished.

Steve glanced at his watch again. "Better not. I'll just take the bill, please." After she'd handed it to him, he turned to Madison. "We can have some dessert during intermission if you'd like."

She just smiled.

"So, how did it go?" Michelle asked, once she and Steve were alone in the kitchen later that night.

He shrugged. "Okay, I guess. We didn't really get to talk much. She was texting with someone at the restaurant, and we had to eat pretty quickly to get to the theater in time."

"Did she eat?"

"Some salad. And one bite of artichoke dip."

"What did you think of that outfit?" Michelle asked.

"I think you know the answer to that one." He paused and then asked, "Don't you supervise her purchases?"

Michelle bristled, and her tone gave him a clear warning. "She's not a little girl anymore, Steve. She doesn't want me following her around in the shops. But to answer your question, yes, I do look at everything she buys with the money I give her. She claims this outfit is something she got with her own money."

He shook his head. "I can tell you one thing—she was turning heads in the restaurant. I felt pretty uncomfortable walking through there with her. Either I looked like an older man taking advantage of a young lady, or like a father who had no control over his own daughter."

Michelle nodded.

"It's just so unlike Madison," he added.

They both sat silently for a minute. Then Steve took a deep breath and placed his hand on Michelle's. "We'll get through this, babe," he said. Then he asked, "Isn't Caleb's game at eight-thirty tomorrow morning?"

"Yeah."

"We'd better get to bed."

Michelle pushed her chair out and stood up. "Yep."

As he followed her out of the kitchen, he thought about how simple their lives were when it was just the two of them. A night like this would have ended very differently, he mused as his eyes grazed the curves of his wife's body. When they slipped under the covers in bed, he wrapped his arm around her and drew her close, and they fell asleep breathing in rhythm with each other.

CHAPTER SIX

Sunday morning, Michelle knocked on Madison's bedroom door to make sure she was up for church. After no response, she pushed open the door to find their daughter sound asleep. "Wake up, honey," she said, gently nudging Maddie's shoulder.

"Huh?" came a muffled reply from the pillow.

"It's past time to get up for church. Did you forget to set your alarm?"

Madison opened her eyes, glanced at the clock on the nightstand, and moaned. "I'm really tired. Think I'll skip it today."

Michelle sat down beside her. "Are you feeling okay?"

"Yeah. Just tired. I was up late last night."

"If you're not sick, I think you should get up and go. You can always take a nap this afternoon," Michelle suggested.

Maddie shot her an aggravated look. "It's not like I don't go every Sunday. Can't I just skip this one time?"

Just then, Steve peeked in through the open door. "Everything okay in here? Caleb's asking about pancakes for breakfast, but it's getting pretty late."

Madison pushed herself up into a sitting position. "I was just telling Mom I'm really tired and would like to skip church today. Is that okay?"

Steve's eyes met Michelle's. She gave a slight shake of her head to indicate her disapproval.

"I'm kind of tired, too, Maddie. But I think it's worth the effort to get up for church. You've missed Thursday night youth group twice this month. Don't you want to stay connected there with everyone?"

She fell back onto her pillow. "Not really. Youth group's not that fun now that Luke is gone."

"What about your other friends?" he asked. "Most of them are still going. Like Lucy," he added.

"It's just not the same." She pulled her covers back up to her chin.

Steve glanced down at his watch and then back at Michelle. She shrugged her shoulders and waited for his response. "Alright. But this can't become a habit."

"It won't, Daddy. I promise," Madison replied, as she closed her eyes and snuggled down deeper into the bed.

Michelle shook her head as they walked out of the room. She really wanted to talk to Steve, but there wasn't time. If they didn't hurry and get some breakfast for Caleb, they'd all be late.

"Can we have pancakes?" Caleb asked, as they entered the kitchen.

"Sorry, sport, but we're running a little late this morning. Here's some cereal," Steve said, grabbing the box from the counter and pouring it into a bowl.

Michelle retrieved the milk and added it to Caleb's cereal. "Eat up, honey."

"Where's the Mad Hatter?" he asked.

"Don't call your sister that," Steve warned.

"Why not? She's always mad at me for something," Caleb replied nonchalantly, as he plunged his spoon into his cereal and began eating.

Michelle raised her eyebrows at Steve, and he nodded. "I'll talk to her about it," he promised their son.

"So where is she? She's going to make us late again, isn't she?" he asked.

"Madison is staying home this morning," Michelle added.

"Why?"

"She didn't sleep well last night," Steve said.

"Do you want me to fix you some toast?" Michelle asked her husband.

"No. As soon as Caleb's finished, we'd better go. I'll eat after church."

"Okay," she replied, grabbing a banana from the counter to eat on their way.

After church, Steve made a point of catching Ben between conversations with other congregants. "Are you free tomorrow for lunch?" he asked. "I could use some advise about Madison."

"Really? Sure. My schedule is pretty light tomorrow," Ben replied. "Coffee Stop around noon?"

"Yeah. Sounds good."

"Okay. See you there."

"What was that about?" Michelle asked, when Steve rejoined her in the hallway, where she was signing Caleb out of his Sunday school class.

"I'm having lunch with Ben tomorrow. Maybe he'll have some pointers about Maddie, and how we should be handling her these days."

She nodded. "Good idea. I've been picking Kelly's brain, too." She paused, and then added, "I never really expected any issues with Madison during the teen years. Guess I was being naïve. But she's always been such a good kid."

"She still is, babe. We just have to learn new ways to bring that out in her."

"I hope you're right," she replied, skeptically.

Caleb walked out of his class and joined them. "Look, Mom," he said, holding up an oversized chocolate chip cookie. "Our teacher brought us treats today."

"Maybe you'd like to share that with your old pop!" Steve said.

"No way, Dad. This one's all mine," he replied with a grin, as he took a giant bite. "Maybe if you're nice, Mom will bake some for you," he added with a sly grin.

"Maybe I will," Michelle said, reaching over and taking Steve's hand.

Steve was eager to meet with Ben the following day. It seemed a little awkward to be getting together with his best friend in more of a pastoral role, but he knew he needed not only friendly advice but godly counsel as well.

"So what's up with Madison?" Ben asked, after they'd settled at their table with sandwiches and coffee.

"It's a lot of things, actually," Steve replied. "She's really changing lately—in the way she dresses, her makeup—even the way she talks to us."

"Sounds like a teenager to me." Ben paused, seeming to study him. "You knew she'd grow up, right?"

"Yeah. Of course. But she's losing her modesty and seems to be trying to emulate the super skinny models in the fashion magazines. She's barely eating, and she runs everyday."

Ben nodded. "It's pretty sad how society pushes this whole image thing on young girls. And Madison—she's such a beautiful girl, just the way she is. I'm sure you've told her that."

"Yeah. Michelle suggested I take her out on a date night, and reinforce how special she is to me."

"Good idea."

Steve smiled, but his heart was heavy. "So, I took her out to dinner and the theater on Friday."

"How did that go?"

"It almost didn't. When Michelle saw what Maddie was planning to wear, they exchanged words. I thought Madison might back out of the whole evening."

Ben nodded, listening intently.

"I just felt it was more important that we go out than to take a stand on her outfit," Steve explained. "But I've got to admit, I felt a little funny walking through the restaurant with her in her high heels, off the shoulder sweater, and mini skirt."

Ben sat back in his seat. "It's hard to imagine Madison dressed like that."

Steve nodded. "Yeah. She was really turning heads in the restaurant."

"I'll bet."

"And then yesterday morning, she balked at going to church. She hadn't even gotten up when Michelle checked on her to make sure she was ready. So we ended up leaving without her."

"Is she still going to youth group?"

"She hasn't the past two weeks. She says it's not the same without Luke."

Ben sighed. "Those two were pretty close. I know Luke misses her, too."

"So what do I do?" Steve asked.

Ben looked him squarely in the eye. "Well, first, you pray. Both you and Michelle. You two pray together, right? I mean besides just before meals."

"Sometimes. But it seems like we've gotten slack about that lately. No reason in particular. Just busy."

"Yeah. I know. So that's where you start. Get back into that."

"Okay."

"And break down the issues one-by-one," Ben continued. "The dieting and running—those are health issues. It's fine for her to try to eat healthy and to get exercise. But you'll know if it starts turning into something more than that."

"I think maybe it's approaching crossing the line."

"Then you need to address that. There are some great Christian counselors I can recommend if you'd like."

"Okay. That would be good," Steve replied.

"As far as the clothes and makeup go, you need to let her feel she has choices and understand that she's going to want to dress like her peers. But that doesn't mean you let her wear just anything she wants. She needs to understand the messages behind her clothes. As a man, and her father, you can explain to her the impact of some of her choices on the males she encounters. Lucy wanted to wear some tight, low-cut tee shirts this summer. She's getting quite a figure, if you know what I mean."

Steve nodded.

"Kelly pulled her aside and said, 'What you are wearing right now is saying to the boys around you—these are available to you.'" Ben gestured toward his chest in imitation of Kelly's moves. "It seemed to help Lucy get some perspective."

"I remember how distracted I'd get in high school by what some of the girls were wearing," Steve replied.

"Me too. They have no idea what is going on in a guy's mind when they dress provocatively," Ben agreed. "It's a little awkward as a dad, but if *we* can't help them understand this, who will? I mean I'm glad our wives are on board to intervene. But we don't get a pass here." He paused, and then continued. "So I get that you didn't want to put a halt to your evening together, but next time I'd take the opportunity to say something. You may get a negative response, but we're not called to be popular with our kids."

Steve nodded in agreement.

74

"We have a small window of opportunity to communicate important truths to them. And while clothes themselves are not inherently bad, the messages they send can get our girls into situations they aren't anticipating."

"Yeah. That's for sure," Steve replied.

"And the youth group thing... I'll have Lucy reach out to her about that. Maybe Madison will have some ideas of things she'd like to see the youth group doing. We're always open to new ideas to make it relevant and fun for the kids without compromising truth. We've been thinking about putting together a short-term mission for the group. Nothing's set up yet, but it's a possibility we may take a group when Luke's home next summer. He'd really like to be part of it. And since he and Madison are so close, maybe it will interest her, too."

"That would be great. I think she'd really benefit from getting out of her comfort zone and seeing what God is doing in other parts of the world."

"Exactly. All the kids would. I'm hoping Lucy will go, too."

Steve nodded, and then glanced at his watch. "I've gotta get going. I have a meeting at one o'clock."

"Okay. Let's just say a quick prayer before you take off." They bowed their heads, and Ben began, "Lord, we come before You now with our kids and all their needs. You've put us in an important position as fathers, and we don't take it lightly. Would You please give us wisdom as our girls grow into teens and then adults? We especially ask for Steve and Michelle to know how to parent Madison through the changes she's experiencing. Help them have the words to say, and give Maddie the ears to hear the importance of her health as well as how she presents herself to the world. Please tug on her heart and give her a renewed hunger for You and for fellowship with the kids in the youth group. And give our youth group leaders and me wisdom to know how to best minister to these teens. In Jesus' name, amen."

"Amen," Steve echoed.

They stood and embraced, Ben clapping him on the back. "Madison will be okay. You'll see. You guys will get through this stage."

"Thanks," Steve replied, hope surging in his heart.

School began that Wednesday, and Madison and her mother had an argument before breakfast. "You are not wearing that to school," her mother declared adamantly.

Madison had carefully selected her outfit for the day. It was a black scoop-neck tee shirt paired with some cute white shorts. "What's wrong with it?" she asked as she gestured down toward the clothes.

"The shorts are too short and the neckline is too low," Michelle said. "If you want to wear that shirt, layer it with a higher neckline tank top. And your white flared skirt would be really cute with it."

"What? That long thing I wore in eighth grade?"

"It still fits you and looks great, honey."

Madison felt so frustrated she could cry. Why was her mother being so overboard with the dress code thing? She looked at herself in the full-length mirror. The outfit was perfect. Just like the ones she'd seen in her favorite magazine. But it was no use arguing. She knew her mother would win. She always did. Madison avoided eye contact and just said, "Fine. I'll just wear my jeans and one of my old shirts."

She began rummaging through her closet and pulled out a pair of jeans with torn knees, grabbing another black top with long sleeves.

"Those look a little warm for today," her mother said softly.

"Well, at least I'll be covered up," Madison replied sarcastically, almost immediately regretting her tone. She watched as her mother's face fell before walking out of the room. Sinking down onto her bed, Maddie fought back the tears. She'd ruin her make up if she started crying now. But she sure did miss the closeness she and her mom used to share.

As Madison slid into her seat in history class, she noticed a tall, thin guy with kind of long brown hair taking a desk in the row to her left. She'd never seen him before, but he was really cute. She caught herself staring, and was just about to look away, when he turned and smiled at her. Her heart froze in her chest, and she could feel herself blush.

"Name's Miles," he said with a slight southern accent.

"Madison," she replied, trying to sound casual as she returned his smile.

"Nice name. I like that."

Before they could go any further, the bell rang and class began. Madison could feel Miles' eyes on her several times during the next hour. She glanced over once and caught him looking her way. Smiling, she turned her attention back to the teacher.

As they exited the room at the end of the period, he held out his schedule to her and asked, "Do you know where room C-30 is?" He pointed to the next class on the list.

"Yeah. It's the portable to the left of the field out back," she replied.

"Great. Thanks." He flashed his big smile at her again. "See you tomorrow."

Madison nodded, hoping she looked friendly without seeming too interested. "See ya."

A moment later, she felt a tug on her arm. It was Lucy. "Who's that?" she asked, pointing to Miles.

"A new guy. He's in my history class. I think he's from Texas or something. He's got an accent."

"Well, wherever he's from, he sure is cute."

Madison smiled and nodded. "Yeah." An image flitted through her mind of walking hand-in-hand with him. *Like that would ever happen,* she thought dismally to herself. She glanced down at her old clothes and thought of how much more attractive she'd felt in the outfit she'd planned to wear that day. Then she remembered some models she'd seen wearing outfits like the one she had on. They'd been really thin and looked cute no matter what they were wearing.

Her parents might be able to censor her clothes, but they couldn't keep her from getting thin. Then maybe she wouldn't care what she wore. She'd look good in anything.

When she got home that afternoon, she found a letter from Luke in the mailbox. She read it as she ate some celery sticks. She'd been hungry since lunch—an apple and a piece of string cheese—but she didn't want to eat much before her run that afternoon.

Luke's letter was basically about school and his classes, although he did mention a few new friends and how much he was enjoying dorm life. He'd also gotten connected with a missions club on campus and was attending their gatherings each week. "College is even better than I imagined," he wrote near the end, and then finished with a mention of missing everyone back in Sandy Cove. He just signed his name at the bottom.

"Like you were expecting him to say, 'Love, Luke'?" she asked herself aloud. Clearly he saw Madison as just a friend.

She folded the letter and slipped it back into its envelope, tossing it on her desk before changing into shorts and a short sleeve tee for running. She laced up her shoes and headed out the door. It was nice being the first one home. By the time she returned from her run, her mother and brother would be back from school, too. Hopefully there wouldn't be any more arguments today.

CHAPTER SEVEN

Miles fell in step beside Madison as they walked out of history class the next day. "So there's a football game tomorrow night," he said casually.

"Yeah," she replied, acutely aware of his arm brushing against hers as they entered the crowded hallway.

"I was thinking of going. Would you like to come?" he asked.

Madison looked up at him and smiled. "Sure!" *Hope this isn't a problem with my parents,* she thought. After all, she really didn't know him.

"Give me your address, and I'll pick you up around six-thirty. The game starts at seven."

"You've had your license for six months?" she asked, thinking about the provisions she was under as a new driver which prohibited her from driving friends anywhere without an adult in the car.

"Yeah. I turned seventeen in July, so I moved here from Dallas with a full license."

"So why are you a junior if you're seventeen?" Madison regretted the question as soon as it left her mouth.

Miles laughed. "I'm actually not a junior. I'm taking history over this year. Didn't do so well with it at my high school last year."

"You're a senior?"

"Yep. One more year, and I'm out of here." He paused and then reminded her, "Wanna give me your address? I should probably have your phone number, too." He pulled out his cell phone and clicked on his contacts.

Madison rattled off her phone number and address as he entered it into the phone. "Cool. Okay, so we'll plan on six-thirty."

"I'll text you when I'm out front," he said.

Madison knew her parents would want to meet him, but she wasn't going to tell Miles that and risk scaring him off. She'd figure something out. "I'd better go. The bell's about to ring," she said, realizing she'd never make it to her locker and class before the tardy bell. Better skip the locker this time and just bring her history book along. Thankfully they were doing a lab in science, so she'd be using the class set of lab books rather than her text.

"See ya," Miles replied with a tip of his head. Turning, he ambled off toward the exit door near the field.

"Was that the new guy you were just talking to after fifth period?" Lucy asked, as she approached Madison at the lockers.

"Yeah." Madison looked really excited.

"You look pretty happy. What's up?"

"He asked me to the football game tomorrow night," her friend replied.

"Really?" Lucy wanted to be happy for her friend, but she secretly always hoped Madison would end up with Luke. She wasn't sure what to think about this Miles guy.

Madison nodded. "Really."

"And I take it you said yes." Madison was clearly interested in this guy. It was written all over her face.

"Of course I said yes! Now I just have to figure out what I'm going to wear," Madison replied. "Want to come over and help me pick something out?"

Lucy hesitated and then replied, "Sure. I'll see if Mom can bring me by tonight for a while."

"Why don't you text her and see if you can just come home with me after school?"

"Okay. Sounds good." Lucy turned to open her locker. Then she remembered what she'd wanted to talk to Madison about in the first place. "Hey, did you get a letter from Luke?" she asked.

Madison nodded. "He seems like he's really happy there."

"Are you going to write back?" Lucy asked hopefully.

"Uh…maybe. Yeah, I guess," Madison hedged.

"You guys are still friends," Lucy reminded her.

"Yeah. Friends."

Lucy noticed something in Madison's countenance dropped a little. "Who knows what could happen when he comes back," she suggested.

Madison smiled, but her eyes looked kind of sad. "Who knows?" she echoed.

When Madison and Lucy met after school, Madison noticed Miles sitting with a few other guys on a wall by the stairs. She recognized three of the girls from the cheer squad passing them, laughing and talking. They all had on short skirts, and one was wearing an off-the-shoulder tee with a tank top underneath. Miles' head pivoted to watch them pass. Madison could see the look of approval on his face.

Hopefully Mom won't be so strict about what I wear out for a date. All I need is her forcing me to wear some junior high outfit, she thought to herself.

"Those girls think they're so hot," Lucy observed.

"Looks like the guys do, too," Madison replied, tipping her head toward Miles and his friends.

"Hey, isn't that Miles?" Lucy asked.

"Yeah," Madison replied. "He's cute. Don't you think?"

Lucy looked over again and then turned back to her. "Sure. And so's that blond guy next to him."

Madison glanced at the other guy. "Miles is cuter."

That afternoon, Madison bypassed her run to spend the afternoon with Lucy figuring out what she should wear to the football game. They pulled out all of Madison's new clothes to try various combinations.

"What do you think of this?" Madison asked, holding up a short white skirt and a red sweater. "School colors," she added with a smile.

"Try it on," Lucy suggested.

Madison stripped off her clothes and pulled the skirt up, fastening it below her waist. Then she pulled the sweater off the hanger and slipped it over her head, easing the arms over hers and then pulling the neckline so that it fell partway down her arm, revealing a bare shoulder with a pink bra strap.

"Do you have a strapless bra?" Lucy asked.

"No, do you?"

Lucy shook her head.

"Would it look better with a black bra?"

"Maybe. That pink strap looks funny."

Madison pulled the sweater off, switched bras and put it back on. "What about now?"

"Better," Lucy replied. "But do you think your mom will let you wear that? My mom wouldn't."

"I sure hope so. Maybe my dad will help her understand. He seemed pretty cool with it when I wore a similar outfit out to dinner and the theater with him." Madison studied her reflection in the full-length mirror. She pulled her skirt down just a little and adjusted the sweater to maximize her revealed shoulder.

"It does look cute," Lucy admitted. "Hope she says yes."

"Me, too," Madison said, smiling.

"So I was thinking of going to the football game tomorrow night," Madison said at dinner, hoping her voice sounded casual.

"Really?" Steve asked. "I'd be up for going, too."

Madison paused. "Well, I was kind of thinking of going with friends."

"Of course," her father replied, but she could see his face fall.

"We could go together another time, though," she suggested.

"Yeah."

"Which friends are you planning to go with," Michelle asked.

"Can I go?" Caleb piped in. "If Logan's going, I want to go."

"He's not going, and no, you can't go," Madison replied.

Her mother shot her a warning look.

"Not this time," Madison said, her voice softening. "But maybe we could all go next time."

Caleb nodded. "Yeah. Whatever."

"So, back to my original question," her mother said. "Who will you be going with?"

"Just a friend."

"Anyone we know?" her dad asked, suddenly becoming more interested.

"Oohh," Caleb said with a sly smile. "Maddie's got a date."

Madison glared at him.

"Is that true, honey?" Michelle asked. "Have you got a date?"

"Well, actually, a guy did ask me," she admitted.

"Do we know him?" Steve wanted to know.

"Uh...no. He's new. To school, I mean. His family just moved here from Texas."

Her mother reached over and put her hand on Madison's. "You know the rule, sweetheart. We need to meet any guys you want to go out with before we say yes."

Madison shook her head and sighed. "You guys are so old-fashioned. No one I know has to do some big interview with their parents before they can go out on a date."

Her dad looked her in the eye. "We may be old-fashioned, but we're not the only parents with that rule. You know Ben and Kelly have the same requirement for Lucy. Besides, even if we were the only parents on the planet who required that, you just happened to be stuck with us." He smiled at her, but she didn't return the gesture.

"I'm sixteen years old, Dad. Come on. Be real."

"I am being real. Your real father. And I need to meet any guy who is thinking about taking out my daughter."

"Mom, help me out here," Madison pleaded.

"Sorry, honey. Dad's right. That's our rule."

Madison pushed away from the table. What would Miles think of having to pass inspection before taking her out? He'd probably just drop the whole thing. Great. Just great. A cute guy finally notices her and she got to tell him she can't go out with him. She didn't mind her parents meeting him. But implying they might not let her go if they didn't like him? That was over the top.

"Don't forget it's your night for the dishes," Caleb reminded her.

"Got it, kid," she snapped, picking up her plate and glass and storming into the kitchen. Tears were pooling in her eyes, when her mother joined her a moment later.

"What's going on?" Michelle asked. "You've known all along that we needed to meet any guys you were going to date. Why is it upsetting you so much tonight?"

Madison tried not to cry, but one stray tear escaped and rolled down her cheek. She wiped it off with the back of her hand and turned away from her mother, hoping she wouldn't notice. "I finally find a guy who actually noticed me and wants to take me out, and now it'll probably never happen because of this stupid rule. What guy is going to want to go through some approval process just to take me to the football game?"

"A guy who's worth it," Michelle replied gently, placing a hand on her shoulder.

Madison pulled away, knowing that her mother's touch could set off a torrent of tears. "Yeah. Well, we'll see about that," she replied under her breath.

Things were silent for a moment, and then she heard the kitchen door swing and her father's voice ask, "Everything okay in here?"

Michelle nodded.

Steve placed some plates on the counter. "Okay, I'll be in my study if you need me. I've got to finish that brief for tomorrow."

After he'd walked out, Madison said, "Maybe I'll just go to the game with some friends that you know. I think Lucy might be going."

"What about your date? Why don't you give us a chance? We're not going to give him the third degree, Madison. We just want to meet him first and talk to him

for a few minutes before we let you drive off with him."
She paused and then asked, "What's his name?"

"Miles."

"All you have to do is invite Miles in when he comes
to pick you up. Let your dad and me talk to him for five
minutes. I'm sure he'll be fine with that, and it will give us
a chance to be fine with him, too."

"And if you're not?"

"Fine with him?"

"Yeah."

Her mother studied her face. "Then you can't go."

"Oh, great," Madison replied sarcastically. "You'll just
tell him to go away?"

Michelle sighed. "What do you want me to say? That
we'll let you go with him even if we have a bad feeling
about him? Is that what you think you'd do if you were the
parent?"

"I think I'd trust my own daughter to know if someone
was okay or not," she said, immediately regretting her tone
but not the message of her words.

"It's not that we don't trust *you*, Madison. It's *him* we
don't know about. Your dad and I have been around a lot
longer than you. We've had more experiences with people
and judging character."

"Doesn't the Bible say not to judge?"

Her mother shook her head, looking exasperated.
"God has put your father and me over you as your parents.
Part of that is to protect you. That means we need to use
our discernment to help us judge the character of someone
you will be dating."

Madison turned away and started rinsing the dishes.

"I hope you'll give us a chance with Miles," her mother
said.

She just shrugged. *So much for dating,* she thought to
herself. There was no way she could ask Miles to get her
parents stamp of approval, and it didn't look like there was

any other way to go out with him. Unless… Her mind began searching for another way. Maybe this could work after all.

"What do you think, Steve? Are we being too old-fashioned?" Michelle asked, second-guessing herself as she felt her closeness with Madison slipping away.

"You're kidding, right? Think of all the stories you've told me about your students. And don't forget Amber," Steve added, referring to the biological mother of their adopted son, who'd gotten pregnant in the eighth grade while a student in Michelle's English class.

Michelle sighed. "I know. I just feel like we are losing our daughter. She and I used to be such pals. Now it seems like we are constant adversaries."

Steve nodded and pulled her close. Resting his chin on the top of her head, he replied, "Yeah. Guess we should be thankful we've made it this far without more confrontations." He gave her a little squeeze and then released his hold on her. "Madison will find her bearings, honey. We just need to hold the line and give her time."

She knew he was right, but suddenly images of Madison and Luke listening to music on his iPod together, talking and laughing and holding hands all flashed through her mind. She needed to get over this whole notion of Madison and Luke being together. *God, You know Your plans for Maddie. Help me trust You to bring them to pass.*

CHAPTER EIGHT

"Are we still on for tonight?" Miles asked before the bell rang to begin history class.

Madison felt her heart pounding. "Yeah."

Their teacher approached the podium and began flipping through his roll sheets.

Madison scribbled Lucy's address on the corner of a piece of notebook paper and tore it out. "This is where you'll be picking me up. Turns out I'll be at a friend's house after school for a while."

He took the paper and nodded, shoving it into his pocket. "See you at six-thirty," he said as the bell rang.

Madison couldn't concentrate on the rest of the class. She was thinking through her plan, and what she'd say to Lucy. She could have just told Miles she'd meet him at the game, but the idea of him picking her up made it more of an official date. It just wouldn't work to have their first date start with a parental inspection.

"So what do you think, Madison?" the teacher's voice broke into her thoughts. She could feel her face turning bright red as students turned to look at her.

"Uh, could you repeat the question please?" She fumbled through her notebook and pulled out the discussion sheet for the lecture. Out of the corner of her eye, she could see Miles laughing quietly to himself. *Great. Now he thinks I'm a fool.*

A couple of other students raised their hands, and the teacher moved on to their responses. She noticed the girl next to Miles glance over at him after she gave her answer. He smiled and flashed her a thumbs up. Grinning back at him, she glanced over her shoulder at Madison, flashing a smile at her, too. Madison noticed her short skirt and long, thin legs. Miles seemed to be checking her out, too.

I need to run more, Madison thought. *Maybe I can start doubling up on weekends.*

When the bell rang, Madison collected her books and headed toward the door. She noticed the same girl flirting with Miles as they walked side-by-side. Filtering into the hall, Miles turned and gave Madison his heart-melting smile. "See you at six-thirty," he said with a wink. And her world was good again.

Thankfully, Madison had no problem finding Lucy at lunch break. "Is that all you're eating?" her friend asked, gesturing to Madison's apple.

"Yeah. I had a big dinner last night."

Lucy shook her head. "You worry me sometimes."

Brushing aside her comment, Madison ventured, "I have a favor to ask."

"Okay. What?"

"I was wondering if Miles could pick me up at your house tonight for the game."

"Why?"

"Because my parents won't be home, and they don't want Miles to know the house will be empty." Madison hoped her voice sounded matter-of-fact and convincing. She wasn't used to lying to her friend.

"Okay. I'm sure that will be fine."

Relief mingled with a sense of guilt, which she promptly brushed aside. "Great! I'll tell my parents." In actuality, she'd just tell them Miles broke their date, and she was going with Lucy instead. That would take care of everything. Then she'd just need to make sure her parents didn't see Miles drop her off. She'd figure that out when the time came. For now, she knew she could go out without being embarrassed by her parents interrogating Miles.

When her mom got home from work, Madison approached her about the evening. "How was school?" she asked, hoping to make small talk first to get her mother off guard.

"It was fine. The kids were taking a test today, so it was pretty uneventful."

"No cheaters using their cell phones to text answers?" Madison asked, remembering a recent account her mother had shared about two girls sending each other answers on their phones.

"Nope. I collect all the phones now before the tests."

"Junior high," Madison replied knowingly.

Her mother smiled at her. "So tonight's the big date," she said. "What time is Miles picking you up?"

"Actually, the date's off. He wasn't feeling well at school, so he cancelled." Madison felt the knot in her stomach tighten.

"Oh, I'm sorry to hear that, honey." Her mother's sympathetic expression didn't help the guilt building inside Madison.

"It's no big deal. I'm going to the game, anyway," she replied. "Can you drop me at Lucy's around six? We're going with some of her friends."

"Sure. No problem. What about dinner? Are you eating here or at the game?"

"At the game." Madison was determined not to eat much dinner. With her stomach in such a knot, she might as well take advantage of her loss of appetite.

"Okay. I think I'll order pizza for the rest of us, then, and I can pick it up on the way home from dropping you off."

"Cool. Caleb will be happy about that," Madison replied.

"Yeah. Your brother could eat pizza every night and never get tired of it."

Impulsively, Madison reached out and hugged her mother. "You're a great mom," she said.

"Thanks! You're pretty great, yourself," her mother replied with a smile.

Madison put on her snuggest fitting jeans and a crewneck sweater, stuffing her off-the-shoulder top into her backpack before she grabbed her jacket. "Let's go, Mom," she called out as she hurried down the stairs.

Her mother came out of the kitchen with her purse slung over her shoulder. "Be right back, Steve," she said as she poked her head into his study. "Caleb's out shooting hoops."

"Is he finished with his homework?" Steve asked.

"Yeah."

"And you're picking up dinner?"

"I'm on it," Michelle replied. Then she turned to Madison. "Okay, I'm ready."

A few minutes later, they pulled up in front of the Johnson's house. "Am I picking you up here after the game?" Michelle asked.

"No. I have a ride home," Madison replied.

"Great. So we'll see you around ten?"

"I was thinking more like ten-thirty or eleven," Madison said. "Just in case the game goes longer. And that gives us time to hang out with our friends afterward."

"Okay. Eleven at the latest. Call me if that is a problem."

"I will." Madison patted the pocket of her backpack where she kept her cell phone.

Her mother watched her walk up to the front door and wave. Thankfully she drove away as soon as the door opened, so Madison didn't have to worry about any conversation happening between Lucy's mother and hers.

"Hi, Maddie," Logan said as he swung the door open wide. "Come on in. Lucy's in her room."

Madison quickly disappeared into her friend's bedroom before her mom showed up to greet her.

"Hi, Luce," she said as she walked in and sat on the bed.

"Hey," her friend replied casually. "So where are your parents going tonight?"

"Some dinner thing for dad's work."

Lucy nodded. "What's Caleb doing?"

"He's at a friend's house overnight." Madison's stomach clenched again. One lie kept leading to another. She hoped this date with Miles would be worth it. "Can you keep a secret?" she asked Lucy.

"Like what?"

"I wanted to wear my new sweater like we talked about, but I was afraid Mom would freak out, and we'd both end up being late. So I brought it in here." She patted her backpack. "I thought I'd just put it on before I leave."

Lucy smiled. "Your secret's safe with me. Just wear your jacket, so my mom doesn't say something to your mother."

Madison nodded. "Good plan." She pulled out her sweater and quickly changed tops, adjusting the shoulders just the way she wanted them. Then she pulled out her makeup bag and added more eyeliner and some glittery eye shadow. "What do you think?" she asked as she glanced at the full-length mirror.

"Perfect," Lucy replied. "Miles will love it."

Madison's phone beeped, and she pulled it out of the backpack. "I'd better go out front. He could be here any minute." She pulled on her jacket, closing it to conceal the revealing sweater underneath. Thankfully, Kelly was in the kitchen cooking when she slipped out the front door. "Tell your mom thanks for letting Miles pick me up here," she said to Lucy as she headed down to the curb. A black Honda was pulling up, and she could see Miles behind the wheel. *Yes! It worked!* she thought to herself, feeling elated to be off on a date with a guy who was starting to make her heart race.

Miles reached across the front seat and opened her door. "Hey, you're ready." He sounded surprised.

"Yep." She slid into the passenger seat and closed her door. As they pulled away, it suddenly felt awkward being alone with him. What would they talk about?

Miles must have been thinking the same thing. He reached over and flipped on the radio.

A few moments later, he asked, "Did you eat dinner?"

"No. I'm not that hungry," she replied. Then noticing his face drop a little, she added, "But I'm happy to stop somewhere."

He glanced over at her and smiled. "Great! Burgers sound good to me. Where's the closest drive-through?"

Madison gave him directions, and soon they had their order in hand.

"Wanna eat in the car?" he asked, tipping his head toward the adjoining parking lot. "Or at the game?"

"This is fine," she replied.

Miles slipped the car into one of the open spaces and shut it off. Madison pulled his two burgers and fries out of the bag on her lap and handed them to him, then got her small order of fries out. *There are probably a ton of calories in these,* she thought to herself, but that was the only food that sounded good to her with her stomach all tied in knots.

Miles shifted in his seat, turning toward her and leaning back against his door. "So tell me more about your family. I thought I might be meeting them tonight."

Madison looked over and tried to offer him a relaxed smile. "It wasn't a good night for that. Everyone was busy."

"Do you have any brothers or sisters?"

"Just one brother. He's eleven. Name's Caleb."

Miles nodded.

"How about you?" she asked.

"Nope. Just me and my mom. My dad split when I was seven."

Madison tried to imagine what it must be like to have only one parent and no siblings at all. "Do you miss him?" she asked.

"Who? My dad?"

"Yeah."

He looked away, gazing out the windshield, then down at his food. "Sometimes," he replied, taking another bite of his burger.

She took a deep breath. Should she ask more or let it drop? Maybe she'd better not pry.

Miles balled up the empty wrapper of his burger and fished the last of the fries from their paper pouch. "We'd better go." He reached for the bag on her lap and added his trash to it. They made eye contact, and Madison saw something in his eyes that she couldn't quite pinpoint. It was a longing of some kind. And it unnerved her a little.

She looked away, trying to maintain her composure. Something told her she was heading down a road that might lead to more than she bargained for. But Miles was so cute. And he seemed to really like her. She pushed away her discomfort, deciding all girls must feel this way on a first date.

After he pulled the car out of the parking lot, she remembered she'd covered up her favorite sweater with her coat. Sitting forward in the seat, she slipped off her jacket and tossed it on the back seat. Shifting her shoulders as subtly as she could, she lowered the neckline on the left side, revealing her black bra strap and bare skin.

Miles glanced over at her and smiled. "Nice sweater," he said.

"Thanks," she replied, a warm rush surging through her body. Then she felt something she'd never felt before—desirable. Physically desirable as a woman. And although it scared her a little, it also felt really good. Her nervousness began to melt away, replaced by a newfound rush of confidence and appeal. Why had she never felt this with Luke? *He's more like a brother to me,* she thought to herself.

Miles glanced over. "Almost there," he said.

As they walked into the stadium from the parking lot, she felt a chill. *Maybe I should have brought my coat,* she thought. But before she could say anything, Miles draped his arm over her and pulled her close. She could feel his hand guide the right side of her sweater off her shoulder, too.

"There," he said. Then he rested his hand on her bare skin. "Let me know if you get cold. We can go back to the car for your coat if you want it." He massaged the top of her shoulder slightly.

Madison could feel herself melting. Her body was responding to his touch in ways that thrilled her. She didn't care if she got cold. There was no way she was going to put that coat back on now. Leaning into him, she replied, "I'll be fine." Wrapping her arm around his waist, they walked past a group of girls he'd been talking to after class.

Several of them glanced over, and Madison could see the envy in a couple of their faces. She lifted her head a little higher and hugged Miles close. He looked down at her with a puzzled smile. "I think this night is going to be a good one," he said.

"Me, too," she replied, looking back over her shoulder to the group of girls, who were now elbowing each other and gesturing toward her and Miles.

Throughout the first half of the game, Madison sat close to Miles. They both had their feet up on the bleacher bench in front of them, and Miles was resting his hand on her knee. Sometimes as he leaned to watch a play, it would slip up her thigh, and she had to catch her breath to maintain her composure.

At half time, he suggested they go to the snack stand, taking her hand, as they climbed down the stairs and through the crowd in the tunnel. While they waited in line, he stood behind her, hugging her to his body. She relaxed back and tipped her head up, looking at him.

He smiled down, and then glanced away. But a moment later, she felt his hands slip under her sweater at her waist. "Mind if I warm up my hands while we wait?" he whispered in her ear, but his hands didn't feel cold to her.

"No problem," she replied as she once again melted under his touch.

After they got some popcorn and a large drink to share, he asked, "So how badly do you want to see the end of the game?"

She turned and looked at him. "I don't really care. Why?"

"I was thinking maybe we could go down by the beach and talk. Have our popcorn there. What do you think?" His voice seemed nonchalant.

Madison paused. Her parents would be livid if they found out. But how would they know? As long as she got home in time, it should be fine.

"Hey, we can stay here if you want," he said in response to her pause.

"No. The beach sounds good," she replied. "I'm not that into football anyway."

He laughed. "Yeah. Most girls aren't." He handed her the popcorn and held onto the drink. Then he draped his arm over her shoulder, and they headed out to the parking lot. As they walked, Madison noticed his limp hand occasionally tapping against her chest. At one point, he fingered her neckline, making some comment about how soft the sweater was.

The parking lot was full of cars but void of people. They navigated their way to Miles car, and he opened the passenger door for her. "Thanks," she said, grinning up at him as she sat down, placing the tub of popcorn on the floor by her feet. It was cold in the car, especially with Miles' body no longer up against hers. She wanted to pull her sweater up onto her shoulders, but that would ruin the look. Instead, she folded her arms across her chest, hugging herself for warmth.

"Cold?" he asked, as he climbed into the driver's seat.

"A little."

"We can fix that," he replied, starting the car and turning on the heater. Then he reached over and rubbed the top of her thigh with his hand. "Better?"

She nodded. "Thanks."

He smiled and turned on the radio. They drove in silence for a few minutes, and then pulled onto a street that led to the shore. It was a dead end, and Miles parked right near the sand, ignoring the no parking sign. Through the windshield, they could see the surf pounding in the moonlight.

"Wanna sit in here where it's warm?" he asked.

"Sure. That sounds good," she replied, leaning down and picking up the popcorn bucket.

Miles unlatched his seatbelt, and she followed suit, turning to face him as she held out the popcorn. He took a handful and ate it, as she picked out a couple of popped kernels at a time. While they enjoyed the salty treat and shared their drink, Miles asked her more questions about her family.

Madison soon found herself explaining about the five-year gap in age between her and Caleb.

"So your brother is adopted?" he asked.

"Yeah."

"Cool."

She nodded. "I think I'd like to adopt a kid when I grow up." As soon as the words were out of her mouth, she silently began chastising herself. *When I grow up? Really? You sound like a little kid,* she thought.

But Miles didn't seem to think anything of it. "That's cool," was his only reply.

When they were halfway through the popcorn, there was a lull in their conversation, and Miles picked up a kernel and tossed it toward her mouth, saying "Catch!" She didn't have time to react before it fell down inside of her sweater.

"Oops, sorry about that," he said with a grin. "Now where did that little bugger go?" he asked innocently, searching in her lap and the seat around her. "Uh oh," he said innocently. "I think I know where it is."

"Oh you do, do you?"

"Yeah." He leaned over and lifted the bottom of her sweater. Out fell the kernel. He snatched it up. "Got it!" he said.

She laughed and threw a piece at him. Amazingly, he caught it with his mouth. "Wanna know where it is?" he asked. Before she could answer, he leaned toward her. "Here, I'll give it to you." He kissed her, parting her lips with his tongue and slipping the popcorn kernel from his mouth to hers.

"Whoa," she replied, so impressed by the trick that she didn't even mind his forwardness.

"Toss me another one," he said, repeating the same trick again. But this time, he didn't pull away from her after the kiss. Instead, he leaned into it, and so did she. One kiss led to another, and soon Madison felt her heart starting to race a little.

"Got any more popcorn up here?" he asked in a throaty whisper as he worked his hand up her sweater, fingering her bra.

Madison didn't know what to do. Her mind said stop but her body yearned for more. A knock on the window startled them both. Miles pulled away, and they both looked out the driver's window. An older man was standing there.

Miles lowered the window.

"Would you guys mind taking it somewhere else?" the guy asked. "You're blocking my driveway, and I need to pull out."

"Uh, sure. Sorry about that," Miles said. He started the motor and pulled his seatbelt back on. Madison adjusted her clothes and belted herself in, too. As they drove off, she pulled out her cell phone and checked the time. 10:45.

"I'd better get home," she said. "My parents are expecting me by eleven."

He pulled over to the curb. "Are you sure? Maybe you could call them and say the game is running late."

She didn't want to sound like she was still under her parents' thumb at sixteen, but she also didn't want to raise any questions that might lead to them discovering her deception. "I'm kind of tired, anyway," she lied. "It's been fun, though," she added with a smile.

"Yeah," he replied, pulling her close for one last lingering kiss. "We'll have to do this again soon."

As they drove up to the front of her house Madison said, "You can just drop me here. My parents are probably getting ready for bed."

"Okay," he replied.

She unlatched her seatbelt and reached over to retrieve her coat from the backseat. "So you have my number," she said.

"Yeah." He didn't say whether or not he'd call her over the weekend, and she wanted to get into the house as quickly as she could, just in case her dad peered out the window and saw an unfamiliar car.

"Well, I'd better get inside."

He nodded. "See you Monday."

Her heart sank a little, but she tried to sound casual. "Sure. Monday." She started to open the door.

"No goodbye kiss?" he asked.

"Oops. Yeah. Of course," she replied, leaning over and giving him a quick kiss then pulling away before it could lead to another.

Miles looked disappointed. "Bye," he said.

She got out of the car and leaned back in. "Bye. Thanks for tonight. I had fun."

He nodded and gave her a half-hearted smile. "Me, too."

Then she closed the door and hurried inside. Her father was sitting in the front room. "Have a good time, honey?"

"Yeah."

"How's Lucy? Did you girls meet up with her friends from school?"

Madison walked past him toward the stairs. "Yeah."

"You're not very talkative tonight," he observed.

She turned and forced a casual smile. "Sorry, Dad. I'm just a little tired."

"Okay. Goodnight, princess."

She cringed inwardly. "Goodnight, Dad."

CHAPTER NINE

Miles didn't call all weekend, although Madison kept her phone nearby at all times, checking it numerous times a day, even during her long runs. She could hardly wait for Monday's history class, replaying over and over in her mind how the other girls had looked at her so enviously at the game. This was going to be her year. The year she finally became someone.

She got to history class early on Monday, but Miles' desk was empty. He slipped into the room at the very last minute, talking and laughing with one of the girls they'd seen at the game. As he slid into his seat, he turned and smiled at her.

Her heart leapt in her chest, and she smiled back. He'd probably put his arm around her as they walked out, right? Just like at the game. Not wanting to embarrass herself again if the teacher called on her, she flipped open her notes and tried to focus. Having Miles in her peripheral vision didn't help. But if he sat behind her, that would probably be just as bad. Then she'd be tempted to turn around all the time.

Mr. Barnes launched into his discussion of the Constitutional Congress, and Madison decided to volunteer an answer before he could call on her. He seemed impressed with her response, and Miles turned and gave her a thumbs up.

"Did you have something to contribute to what Madison just said?" their teacher asked him.

"Nope. She hit it on the head," he replied.

After class, the same girl he'd been talking to on the way in started walking beside him and asking him something. Madison moved to his other side but had to back off when they got to the door, which would only allow two people through at a time. She was a little disappointed that he didn't wait and walk through with her. Once they were out in the crowded hall, he looked over his shoulder and tipped his head to the side to indicate she should come alongside him.

Moving next to him, she felt a rush go through her body again.

He looked down at her and said, "How was your weekend?"

"Good. How about yours?"

"Fine," he replied without putting his arm around her or taking her hand.

When they got to his locker, he turned to her and said, "Have a good one. See you tomorrow."

She felt confused and rejected, even though he'd at least wanted her to walk with him. Her face must have shown it, because he asked, "Are you okay?"

Nodding, she turned to head for her locker. "See ya," she said over her shoulder.

As she walked away, she felt a hand on her shoulder. Turning she found herself looking into his face. "Hey, are you upset that I didn't call you this weekend?"

She shrugged.

He leaned down and kissed her. "Sorry about that. I'll call you tonight."

Her heart raced and her spirit soared. She couldn't believe he just kissed her right there in the hall where everyone could see it. He must like her after all. "Okay," she replied with a smile. "Talk to you then."

He studied her for a moment. "You should get more sweaters like the one you wore to the game," he said with a wink.

She just grinned. *I think I will,* she promised herself silently, planning on how she could always change her top once she got to school.

After dinner, Madison went up to her room to wait for his call. She worked on homework, answered some emails, got ready for bed, and spent a half hour on Facebook before he finally called at ten.

He sounded down, apologizing for calling so late.

"No big deal," she replied. "Is everything okay?"

"Yeah. I'm just a little worried about my Mom."

Madison's heart swelled. What a sweet guy to be worrying about his mother like that. "Why?" she asked.

"She's been going through pictures of my dad again. She does this every year around their anniversary."

Madison didn't know what to say. "She must miss him."

"Yeah."

The phone was silent for a moment then he said, "I'm not much in the mood for talking."

"Okay," she replied. "I understand. Well, I'll see you tomorrow."

"Yeah. Bye."

As she put the phone on the nightstand, she found herself praying for Miles and his mother. A thought came to her —maybe she should invite them to church. But first, she should probably figure out a way to talk to her parents about him again.

Her mind flashed to their date and the popcorn game, and she felt conflicted. Time alone with Miles was her first priority, but then once they were established as a couple, she'd figure out how to introduce him to her mom and dad.

"Want a ride home from school today?" Miles asked her after class on Tuesday.

"Uh, yeah! Sure," she replied. Since her mother and brother didn't get home for at least an hour after she did, it would give them a little time alone together. *Remember what Amber told you,* a voice within said. She flashed to a warning Caleb's birthmother had given her when she'd been out to visit a couple of years ago. She'd told Madison about how she and her boyfriend, Caleb's father, had spent a lot of time alone together at the beach after school. That was where Caleb had been conceived.

I'm not Amber, Madison thought to herself. *I'm not going to do something stupid like that.*

"I'll meet you in the parking lot," Miles said. "Right after sixth period."

She nodded and smiled. "See you then."

He didn't kiss her this time before walking away, but he did look over his shoulder and give her a big smile.

The next period seemed to drag on forever. Finally the last bell rang, and the halls filled with students eager to vacate the premises. Madison made a quick stop at her locker and then headed out to the parking lot. Searching for his car, she spotted Miles in the far corner of the lot, talking to some guy. As she approached them, the guy took off.

"There you are," Miles said.

"Sorry. I had to stop at my locker," she replied.

"No problem." He clicked the key fob to unlock all the doors but didn't come around to her side to open hers. "Wanna stop for something to eat?" he asked.

"Whatever you want to do is fine with me." She noticed she was starting to feel more at ease with him, more confident of their new relationship. After all, hadn't he confided in her about his mom? He must feel pretty safe with her. And she felt safe with him, too.

"Let's go get some ice cream," he suggested.

Madison remembered a new place beside Jessie's that had lots of flavors. She could look at some clothes while they were there. But she'd have to keep track of her time. She gave Miles the directions, and they headed over.

"Rum and coke, now that sounds good," he said with a grin as they perused the various ice cream flavors.

They each sampled several, and then Madison asked if she could just have a couple of bites of whatever flavor he chose. "I'm not that hungry," she explained, thinking again about how she'd normally be running right now, not eating something fattening like ice cream.

"Sure," he replied, ordering a double scoop cone of the rum and coke.

It was funny to think that just a couple of weeks ago, she would have felt really awkward licking off of someone else's cone, especially a guy's. But after Friday night, it seemed like just one more way to solidify their relationship as boyfriend and girlfriend. She only took a few licks as they walked toward Jessie's. Then she boldly took his hand and led him over to the window of mannequins.

"This is one of my favorite stores," she said.

Miles studied the frozen models. "I like that black top," he said, pointing to a low cut clingy tank. "And those shorts," he added.

Madison's eyes followed his to a mannequin wearing black short shorts. She nodded. "Cute. I like those, too."

"You should get them," he replied. "They'd look good on you."

She felt herself flush. Looking away, she said, "Thanks."

Her phone buzzed and she pulled it out of her purse. There was a text from her mother. *I'll be home a little late today. Meeting with my department. Dad's picking up Caleb at Kelly and Ben's on his way home.*

Madison texted her mom back and then dropped the phone into her purse. *Perfect. Now she wouldn't have to hurry home.*

"Everything okay?" Miles asked.

"Yeah. My mom's just running late today."

He nodded. "Want to go to your house? Or we could go to the beach if you want."

She thought about it for a minute. "Let's go to my place so I can change. Then we can go to the beach."

"Sounds good," he replied, draping one arm over her shoulder as they walked out to the car.

Madison was a little nervous about him being at her house, but she really wanted to change into one of her other new tops and some shorter shorts her mother wouldn't let her wear to school.

She unlocked the front door and called out, "Anyone home?" just to make sure they were alone.

Silence.

They walked into the living room and Madison said, "I'll be right down."

"Need any help changing?" he asked her with a grin.

She looked at him with a smile and shook her head. "I think I can manage."

"Just asking," he replied, holding his hands up in surrender.

She hurried up the stairs, went into her room, and changed. Checking her image in the mirror, she hoped her legs didn't look too fat. The shorts rode up pretty high in the back, so she adjusted her underwear to make sure it wouldn't show. She'd bought a low cut tank similar to the one they saw at the mall, so she pulled that out and put it on. Then she grabbed an off-the-shoulder sweatshirt she

110

could layer over it if she got cold down at the beach. Pulling her cell phone out of her purse, she headed downstairs.

I should take my running shoes, she thought. *That way if Mom or Dad are home when we get back, I can tell them I was out running.* She retrieved the shoes from the bottom step where her mother had put them the day before.

"Okay, I'm ready," she told Miles, who was still standing where she'd left him.

"Planning on going running?" he asked.

She hesitated before answering. "I'd rather not answer a bunch of questions if we get back after my parents do. I'll just tell them I've been out running. You know how parents can be," she added. "They're pretty old-fashioned about knowing where I am all the time."

"Got it," he replied, adding, "Nice outfit."

"Thanks." She grinned. It felt so good to be appreciated. And he didn't seem to notice her fat legs.

The beach was empty when they got there. Miles led her by the hand as they walked to a wide stretch of sand and sat down. "What's this?" he asked, reaching over and fingering the silver ring on the chain around her neck.

"Oh, it's just something my great grandfather left for me when he died," she replied. "Actually, he gave it to my dad to give to me. We went out on a special date when I was twelve and he gave it to me then." She flashed on a memory of her father taking her out to dinner giving her the purity ring, all wrapped up in a pretty box. She'd worn it on her finger for a while, but then she decided she liked it better on a chain.

"Cool," Miles said, placing it gently back in place on her chest. Gazing out to sea, he rested his elbows on his raised knees. Then he clasped his knees with his hands and leaned back, lowering himself to the sand. Madison looked over at him lying there beside her. He grinned up at her. "It's warmer down here," he said, patting his chest to indicate a pillow for her head.

She scooted down in the sand and stretched out beside him, following his lead by resting her head on his chest. He pulled her body close, and they lay there quietly for a few minutes, his heart beating in her ear. "This is nice," he said.

She nodded. "Yeah."

Everything seemed just perfect. The sound of the waves, the warmth of the sand, and the rhythm of their breathing in harmony. Madison felt happier than she remembered feeling in a long time. And to think how upset she'd been when Luke left. Everyone was right. That had just been puppy love. This was different. The way Miles touched her and kissed her. It was the way a real boyfriend acted.

"What are you thinking about?" he asked her.

She smiled to herself. "Nothing. How about you?"

He shifted onto his side, stealing her pillow away. Leaning over, he kissed her. "I was thinking how glad I am that we moved here." Before she could respond, he kissed her again, wrapping both arms around her and pulling her body tightly up against his. She melted into him and didn't resist when he reached his hand up under the back of her tank top and unhooked her bra.

As they drove to her house an hour later, Madison reminded herself about the running shoes. She made sure her clothes were all in place. Although she felt a little guilty about how physical she and Miles were getting, she knew her limits and was not about to get herself in too deep. Miles seemed fine with it when she'd pushed his hands away from trying to open her shorts. Now he knew what she would and would not let him do.

She could see her mom's van in the driveway, as they turned onto her street. "Why don't you pull over here," she said, pointing to the curb half a block from the house.

"Got it."

She reached over the seat, grabbed her running shoes, and put them on. "See you tomorrow," she said, leaning over to kiss him goodbye, and completely forgetting about her sweatshirt. Getting out of the car, she closed the door and waved as he drove off. Then she jogged toward the house, thinking about how she'd manage to get a real run in that day. *Maybe I'll ask Dad to go with me. He's been wanting us to run together.*

As she opened the door, she called out, "Mom?"

"In here, honey," her mother's voice replied from the kitchen.

Madison mussed her hair a little and then walked in. "How was your day?" she asked.

Her mother was sorting the mail. "Fine," she replied. "Been out running?"

"Yeah. I did a short run, but I'm going to see if Dad will run with me after dinner, too."

Her mother looked at her and smiled. "He'd like that."

"When's dinner?" Madison asked.

"Dad's picking up tacos after he gets Caleb. Probably around six-thirty." Her mother's face lit up. "Hey! There's a letter for you from Luke." She handed Madison the envelope.

"Cool. Thanks." Madison headed out of the room. "I'll be upstairs doing homework."

Her mother nodded. "Okay. I'm making chocolate chip cookies for dessert," she added.

"Great. The guys will be happy about that," Maddie replied. Up in her bedroom, she stretched out on the bed with Luke's letter.

Hi Maddie,

So how's life at SCHS? Hope you like Mr. Barnes. Great discussions, huh? Most of his tests will come from those, so be sure you pay attention. The book's a guide, but Barnes always talks about the stuff that matters in his opinion. If you're ever absent, be sure you get good notes from someone. Hopefully you've got some friends in there.

Madison smiled, thinking about Miles. Not exactly what Luke probably had in mind, especially since Miles was more of a distraction than a help, at least as far as class discussions went. She glanced back at the letter. A couple of weeks ago, just the sight of Luke's handwriting would have made her happy. Now she had to keep pulling her thoughts back to him rather than to the images of Miles that Luke's comments about her history class evoked.

Things are good here in the Ozarks. ☺ Not sure if I'll ever get used to that name, though. Sounds like I'm out in the backwoods of nowhere. But it really is nice here and not at all backwoods, if you know what I mean. My roommate's pretty cool. We've got a couple of classes together, so that helps with studying for tests etc. My favorite class is global missions. The professor's been all over the world with various missionary teams. He's really an inspiration. Makes me want to consider the mission field.

Great, Madison thought. As if Missouri wasn't far away enough. Now he was talking about going to some remote country as a missionary. She could never see herself doing that. Miles was more her speed. He loved Sandy Cove, and so did she. Glancing back at the piece of paper, she was about to gloss over the rest, when she read:

So I was talking to Lucy tonight, and she told me you had a date for the football game. Some new guy, she said. Hope you two had a good time. Write me back and tell me about him.

Really? Like she was going to write to Luke about Miles. Not. *Well, let's see how he finishes off this letter,* she thought, her eyes traveling to the bottom of the page.

I miss you. Seems like a long time until Christmas break. But I'll be pretty busy this quarter, so I'm sure it'll go by fast. Tell everyone I said hi. Can't believe Caleb is in middle school now. Must be easier for your mom, though, just taking him to school with her.

Okay, well I've gotta run. Take care, Mad.

Yours,
Luke

She read through the letter one more time, looking for hints of his feelings about her. But all she saw was the brotherly affection she'd kind of figured was the case. No worries. Her focus was on Miles now, anyway. *Luke will probably find a girl out there, too,* she thought.

Pulling out her notebook, she tossed the letter aside and looked for the discussion homework questions for history. She was just about to begin working on them when her mother called from downstairs. "There's someone here to see you, Maddie."

Wonder who that could be? She pushed aside her backpack and headed down. Standing in the entryway was Miles, her sweatshirt in his hand.

CHAPTER TEN

"Your friend was just telling me about how much he enjoyed your date Friday night," Michelle said.

Madison cringed inwardly but tried to maintain her composure. "Well, it wasn't exactly a date, Mom. We just sat together at the game."

Miles must have read her signals because he piped in with, "Yeah. Just warming the bleachers with a bunch of friends."

Madison's mother studied her face.

"You left this in my car," he said, handing her the sweatshirt.

"Miles gave me a ride home today," Madison quickly explained.

"I see," Michelle replied. Then turning to Miles, she said, "That was nice of you."

"No problem," he said with a nervous smile.

Michelle nodded. "Well, I'd better go check on my cookies," she said. "Do you like chocolate chip? You could stay for dinner if you'd like."

"Thanks, but I'd better get going," he replied.

A wave of relief washed over Madison. "I'll just walk Miles out to the car, and then come set the table," she told her mother.

Once they were outside, Miles said, "Guess you didn't tell your parents about our date the other night."

She gave him a coy smile. "I was just trying to spare you the third degree from my dad. He's pretty paranoid about me dating."

He nodded and returned her smile, his eyes caressing her form. "I can see why."

Madison blushed. Pushing him away playfully, she said, "I'll see you tomorrow." Holding up the sweatshirt, she added, "Thanks for bringing this by."

"Sure. Anytime." He grabbed her hand and pulled her close, locking his lips on hers.

She started to pull away, but found herself kissing him back instead.

"Mom, some guy's out front playing tonsil hockey with Maddie," Caleb called from the front room.

"What?" Michelle asked as she turned off the oven.

"They're making out," Caleb replied.

Making out? Michelle headed out to join her son. "Who's making out?"

"Maddie and some guy."

Michelle looked out the window. Madison and Miles were standing close to each other by his car door. "They're not making out," she said, feeling relieved.

"They were a second ago," he replied. "Wait 'til I tell Dad about *this*," he added with a grin as he bounded toward the stairs.

"Hold it buddy," Michelle said, cuffing him. "I'll handle talking to your father. Got it?" she asked, making sure he made eye contact with her and understood that she was serious.

His smile faded as he mumbled in reply, "Got it."

When Madison came back inside, Michelle was waiting. "We need to talk," she said.

"Okay. About what?" Madison wore an innocent look.

"About Miles. And exactly what is going on between you two."

"We're just friends, Mom."

Michelle sighed. When did Madison start lying to her? "Caleb saw you kissing just now."

Her daughter's face flamed. "What business does he have spying on me?" she asked furiously.

"It won't work, Madison."

"What won't work?"

"Trying to shift the focus to your brother. He was walking through the living room and saw you right there." Michelle pointed to the window with the open blinds. "Before you say anything else, let's get a few things straight. First, I understand what it's like to be attracted to a guy. And wanting to go out on dates is part of being in high school." She took a breath and then continued, "I'm not mad that you like this guy. I have nothing against him. Yet. But I don't like lying, and I have a feeling you haven't told me everything about Friday night and the game." She paused, waiting for Madison to answer.

"Okay, so maybe it was a date," she admitted. "But I didn't know if I'd even like him, and I didn't want Dad grilling him with questions before I even got a chance to find that out."

"How did you get to the game?" Michelle asked. "And don't lie."

"I had Miles pick me up at Kelly and Ben's."

"Did they know you were going on a date? I can't imagine Kelly not calling me to check to make sure it was okay."

Madison hesitated.

"You might as well tell me, honey. I can easily call them and find out," Michelle warned.

"Alright, alright. I'll tell you. Just don't get Lucy in trouble. She didn't know. I told her you guys were out for the evening, and so you wanted my date to pick me up at their house. Like you didn't want him to know I was home alone. That's what Lucy told her parents."

"And Kelly didn't ask you to bring him inside to meet them?"

"No. She didn't have a chance. I went outside while she was fixing dinner and met Miles at the curb when he pulled up."

Michelle studied Madison, searching for the truth and looking for the girl she used to trust.

"Why are you staring at me like that?" her daughter asked.

"This just doesn't seem like you, Madison. You've always been honest with me in the past. At least I think you have."

Madison sighed, looking her in the eye. Michelle could tell her daughter was on the verge of tears. "I really like this guy, Mom. And amazingly enough, he likes me too. Please don't mess this up for me."

Michelle's heart ached. She could remember the thrill of young love, and she wanted Madison to be happy. It seemed like Maddie struggled so much with her body image and confidence, and the attention this Miles guy was giving her probably made her feel attractive. But Michelle didn't want her daughter getting her sense of worth from some high school boy who was here today but could be easily gone tomorrow.

As if reading her thoughts, Madison said, "Miles really cares about me. He makes me feel special. Like I'm attractive."

"You are attractive, sweetheart," Michelle replied.

Madison laughed half-heartedly. "To you and Dad, maybe. But not to the guys. At least not until now."

"What about Luke? He's always had an eye for you."

Maddie shook her head. "As a sister, maybe, but not as a girlfriend."

"I think you've misread him, honey. You two have a special bond, and he's a great guy."

"Whatever. But he's gone now, and Miles is here." Madison paused and then asked, "So can I go out with him now without having to make up stories and sneak around?"

"Let us get to know him a little, and then we'll decide," Michelle said. "But for now, let's say no alone time together. And no more lies."

"Are you going to tell Dad everything?"

"Yes."

"He'll probably blow a gasket about Friday night and never let me see Miles again."

"I can't promise you anything, Madison, but I'll talk to him and try to get him to give your friend a chance. No guarantees there won't be consequences for the lying, though."

"Miles didn't know about that, if it helps anything."

"I'm glad to hear that much at least," Michelle replied. She put her hands on Madison's shoulders. "Your dad and I love you, honey. We want you to be happy. But we want you to be safe, too."

Madison nodded.

"Your father and I will discuss all this tonight, and we'll let you know what we decide. For now, let's just get the table set so we're ready for dinner when he gets home."

"Okay."

They embraced, and Michelle hoped her daughter could feel the love going from her mother's heart to her own.

Michelle peered over her raised coffee mug at her husband, who was busy on his laptop. "Steve?"

No answer.

She cleared her throat. "Honey?"

"Yeah?" he replied without glancing her way, his fingers still tapping at the keyboard.

"Sorry to interrupt, but we need to talk about Maddie again."

Pausing, he looked up. "Okay, hold on a sec." He typed for a moment longer and then closed the laptop. "What's up?"

"She lied to us about the football game."

"There wasn't a game?"

"Oh, there was a game alright, but she didn't go with Lucy."

Now Steve looked as concerned as she felt. "Not that guy she was telling us about."

Michelle nodded. "Yeah."

He shook his head. "Why wouldn't she just be up front with us? She must think we wouldn't approve of him."

"She claims she didn't want the third degree from us before she even got a chance to get to know him a little more herself."

"Really. Well, now she's backed herself into a corner where it's going to be even harder to spend any time with him," he replied.

Michelle searched for the right words. "Go ahead. Tell me what you're thinking."

"I'm suggesting our daughter lose her freedom for a few weeks. Maybe then she'll think twice before lying about her whereabouts and companions." He paused and then asked, "How did you find out about all this?"

Michelle took a moment to figure out how to tell Steve. "Actually, the boy, Miles is his name, anyway he came by here to return her sweatshirt. Apparently she left it in his car."

"Great. I wonder what else she left in his car," he muttered under his breath, standing up and thrusting his hands into his pockets. Although he looked pretty angry, she could tell he was also hurt and worried.

"Come here," she said, patting the seat on the sofa beside where she was sitting.

He looked at her and shook his head. "I'm going up to talk to that girl."

"No you're not. Not like this," she replied. "Sit down with me and let's discuss it together. The last thing we want to do is push her to the point where she's sneaking behind our backs all the time."

"How do we know she's not already doing that?"

Michelle sighed. "You know Madison, Steve. She's not a bad kid. She just wants what most girls her age want—a guy who likes her and wants to go out with her."

"I get that. But I was that guy in high school, and I know what those guys are looking for. Ask Ben. He'll tell you."

"I know all about Ben, honey. But just because he was a womanizer before he got saved, doesn't mean this Miles guy is, too. We don't really know anything about him."

"My point exactly. That's why we required her to bring any potential dates here first. So we could meet them. We've got a responsibility to protect her, not be her pals." His tone was almost patronizing, and Michelle had to fight the urge to snap back at him.

"You're right," she said softly. "But can we please just talk about this before you go upstairs to confront Maddie?"

He studied her face, and she could see the hard edges on his soften. "Okay, babe." Walking over, he sat down by her side, turning so that he was facing her. "What do *you* think we should do?"

"I don't know. Probably grounding her for a couple of weeks is a good idea. But I also think we should talk her through this calmly. You know, try to help her see our perspective." She hesitated and then continued, "We've

123

always been able to talk to her in the past. I don't want to lose that."

He nodded. "Me neither. But I want her to understand that sneaking around and lying isn't going to get her what she wants."

"What if we told her Miles was welcome to come over here, even while she's grounded—when we're home, that is. Maybe even encourage her to invite him to some youth group stuff at church?"

"Fine by me," he replied. "It would be interesting to see if he'd come over. Plus, we want her dating guys who are Christians, so the youth group idea would be a good test for where he stands spiritually. But I've got to say, I doubt if he's a Christian, especially since he was good with taking her out without meeting us."

"Well, that might actually be Madison's fault, not his. She told him he needed to pick her up at Lucy's because you and I were out for the evening."

"Great. One lie leads to another," he said.

She nodded. "Yeah. Isn't that the way it always is?"

"So how long do you think we should ground her for? How about three weeks?"

"Three weeks sounds reasonable to me."

Steve slapped his hands down on his knees. "Okay. I'll go talk to her." He stood up, then bent down and kissed her. "It all begins," he said, and Michelle smiled in return. The teens had started smoothly with their daughter, but clearly this year was going to be tougher.

"Want me to go with you?" she asked.

"No. Let me try talking to her first from a guy's perspective. I don't want her playing on your sympathies with those sad eyes of hers."

She smiled. "Okay. Go for it. I'll be down here praying."

"Thanks, babe," he replied with a smile.

Twenty minutes later, he reappeared.

124

"How'd it go?" she asked.

He looked weary. "Fine, I guess. She seemed pretty defensive, but hopefully she understood what I was trying to tell her. And she definitely knows lying is out."

"Did she say anything about having him come over here while we're home?"

"She said she'd think about it."

"What about the youth group idea?" Michelle asked.

He shrugged. "She didn't seem too hot on that. She's been resisting youth group herself lately, so it didn't really surprise me."

"I know. Ever since Luke left, she's pretty much lost interest in it," she replied. "I'll try talking to her, too. Maybe I can get her to give it another try. What about the concert the youth group is going to this coming weekend? We'd told her she could go if she wanted. Maybe we should make an exception on the grounding. Just for that event, that is."

Steve nodded. "Good idea." He paused and then added, "We need to pray, honey. I think we've got a battle ahead this year." Sitting down again by her side, he took her hand in his and together they prayed for wisdom and strength to be the kind of parents who held fast to what they knew was right while still showing unconditional love.

"Sometimes I see how Grandpa rubbed off on you," Michelle said.

"Now that's about the best thing I've heard all day," he replied with a warm smile as he drew her into his arms.

When Miles asked Madison about going with him to the next football game that coming Friday, she explained that she was grounded. "Bummer," he replied. "What happened?"

"I didn't do something they wanted me to do," she said, telling a half-truth. "You can still come over," she added. "I just can't go anywhere for three weeks."

"Okay. Want a ride home?" he asked.

She thought for a minute. Her mom never got home before four o'clock. That gave her an hour and a half after school let out. "Sure," she replied. Maybe she could talk to him about the youth group concert at the same time.

"Cool. Meet you in the parking lot," he said, as he walked away.

While they drove to her house that afternoon, she said, "So this morning, my mom was saying that even though I'm grounded, I can go to the church youth group concert thing next weekend if I want to. Would you want to go?"

"What is it?"

"It's a couple of Christian bands playing at the college. Our church is taking the youth group for pizza first and then over to the concert."

"Oh." He didn't seem impressed.

"No problem if you don't want to go."

"It's not really my thing," he said. "Church, I mean."

She nodded. "Okay. Just thought I'd ask."

He reached over and put his hand on her thigh. "Wanna stop for ice cream?" he asked, clearly changing the subject.

"I'm not really that hungry. But if you want to, it's fine with me." She smiled reassuringly.

"Got any food at your house?"

"Yeah. My brother's an empty pit when it comes to food, so we always keep tons of stuff around. We could just go straight there and have something."

"Sounds good to me," he replied, giving her leg a squeeze.

After having a snack, they wandered into the living room. "You guys have a pretty big house," Miles said, glancing up the stairs.

"Yeah," she replied. "Wanna see the rest of it?"

"Sure."

She took him upstairs, a feeling of forbidden pleasure surging through her. When she and Luke were kids, he'd been in her room a few times, but she'd never had any other guy even come to her house. Thankfully she'd picked up her room the night before, so she didn't have to worry about what might be on the floor, like underwear.

Miles just glanced into her parents' room but walked freely into Caleb's. "So this is your brother?" he asked, pointing to a picture on the bookcase.

"Yeah. That's him."

"Cute kid." He looked around the rest of the room. "He's into sports," he observed.

"Yep."

Miles nodded as he studied the posters on the walls. "So where's your room?"

"Right down here," she said, leading him out into the hall and pointing to the end.

He followed her through the door into her sanctuary. "I've never been in a girl's room before," he said with an awkward smile.

"What do you think?" she asked, gesturing to the décor.

"I like it," he said. He sat down on the edge of her bed, and Madison suddenly felt very nervous. She knew her parents would freak out if they could see what was happening.

"Come here," he said, patting his knee for her to sit down.

She didn't want him to know she was suddenly feeling uneasy. *It's fine*, she told herself as she sat down on his lap. She'd have to figure out a way to get him out of the house by the time her mother got home. Then everything would be okay.

"Sometime I'll have to show you my room," he said. "It doesn't look anything like this. In fact, it's pretty hard to find the floor in there. You might say I could be a little neater."

She laughed, starting to relax a little.

He looked at her and said, "I could just kiss you right now."

"Go ahead," she replied.

As their lips met, she immediately felt her body beginning to respond.

Get out of there! A voice in her head urged. But she had a hard time pulling away. As Miles' hand began to move over her body, she heard a sound that broke the spell. It was the garage door opening.

CHAPTER ELEVEN

Madison dragged Miles by the hand down the stairs as quickly as she could make her feet move. She heard her mother and Caleb's voices in the kitchen. Catching her breath, she smoothed her clothing and released her hold on her boyfriend right before Michelle walked into the room.

"Hi, Mom," she blurted out.

Her mother glared at her. Then she turned her attention to Miles. "Can I have a moment with my daughter, please?" She walked over and opened the front door, gesturing to the porch.

"Sure thing," he replied, glancing at Madison with a questioning look before walking outside.

Michelle turned to face her. "I thought we had an understanding," she said.

"We do. Miles got here right before you did," Madison replied. "Remember, you said he could come over here."

"When *we* are home," Michelle replied emphatically.

"So I should have left him waiting outside until you pulled in?" she asked defensively.

"Yes. Or asked him to come back later."

Madison sighed. "Fine. Do you want me to send him home now?"

Her mother stared at her.

"What?"

Michelle gave her a disappointed look and shook her head. "I feel like I don't even know you anymore, Madison. Sneaking around behind our back, and your attitude. What's up?"

She felt herself starting to crumble, hating how her relationship with her mother was so strained now. If her parents weren't so outdated and overboard about the whole dating thing, none of this would have happened. But how could she risk losing what was happening with Miles? He made her feel like she was as pretty as the other girls— the popular girls—at school. Although she wanted to just sit down and cry and make things right with her mother, Miles was right outside the front door waiting for her.

"I'm sorry, Mom. I promise no more sneaking around." She watched her mother's expression and was relieved to see it soften.

"Okay," Michelle replied, stroking Madison's arm and then clasping her hand.

"So can he stay?"

She nodded. "I guess. Would you like to invite him for dinner?"

Madison hesitated. That seemed like it would be pretty awkward. But she knew her dad would have to meet Miles if she had any chance of really dating him. "Uh, yeah, sure."

"Alright. Good," her mother replied.

Madison gave her a hug. "Guess I'd better go out and get him." She found Miles sitting on the porch step, elbows on his knees studying the cell phone in his hands. "You can come in now," she said.

He looked up and smiled at her. "Everything okay?"

"Yeah. In fact, my mom suggested I invite you to stay for dinner."

"Really? Cool. I'll text my mom." He glanced back down at his phone and sent a message. "So what do you want to do until we eat?" he asked.

130

She hadn't thought of that. Now that her mother and Caleb were home, it was a little awkward being with him at the house. "How about watching something on television?" she suggested.

"Okay." He stood, following her back into the house. Madison flipped on the TV, and they watched an old rerun of a sitcom. "Maybe I'll do some homework while we watch," she said, unzipping her backpack that was beside the couch on the floor. "Want to do our history questions?"

"Sure. Be right back." He went out to the car and got his notebook.

By the time they'd finished, Steve was pulling into the driveway. He came in through the front door and looked surprised to see Miles there. Madison introduced him. "Mom said he could stay for dinner."

"Looks like you've been doing homework together," he observed.

"Yeah, history," Miles replied.

Madison noticed her father studying Miles. She cleared her throat to get his attention and shot him a pleading look.

"Well, I'd better see if your mom needs any help in the kitchen," he said. "Nice to meet you, Miles. I'm glad you're staying for dinner."

After he'd left the room, Miles said, "Are you sure this is a good idea? My staying, I mean? Your dad seemed a little...I don't know, not thrilled about it."

Madison winced inside. She'd picked up the same vibes from her father. Why did parents have to be so impossible about everything? "It'll be fine," she said, hoping she sounded more convincing than she felt.

As they sat down for dinner, she could tell Miles was a little nervous. Especially when everyone joined hands before her father prayed over the meal. The only redeeming part was that he kept holding her hand for an extra second or two after the prayer was over.

"So tell us a little about yourself," Steve said, his eyes on Miles.

"Well, my mom and I just moved here from Texas. We live in the apartments over on Second Street," he said.

"Do you have any brothers or sisters?" Caleb asked.

"Nope. Just me."

Madison's brother nodded. "Oh."

There was an awkward silence for a few moments as everyone started eating. Then Michelle asked, "Does your mother work?"

"Not right now. But she's looking for a job."

"What kind of work does she do?" Steve asked.

"She's a bartender. And she's done some waitressing. But bartending pays better," he replied.

Madison felt her stomach tighten. Probably not the best conversation to impress her parents. "Miles loves Sandy Cove, don't you?" she said, changing the subject.

He nodded. "Yeah. It's a really pretty town. And I love the beach," he added, glancing over at Madison and smiling.

Steve cleared his throat as if to pull Miles attention away from her. "So do you and your mother attend church around here?" he asked.

Great, Madison thought. *One more thing not to like about him.*

"Uh, no," Miles replied, shifting uncomfortably in his seat. "My mom grew up Baptist," he said. "Madison says you guys have a great church you go to," he added, turning to Maddie and smiling knowingly.

Steve nodded. "You'd be welcome to join us anytime. It's a good way to get to know people in the community. Madison's been pretty involved in the youth group there, so she could introduce you to all of her friends."

"Thanks. I'll keep that in mind," Miles replied, turning to Madison again and giving her a wink. Then he turned his attention to Caleb. "So I've heard you like sports."

Madison flashed back to the two of them up in Caleb's bedroom and then her own.

"Yeah. I play baseball, soccer, and basketball," her brother replied. "How about you?"

"I like to watch. But mostly I just skateboard myself," he said.

Caleb nodded. "Cool."

It seemed to Madison that dinner would drag on forever. Finally, her mother said, "Dessert anyone?"

"Not for me," she replied. Then turning to Miles she asked, "How about you?"

"I'm fine." He seemed to be as eager to get away from the table as she was. "But thanks anyway. And thanks for dinner." As they stood up, he added, "I'd better get going."

Madison turned to her mother. "I'll walk him out to the car and then help you with the dishes."

Michelle smiled. "Okay, honey." Then she turned to Miles. "It was nice getting to know you," she said.

"You, too," he replied a little awkwardly.

As they walked out the front door, Madison surprised herself by taking his hand. "Sorry about all that," she said.

"What?"

"The third degree."

He laughed. "No problem. I'm not sure your dad approves of me, though."

She didn't know what to say. *I hope Dad doesn't ruin this for me,* she thought. "Try not to let him get to you," was her final reply.

Squeezing her hand, he replied, "See you at school tomorrow." Then he got into the car without giving her a kiss goodbye.

When she came back into the house, her mother and father were waiting for her. "We need to talk, honey," her mom said.

Madison felt her heart sink. "You don't like him, do you?" she asked.

"It's not that we don't like him," her father said, "it's just that we're pretty sure he's not a Christian, Madison, and you know what we think about dating non-believers. It'll just lead to heartache later."

Madison looked to her mother for support, but she didn't find any.

"I agree with your father. Have you even discussed it with Miles?" she asked.

"Kind of."

"And?" Michelle asked.

"And I'm fine with him. We even talked about the youth group concert." She didn't add the fact that he wasn't interested in going.

Her parents exchanged glances. "Keep this relationship light, Madison," her mother said. "I really don't think it's going to be one for the long haul."

"And remember, we don't want you two together here unless we're home," her father added firmly.

"Got it," she said, as she headed for the stairway.

The next day, Miles wasn't in history class. Madison kept expecting him to walk in late, but he never showed up. Later, she saw him in the hall talking to some senior girl. The girl was smiling and laughing and gave him a playful nudge.

Should I walk over to him? Maddie wondered. *Or just act like I didn't see him?* She opted for the latter and was passing him when she heard her name. Turning, she saw the other girl waving as she left.

"Hey," Miles said.

"Hey," she replied, trying to act casual. "You weren't in class this morning."

"No. I got here late. Flat tire, so my mom dropped me off."

134

She nodded. "Is she picking you up after school?"

"Yeah. We're getting the tire replaced. She's got some job interview this afternoon, so she might be a little late."

Madison thought for a moment and then offered, "I could hang out with you for a while if you want. I just need to be home before my mom gets there."

"Okay, cool," he replied. "Meet you by the gym?"

"Sure," she said, waving as he headed out the door to the portable classrooms. He seemed different somehow. More distant. Probably because of her parents and all the church talk last night.

When she went out to the gym after school, he was talking on his cell phone. He glanced up at her and made eye contact, then she heard him say, "Okay. Ten minutes. Got it."

"What's up?" she asked.

"That was my mom. The interview was shorter than she thought. She's heading over here to get me, so I only have a few minutes."

Madison's heart sank a little. Oh well. Her bus was about to leave. Maybe she should hurry and see if she could still catch it. When she mentioned that possibility to him, he didn't offer his mom to give her a ride. Instead he just nodded. "Good idea. See you tomorrow."

As she rushed to the bus stop, she spotted the girl he'd been talking to that morning in the hall. Her outfit was edgy. *Think tomorrow I'll wear that sweater Miles likes so much,* she thought. Being cute was important, and being sexy was part of being cute.

That night, she pulled out the sweater and her tight jeans. She'd wear knee high boots over them and pull the sweater off her shoulders before history class.

Thankfully, her dad left for work really early, and her mom was super busy the next morning so there were no discussions about what she was wearing. When Miles came into class and spotted her, he smiled. The old Miles was back. Whatever had been going on the day before seemed to have evaporated. Now she had his attention again.

"Did you get your new tire?" she asked as they strolled out of the room.

"Sure did," he replied. "You've got my favorite sweater on today," he added, draping his arm over her shoulder.

It felt good to be close again. She nodded. "Just for you."

"Want me to drive you home today?" he asked, absentmindedly fingering the exposed bra strap on her shoulder.

"Sure. But I think you'd better leave before my mom gets home. You can come back if you want. But she's freaking out about the grounding thing. You're not supposed to be there when she's not home."

"No problem. I've got some stuff to do this afternoon anyway. I'll just hang out for half an hour or so and then split before she gets there." He leaned over and gave her a kiss before taking off for his next class. "See you in the parking lot."

Madison was elated. He really did like her after all. "See ya," she replied with a smile.

Much as Madison wanted to comply with her parents' wishes, she knew Miles better than they did. And she liked him. Plus, he really liked her. That must mean something. She'd get him to go to church with her eventually. She was sure of it. She just needed time. Time to build their relationship to a point where she could share her faith with him and convince him to give it a try. In the meantime, she couldn't bear to give up the relationship and how special he made her feel.

That afternoon they began a pattern that would continue throughout the remainder of Madison's grounding period. They'd meet at his car each afternoon, drive to her house, grab some food out of the kitchen and take it up to her room, sit on the floor by her bed and eat and talk. They could talk about anything and everything. But when Madison brought up the youth group or church, she could feel him begin to shut down.

Usually after about a half hour of talking, they'd end up making out. Madison felt so loved when she was in his arms, and she had to repeatedly remind herself to watch the clock and keep directing his hands away from places she wasn't comfortable with them going.

She knew her boundaries, and for the most part, Miles seemed to respect her limits. He'd sometimes give a little moan of disappointment when she stopped him from unzipping her jeans or from reaching up under a mini skirt she was wearing. But the time factor helped, with both of them knowing he'd have to leave by three forty-five. If Madison's mom called or texted and told her she'd be a little late, they'd stretch it to four. But never beyond that.

"It's just not worth it," Madison would say. Her parents would end it for sure if they caught them there alone together, no matter what was going on.

Then one day, everything changed. Michelle had a department meeting that would include dinner, Steve had a deposition late in the afternoon, and Caleb was going home with a friend for the afternoon and evening. Madison's phone rang as she and Miles walked into the house.

"Hi Maddie. I'm going to have to stay late today for a department meeting," her mother said. "We're actually ordering pizza because we've got a few hours of restructuring to do to accommodate some new standards. I tried to get a hold of your dad, but he's tied up in a deposition. So you'll be on your own for a while."

"What about Caleb?" Madison asked, pushing Miles hand away from her top.

"He's going home with a friend for the afternoon and dinner. I'll pick him up after my meeting."

"Okay."

"Maddie, you know the rules right?"

"Yeah. I know them," she said, as she again pushed away her boyfriend's probing hand.

"I can trust you, right?" Michelle asked.

"What do you think?" Madison replied defensively. She heard her mother sigh.

"Alright. I'll see you around eight. There's leftover chicken and vegetables in the fridge."

"Got it. See you at eight."

Madison and Miles had the house to themselves.

Across town, Joan was awakening from her afternoon nap. As she shuffled into the kitchen to prepare a cup of tea, the photo of Madison appeared on the screen of the slideshow picture frame. Gazing at her face, Joan suddenly felt a prompting to call her great granddaughter. She glanced up at the kitchen clock. Three-thirty. She should be home from school by now. Reaching for the phone, she dialed the number.

Miles pulled Madison into his arms. "Eight o'clock, huh?"

"Yeah," she replied with a smile.

"I guess we'll have to find a way to fill the time," he mused, taking her by the hand and leading her to the stairway.

A voice in Madison's head warned her not to go, but Miles gave her the sweetest smile and leaned over to whisper in her ear, "We'll just relax and snuggle a little, okay?"

She nodded and began following him upstairs. Her phone rang again, and she glanced down at the screen. Grams? Why would she be calling.

"You aren't going to spend the afternoon on the phone, are you?" Miles asked, a pleading puppy-dog look on his face.

Madison hit the silence button and made a mental note to call her back later, after her mom got home.

As they stretched out on the floor of her bedroom, Madison nestled down beside him, resting her head on his chest. "I like this room," he said.

"Really?"

"Yeah. It's pretty. Like you."

She smiled. "I'm glad you think so."

He shifted his body and eased her head onto the floor then bent down and kissed her. "You taste good," he murmured softly. "It's that cherry lipgloss isn't it?"

"Yep."

"Think I'll have a little more," he replied, his kiss turning to a deep, passionate one.

She rolled onto her side, and they lay facing each other, entwined in a close embrace while they continued to kiss. Soon he was unhooking her bra and removing her top. As he gazed at her, he leaned forward and whispered in her ear, "I love you, Madison. You're the most beautiful girl I've ever known."

Her heart soared, and as their lips met, her resolve melted away. The boundaries dissolved completely, and soon they were both undressed. As his hands explored her body, Madison experienced feelings she'd never felt before. She gave all of herself in spite of her reservations. It wasn't until afterward that she realized the full implication of their actions.

And then she felt another sensation she'd never experienced before. A feeling of utter panic coursed through her veins. She felt her throat close tight and her stomach clench as her heart pounded loudly in her ears.

"Are you okay?" Miles asked, as he pulled on his jeans.

She forced a smile, feeling lightheaded and afraid to stand. "Sure. Yeah, I'm fine." She struggled to get dressed, took a deep breath, and then the panic seemed to subside.

As she stood up, Miles drew her into his arms. He bent down and looked into her eyes, giving her a long, deep kiss. "I've been waiting for that for a long time," he said.

"Me, too," she lied.

"Well, maybe I'd better leave," he said after another kiss. "We don't want your parents to show up with me here."

"Right." *Besides,* she thought, *what would we do now?* It didn't seem like the time to watch television together or pull out homework. Something had changed. Everything. Now Miles loved her. But was she ready for that? Madison wasn't sure.

Joan sat in her rocking chair with her tea, her spirit unsettled. *Oh, Lord, what is it? What's happening with Maddie? Should I call Michelle?* Waiting for an answer, she rocked and continued to pray. *Please protect her, Father. Give her wisdom, and help her know You are always there, watching over her.*

The doorbell rang, and it was Margie. After offering her a cup of tea, Joan confessed her concerns. "Something's not right. I can feel it in my bones," she told her friend.

"Well, then let's call the Sisters and step up our prayers," Margie replied.

And that is exactly what they did. Silver-haired Sisters swung their swords of faith as they leveled scriptures against the forces of darkness.

The next ten days seemed to drag on for eternity as Madison waited for her period. All she could think about was her brother's birthmother, Amber, and how she'd gotten pregnant in eighth grade. *At least Miles is almost eighteen,* Madison thought. *And he says he loves me.*

She tried to picture what it would be like if she were pregnant. Would they get married? Would they live here with her parents while they finished school?

And what would *Luke* think of her?

"What difference does that make?" she asked herself aloud. "Luke is my past. Miles is my future."

But she'd noticed some things about Miles lately that concerned her. For one, he seemed to always be trying to figure out ways they could be alone somewhere. And even when they were around other people, he found ways to secretly sneak in a caress of her breasts. His kisses in the hall, which had meant so much to her at the beginning, were now prolonged almost to the point of embarrassment, and she'd ended up late to more than one class.

Although he continued to drive her home everyday, she managed to keep him out of her bedroom, explaining that they couldn't take another chance at being discovered. He'd even taken her out for a drive one afternoon to a pretty secluded area where they could be alone, but as they kissed and he began working her clothes off, she stopped him. "Not here. This doesn't feel right," she'd said.

Another thing that bothered her was that he'd sometimes make a comment indicating he was getting more open to going to church, but in the end, he always had some excuse when the weekend rolled around. Until they got that issue settled, she needed to keep the relationship low key with her parents. Since they didn't know she was hanging out with him every day after school, she just brushed aside their questions about him, focusing more on talking about how she kept inviting him to church but it hadn't worked out yet.

Finally, the day her period was due came and went. That night the same panic returned that she'd felt with Miles that afternoon in her bedroom. She was lying on her bed listening to music and trying to convince herself that everything would be okay, when it hit again. Her heart raced, pounding so loudly she couldn't even hear the song that was playing. She felt out of breath, and her throat and stomach were tight.

She was terrified. *What's happening to me? Am I going crazy?* She wanted to call Miles or to go and talk to her mom. But she didn't have the nerve to share her fear with her boyfriend, and there was no way she was telling her mom about what had happened between them.

She forced herself to breathe, and a few minutes later, it subsided just like the last time.

Over the course of the next two days, she had two more panic attacks. Finally, her period started. *I'll be okay now,* she thought.

But the following day, when Miles was driving her home from school, it happened again. The world seemed to stop as the panic took over her senses. She lost touch with what was happening around her, every thought directed to just breathing. As it eventually subsided, she heard him say, "Right?"

"What?"

"I said, this is good news, right? That you started your period, I mean," he said. "Now we'll just be careful, and everything will be fine." He leaned over and kissed her tenderly.

She nodded, fighting the nausea that accompanied these attacks, and wondering if she should tell him there wouldn't be any other times they'd be together like that. At least not for now. Instead she just said, "Yeah. You're right."

"Wanna go get a burger?" he asked.

Her stomach clenched. "Not for me. But if you want one, that's fine. I don't mind stopping," she said, all the time thinking how much she wanted to get out of the car. It suddenly felt claustrophobic in there.

"Okay, cool," he replied, turning down the street toward the fast food drive-through.

The smell of his burger and fries just added to her nausea. "I think you'd better just drop me off at home," she said. "My stomach's not feeling so good."

"Maybe you need to eat. You hardly had anything for lunch," he said, holding his half-eaten burger out for her.

Swallowing the bile in her mouth, she replied, "No thanks. I think I might be getting sick." She put her hand over her mouth.

"Oh man. You're not going to barf are you?" he asked, dropping the burger into the wrapper on his lap and focusing on getting her home.

She shook her head and pulled her hand down. Now that they were headed to her house, she was feeling a little better. She just needed some time to herself to sort through everything. She knew she loved Miles, but their physical relationship was beyond what she'd planned.

As she was resting alone in her room that afternoon, Luke called. Madison's first thought was that she was glad Miles wasn't there. Luke's voice tugged at a part of Madison's heart that she wanted to deny existed. She felt excited and happy and nervous and guilty all mixed together.

"So how are things with you?" he asked.

"Pretty good," she blurted out, knowing that was far from the truth.

"Lucy said you've been dating that guy, Miles, quite a bit. Are you two getting serious?" he asked.

She paused. Whatever she said would probably get back to Lucy and then maybe to Miles. "I guess," she replied.

"So tell me about him."

Madison started with a physical description and then led into telling him about Miles' mom and the struggles they were having with her out of work.

"Maybe he should get a job after school," Luke suggested.

Madison hadn't really thought about that idea, especially since that was their time together, in more ways than one. But Luke was right. That would really help Miles' mom out. "I'll mention that to him," she said, wondering if she really would. Then changing the subject, she asked, "How about you? Are you dating anyone?"

"Not really. Nothing serious." He paused for a moment. "There's a girl I've become good friends with. But there's nothing else to it. At least, yet."

Surprisingly, Madison felt her heart flip flop over the word *yet*. So Luke was thinking this girl might become his girlfriend. *Why should she care about that? After all she had Miles.* "Cool," was all she said in return.

They talked for a while longer about school and their families, and Madison noticed how comfortable it was to just talk to him. She and Miles didn't seem to do much talking these days. By the time they hung up, she had to admit she really missed having Luke around.

CHAPTER TWELVE

Stepping on the bathroom scale, Madison was surprised to see she'd lost another five pounds. Her clothes were getting looser and looser. She'd probably have to ask her mom for some money to buy new jeans and shorts. Although her panic attacks really scared her, they also curbed her appetite almost completely. The extra weight her jogging hadn't been able to budge was now dropping off so easily.

Miles noticed it, too. "You're looking really hot these days," he said with a smile as he rested his hand on her rear end while they walked down the hall.

"Thanks," she replied, looking up and smiling. It felt good to be thin, and she could see the envy in other girls' eyes as Miles fawned over her on campus. He seemed to always have a hand on her when they were together, and he never walked away without giving her a deep and lingering kiss. Although she sometimes felt embarrassed, she also found herself feeling a little more confident and attractive.

But the anxiety and panic attacks continued at a steady pace. Miles was pushing for more "alone" time. And she knew what that meant. He promised he'd use protection, but she'd heard of a senior who got pregnant and swore she and her boyfriend had used condoms every time. When Madison casually mentioned that to her mother, she was surprised by the response.

"You know, honey, I think condoms are only about eighty-five percent effective in preventing pregnancy."

"Really? I thought it was more than that. They kind of push them in health ed as being pretty safe."

Her mother rolled her eyes. "It really irks me that the schools are giving kids that impression. One little tear or pinprick hole, or even just not using them correctly is all it takes for a baby to be made."

"Well, at least they protect against AIDS, right?" Madison asked.

Michelle shook her head. "Think about it, Maddie. If condoms only prevent pregnancy eighty-five percent of the time, and pregnancy can only occur one day per month, but AIDS can be transmitted anytime, how smart is it to rely on them for safe sex?" She took Madison's hand in hers and looked her in the eye. "I'm glad you've got the common sense to wait until marriage, Maddie. Unfortunately, most kids buy into the mentality that everyone's doing it, and all they need is to be sure to use a condom."

Madison felt a wave of nausea and the beginning of another panic attack. She just nodded to her mom and then said, "I've gotta go do my homework." By the time she was in her bedroom with the door closed, her heart was pounding so loud she thought it would explode. She was sweating all over, and she could barely catch her breath. It took a full five minutes before her symptoms began to subside. She nearly bolted for the bathroom once, thinking she'd throw up any second.

When Caleb knocked on the door an hour later and announced, "Dinner's ready," Madison knew she couldn't face her mother or food for that matter.

"Just tell Mom I'm not feeling good. I'll have something to eat later," she said.

"Suit yourself," he replied, shaking his head and walking away.

A few minutes later, her father appeared at her doorway. "What's going on?" he asked.

"Nothing," she replied. "I'm just not hungry. My stomach's a little upset."

He studied her. "You've got us worried, sweetheart. Your mom and I have both noticed how thin you're looking."

"I just haven't had that much of an appetite lately," she said, trying to sound reassuring.

"Maybe you need to see the doctor. Just to be sure there's nothing wrong," he suggested, sitting down on the bed near her.

Madison's stomach clenched again. The last thing she wanted to do was see a doctor. He'd probably figure out she'd had sex. Or he'd find out about her attacks and put her on some psych meds or something. Why couldn't her parents just leave her alone?

"I'm fine, Dad. Seriously. It's probably just girl stuff. Ask Mom. She'll tell you. Sometimes it just makes us not feel right."

He pursed his lips and looked her in the eye. When he put his hand on her arm, she almost let her guard down and spilled everything. But something held her back. He'd never understand. No one would. Even Miles thought everything was great. No one really knew that she was losing herself and terrified she was losing her mind at the same time.

Thankfully, her mother's voice called up from downstairs. "Are you two coming? Dinner's getting cold."

"Be right down," Steve called back in reply. Turning to Madison, he added, "If you don't start feeling better soon, I think the doctor is our next step. Girl stuff or not. This isn't healthy." He gave her a hug and then stood and left the room.

As soon as he was gone, Madison picked up a magazine and started flipping through it. Maybe looking at ideas for new outfits would get her mind off of everything. As she perused the pages, she started relaxing. Noticing a couple of pairs of jeans with decorative back pockets, she nodded. "These would look good on me now," she said in a soft voice. Panic attacks or not, she was happy to have her new figure. And so was Miles.

"I was thinking maybe we could go shopping today after school," Madison suggested to Miles the next day. His hand was in her back jeans pocket, his new way of attaching himself to her in the hallway.

"Why?" he asked.

"I need new jeans. These are getting loose on me."

"Yeah, I noticed that," he replied, giving her cheek a little squeeze inside the pocket. "I guess we could stop by there on the way to your house," he added, pulling his hand out of her pocket and sliding it up under the back of her top to rest it on her skin. "What time does your mom get home today?"

"The usual. By four at the latest."

"Maybe we should go there first, and then I could take you shopping when she gets there," he suggested, caressing the skin on her side.

She leaned into him and his hand slipped around to her abdomen, the fingers nudging into the front of her pants. Hugging his arm against her body, she aborted his effort. "There's a teacher right up there," she murmured, tipping her head in the direction they were walking.

He laughed and pulled his hand away, coming out from under her shirt and draping his arm loosely over her shoulder. "We'll figure it out after school, okay?" he said, as he leaned down, gave her a quick but intimate kiss, and peeled out the side door.

"Okay," she replied to the air he left behind. She really wanted to talk to him about the condom thing. If it really was only eight-five percent effective, maybe they should cool it a little. She wasn't ready to go on the pill or anything, and she sure didn't want to get pregnant.

When she met him at his car after school, he seemed a little down. "What's the matter?" she asked as they drove out of the parking lot.

"Nothing," he replied with a deep sigh.

She could tell something was really wrong, but he clearly didn't want to talk about it. As he began driving toward her house, she asked, "What about shopping?"

"Could we skip it for today?" he asked, staring out the windshield with a brooding expression.

"Sure."

They drove on in silence for the last few minutes. As he pulled up to the curb in front of the house and shut off the motor, he turned to her and his expression really frightened her. His eyes were dark and hopelessness shrouded them.

"What is it?" she asked. "What's wrong?"

He leaned over and kissed her, gently at first and then almost desperately. "I need you, Maddie. You are the only good thing in my life."

The intensity in his voice and expression scared her. "I love you, Miles. You know I'm here for you," she replied, fighting back the wave of anxiety threatening to overtake her.

He pulled her close and kissed her again, his hands groping for her as if he couldn't get close enough. "Not here. Not in the car. The neighbors might see," she said. She reached over and opened her door. "Come on. Let's go inside." Shopping was definitely not going to be a happening thing today. And neither was the condom discussion.

Pulling him over to the couch in the living room, she tugged on his hand to sit down beside her. "Do you want to tell me what had you so upset?" she asked softly.

"It's my mom. Her jerk of a boyfriend from Dallas just called. He's on his way here."

"Really? How does your mom feel about that?" she asked.

"She says she couldn't care less, but I know differently. As soon as Buck shows up on the doorstep, she'll be back under his thumb. The guy's a total control freak, and she lets him take over her life every time they get back together."

"How does he act toward you?"

"Like I'm in the way. A bother." He paused. "But I don't care what he thinks about me. It's my mom I'm worried about."

Madison nodded. "Can't you tell her that? I mean really explain how concerned you are?"

He shook his head and gently pushed her away as he sat up. "She won't listen to me. Or to anyone else for that matter. Her best friend tried to tell her what a loser the guy is, but mom just told her she didn't know him—the real Buck. Right." He stood and pulled on his jeans. "I'd better get home," he added.

Just then the sound of the garage door opening caused Madison to glance at the clock. "My mom's here."

Michelle walked into the kitchen and called out, "Maddie? Are you home?"

"In here, Mom."

As her mother came through the dining room, Madison stood to her feet. "Miles gave me a ride home."

Michelle greeted Miles and asked, "Would you like to stay for dinner? We're eating early because I'm having coffee with my mom this evening."

"Oh, no, I'm leaving in just a few minutes," he replied. Glancing over at Madison, he added, "In fact, I'd better get going right now." He stood and held out his hand to her. "Walk me to the car?"

"Sure," she said, lacing her fingers through his. "Be right back," she told her mother.

Sheila Chambers glanced at her watch. Michelle was ten minutes late. She and her daughter tried to meet for coffee twice a month to keep up with each other's lives. It seemed like Thursday nights were best for both of them. Sheila's husband, Rick, taught a night class on Thursdays, and Michelle liked the idea of Thursdays since her classes usually had tests Fridays, meaning she had a fairly easy routine the following day. So they'd set aside the first and third Thursdays as their mother-daughter date nights.

Sipping her hazelnut latte, Sheila thought about her afternoon and her visit with her mother. Sheila was struggling to find the right part-time caregiver. Eighty-nine-year-old Joan was still full of life and love, but her memory was slipping more and more. The important things were still there—the names of all her loved ones, the basic routines of daily living, and of course all of the past. But she'd become increasingly forgetful about appointments and had left the stove or oven on several times. It worried Sheila, knowing her mother was alone and might actually start a fire by accident.

A bell chime signaled the opening of the front door of the Coffee Stop, and Sheila looked up to see Michelle hurrying inside. "Hi, Mom," her daughter said breathlessly. "Sorry I'm late." She pulled out her wallet. "I'll grab my coffee and be right back."

Sheila smiled and nodded. "Take your time, dear. No rush."

ROSEMARY HINES

When Michelle returned a couple of minutes later, she was carrying a tray with her coffee and two slices of pecan pie. "I couldn't resist," she said with a wink, placing one plate in front of Sheila as she settled into the seat across from her. "And no fussing about any diets," she warned. "I get enough of that with Madison."

"How *is* Maddie these days?" Sheila asked, sharing her daughter's concern about Madison's obsession with diet and exercise.

"You know, Mom, I'm not exactly sure." Michelle paused before continuing. "I guess right now, her boyfriend is my biggest concern."

"Really? That new boy...Mike?"

"Miles."

"Oh, yes. Miles. So tell me what's got you so worried." Sheila took a bite of her pie, and then studied her daughter's face.

Gazing off into space as if searching for answers, Michelle finally replied, "I just don't trust him."

"But you trust Madison, right?" Sheila asked.

Michelle turned and looked her in the eye. "You know, Mom, I'm not really sure." She hesitated a moment and then added, "I've just got a gut level feeling that something's not right with Madison. And I think it has something to do with her relationship with Miles."

"Have you talked to her about it?"

"Not really. There's nothing specific I can say, yet. But she just doesn't seem like herself. She's edgy and more quiet than normal. Plus, she doesn't seem to have much appetite. It was one thing when she was trying to diet. I could see her fighting her appetite then. Now, it's like she has to fight to eat instead."

A shadow of concern settled on Sheila's spirit. Madison was her only granddaughter and the first grandchild. She held a special spot in Sheila's heart. "Have you discussed this with Steve?" she asked.

"Numerous times. But he's got a lot on his plate right now at work. We've both talked to her, and she knows she's not allowed to be alone with Miles, other than to get a ride home. We've urged her to keep the relationship light, especially since Miles is not a Christian. As far as I know, she's taken that to heart. But I've got this feeling something's really troubling her. Mother's intuition, I guess."

"Well, don't downplay that, Mimi. God often reveals things to mothers in ways we can't always explain. I think you should have another heart-to-heart with her. Just approach it casually and see where it leads," she suggested.

Michelle nodded. "You're right. I do need to talk to her again." She sank back in her chair, cupping her coffee in her hands. "So how are things with you and Rick?"

Sheila smiled, thinking once again about how thankful she was for the unexpected joy of a second chance at love and marriage. Although she was a grandmother to a teenager, she often felt like a young girl herself, as she reveled in being a newlywed. The past few years had gone by so quickly, but she still eagerly looked forward to Rick's smile and kiss when he returned home each day.

"We're doing well," she said. "Rick spoils me with his attention. Not that I'm complaining," she added with a grin.

"You two are like little lovebirds," Michelle replied. "I'm jealous," she added, teasingly.

Sheila felt herself blush. "I guess we are," she admitted.

"You deserve it, Mom. Really. After all you went through with Dad, I'm so glad this has worked out for you."

"Thanks, honey. You know how much I loved your father. But Rick and I have something that's...well...it's hard to explain. There was a part of your dad that I could never quite reach. Even after everything that happened," she said, thinking about John's final years and how much closer they'd grown. "It's easy with Rick. We don't have any walls." She paused, grasping for the best way to convey what she had with her new husband. "It's like we are too old for games, and we want to know each other completely and honestly."

"That's wonderful. I can see he feels the same way as you do. Whenever he's around, he is so attentive and interested in all that you say and do. It really makes me happy," Michelle said. "I'm sure he never thought he'd find this kind of love either."

Her daughter's words meant so much to Sheila. To know that someone else could see the unique treasure of her relationship with Rick made it all the more real and special.

"So how's Grandma doing?" Michelle asked.

And the cloud of concern returned. "She's okay, physically. But I'm noticing more and more memory issues with her," Sheila confided. "The other day when I dropped by to pick her up, I went to get a glass of water in the kitchen and discovered that the oven was on. When I asked your grandmother about what she'd been cooking, she couldn't remember. I saw a plate with some cookie crumbs on it, and asked if she'd been baking. Then she remembered that she'd made cookies the night before. So that oven was on all night."

Michelle winced. "Not good."

"Not at all," Sheila agreed. Much as she wanted to encourage her mother to keep her independence, safety was another issue altogether.

"I could try to go by there on my way home from school to check on her if you'd like," Michelle offered.

"You've got enough to deal with, Mimi. I just need to figure out the best way to provide caregiving. Your grandmother never wants to inconvenience anyone, and I know she'll be worried about that if I'm over there all the time."

"How about if I go by twice a week. That would break it up a little. And you could go two or three times. Then maybe we could arrange for someone else to help out in between our visits. I've been telling Grandma she should get a housekeeper. Maybe my gal could go once a week and clean and check on things."

"Oh, that sounds like a great plan. But are you sure you want to commit to going over there twice a week? I don't want this to become a burden for you, honey." Sheila looked her daughter in the eye, and Michelle nodded.

"I want to do it, Mom. I wouldn't offer otherwise. Grandma is one of my favorite people. It'll be good to have the discipline of a regular schedule to keep me seeing her during the school year. Sign me up for Tuesdays and Fridays. And I'll ask my cleaning lady about what day would be good for her."

The cloud lifted, and Sheila felt a surge of relief. God was certainly good to her. She could never thank Him enough. But as she drove home, Michelle's concerns about Madison resurfaced. "Rick and I need to pray for Maddie," she said in a whisper. *Wow. What a gift to have a husband I can pray with*, she thought as she pulled into their driveway.

CHAPTER THIRTEEN

"So how serious are you and Miles getting?" Lucy asked on Saturday afternoon, as she and Madison paged through some magazines in her room.

Madison seemed to be trying to figure out what to say. "I guess we're pretty serious, why?"

"Just wondering. I mean I hardly ever see you after school anymore. You two disappear pretty quickly right after class ends." She missed hanging out with Madison after school, but didn't want to be a drag about it.

"Yeah. He likes to get off campus before the parking lot gets crowded."

"So what do you do when you leave school?" she asked.

Madison turned away from her, standing up and walking over to her closet. "Just stuff. We come over here and hang out usually. You know, watch TV. Stuff like that."

"Oh. You're lucky your parents don't make a big deal about you two being alone together. My parents are so strict. They'd freak out if I had a boy at the house when they weren't home."

Madison nodded. "Yeah. Well, my mom gets home about an hour after we do, so it's not like we are here that long by ourselves." Without going on to explain that Miles usually left before her mother got home, she changed the subject by handing a magazine to Lucy. "So what do think of this outfit?" she asked, pointing to a model wearing a tight, shimmery dress.

"Looks good on *her*," she replied. "It's a little too fitted for my taste," she added. "Now this is more like me." She pointed to a picture on the opposing page, and soon they were lost in a fashion discussion.

That night, Lucy decided to write to her brother. She told Luke about Madison's relationship with Miles getting pretty serious. *Why am I telling him all this?* she thought to herself. But something nudged her to tell him she was concerned. Even though Madison seemed happy, she also seemed different. Somehow more serious. Older or something. She tried to explain it in the letter, knowing that Luke really cared about Madison, too.

Five days later, Luke was walking back to his dorm room with his new friend, Autumn, when he decided to stop by the mailboxes in the student union. Their relationship had progressed faster than he intended, and although he liked her a lot, he wanted to be sure they didn't get ahead of themselves or rush into a commitment because of their obvious chemistry. So far, the relationship had not progressed beyond holding hands and spending much of their free time together. But he knew she wanted to take it to the next level.

His goal was to focus on school as much as possible, and to avoid being alone with her for any significant periods of time. His attraction to her was compelling, and he could easily be drawn into a serious physical relationship if he didn't keep his guard up.

As he pulled the mail out of his box, he found himself hoping to see something from Madison. He'd written her over a week ago and was still waiting for a reply. Instead he found an envelope from Lucy. *Interesting, he thought. She usually just emails me.*

"What is it?" Autumn asked, leaning in to look at the envelope.

"Just a letter from my sister."

She smiled and looked relieved. "Oh. That's nice."

They walked across the campus toward the dorms. The mid-western brilliant fall colors were beautiful as they crunched dried leaves under their feet. Much as Luke was coming to love this place, he suddenly felt homesick. Maybe it was the letter from Lucy. Or the absence of the fragrance of salt air. But in his loneliness, he pulled Autumn close, and she wrapped her arm tightly around his waist.

"Wanna go get burgers?" she asked.

"Yeah. That sounds good," he replied. They strolled over to her car, and he stuffed his mail into his backpack, tossing it onto the back seat.

They spent an hour at the burger joint, eating and talking. But Luke's spirits were still down. "We'd better get back," he said. "I've got homework I need to get started with."

"Are you sure? We could go somewhere else and just be alone. You know, to talk," she suggested.

He shook his head. "Thanks, but I'd better get back to the dorm."

"Okay," she replied, sounding disappointed.

When she dropped him off at his dorm, she said, "Call me later, if you need a break, or just someone to talk to."

"I will," he promised, grabbing his backpack and heading to his room.

As he settled on his bed and pulled his books out of his backpack, he spotted Lucy's letter. Pushing everything else aside, he sat back and opened it. As he read the familiar handwriting, his stomach began to tighten.

So Madison and her boyfriend are getting really serious, I guess. He drives her home from school everyday and they hang out at her house. Madison's changing. She seems different, like she's suddenly older or something. I can't exactly explain it. But she doesn't seem like herself. I still like hanging out with her whenever she has time for me. But you should see her, Luke. I mean she dresses differently and everything. I hope she doesn't get into some kind of trouble with this guy. He's nice, but I just don't trust him. Maybe I'm crazy. Madison says she's really happy, so I guess that's what matters.

Just the mention of Madison triggered an onslaught of images in Luke's mind. Her sweet smile, her wide-eyed innocence, and her lighthearted ways. What was happening to her? Not too long ago, Lucy had emailed him about Madison's dieting. Now it was her boyfriend and her new ways of dressing. Lucy wasn't perfect, by any stretch of the imagination. But she was pretty savvy about people. If she didn't trust Miles, there was probably a good reason. And her concerns about Madison made him even more homesick.

Why was that? And what exactly did he feel for her? Closing his eyes, he tried to think back over their friendship. There'd been times he'd felt something special, a spark of some kind between them. But there was also such a familiarity and playfulness to their relationship, like brother and sister combined with best friend. He'd shelved any feelings of attraction when he'd moved from middle school to high school. Their lives were in such different realms at that point. And with their families so close, being pals seemed more appropriate.

But was that what he really wanted? And what about her? Lucy said she was pretty hooked on this Miles guy. But if he wasn't good for her, like Lucy insinuated, should Luke reach out and say or do something?

And what about Autumn? Where did she fit into all of this?

He stood up and raked his fingers through his hair. Pacing the room, he finally grabbed his jacket and headed outside to walk and pray. For the next hour, he searched his heart and pleaded with God for answers. By the time he got back to his room, he had one of them. He needed to halt his relationship with Autumn. At least until he better understood the feelings toward Madison he was now beginning to acknowledge.

He'd talk to Autumn the next day. But for now, he wanted to reach out to Madison. Picking up his phone, he punched in her number.

Madison looked at caller ID on her cell phone. Luke? Images of Miles flashed through her mind. Images of him lying naked beside her on the floor. And panic surrounded her. The air felt thin and all she could hear was her heart pounding as nausea welled up inside. She pushed the silence button on the side of the phone, sank to the floor, and tried to breathe. Gradually, the sound of her heart diminished and her sea legs returned. Using the sleeve of her shirt, she wiped the sweat from her brow.

"Everything's okay," she told herself softly. "Everything is going to be fine."

She looked down at her phone again. The screen reported one missed call from Luke. When she checked the voicemail, it was empty.

Rick listened as his wife explained her concerns about her mother and granddaughter.

"We need to pray, honey," she said.

He knew she was right, and he wanted to be the kind of husband she needed. But it made him nervous when she asked him to pray with her. After all, he was still getting his bearings in his new faith. Praying over meals and things like that were fine. But Sheila's father had been a pastor. He was the example she grew up with, and Rick had experienced that man's prayers. They were powerful and flowed so easily from Phil. He wished Phil were still alive, to give Sheila the prayer support she needed, and that Rick felt so inept in providing.

"Rick?" Sheila's voice asked, cutting into his thoughts.

"Yeah. Sure. You're right, sweetheart. Why don't you pray and I'll pray right along with you?" he suggested.

She paused, studying him before agreeing. "Okay." Reaching over and taking his hand, she bowed her head and began to pray. And while she interceded for her mother and granddaughter, Rick also prayed for his role as her spiritual partner, asking God to grow him into the kind of man her father had been.

Luke tried to call Madison again the next day. And the day after that. But he never got an answer. Leaving a message just didn't feel right.

He thought about calling Lucy and asking her to watch out for Madison. But then he thought better of it. Who was he to tell his sister to do something like that? Besides, Lucy was a year younger than Madison. She was in no position to be monitoring or trying to counsel her older friend. And what kind of impression would it give his sister if he acted all concerned about Maddie? Sure they were friends, but he had no other claim to her than that.

If Madison wanted to talk to him, she would have answered the phone or at least called him back when she saw that she'd missed his calls. For now, he'd just pray and ask God to protect her. And he'd seek wisdom and clarification about his feelings for her.

Thankfully, the break up with Autumn had gone better than he anticipated. She looked a little sad and disappointed, but she said she understood and still wanted to be his friend. Who knew? Maybe someday it would work out after all. But not until he saw Madison again.

CHAPTER FOURTEEN

Madison stared at the numbers on her math assignment. Math had always been an easy subject for her. It was clear cut and step-by-step, with only one right answer. If she just followed the rules, she'd find it.

Now the numbers suddenly looked like a hodgepodge of sticks and curves swimming on the page. She closed her eyes tightly, trying to clear her mind and focus. A tap on her shoulder from behind caused her to flinch ever so slightly.

"Do you get number five?" a whisper asked.

She glanced down at her paper. She hadn't completed a single problem. Without turning around, she just shook her head.

And then it hit.

The rush of heat over her body, the pounding in her ears, and the shortness of breath. Panic surged, once again threatening to swallow her alive. Was she going to pass out? What would everyone think?

Her stomach clenched, and covering her mouth with her hand, she forced herself to stand. Walking unsteadily to the teacher's desk at the front of the room, she swallowed back the bile in her throat and forced out the words. "May I go to the bathroom?"

Thankfully, the teacher barely glanced from the stack of papers he was grading. He reached into his drawer, pulled out a hall pass, and handed it to her. As she hurried out the door and down the empty hall, she began to feel the suffocating sensation subside. She was relieved to find the bathroom empty, and she stood at the sink, gripping the white porcelain as she stared in the mirror.

The face that looked back at her was the face of a stranger. Gaunt eyes and pale skin gave a ghostly appearance. She took a deep breath and let it out. Then, turning on the faucet, she let the cool water caress her hands and wrists. She grabbed a paper towel, wet it and wrung out the water, then lifted her hair and wiped the back of her neck. Not wanting to wash off her make up, she just gently dabbed her cheeks and forehead.

After another deep breath, she straightened up to the best of her ability and forced a façade of happiness. Her eyes gazed back at her, the fear still clearly present behind her smile. *What is happening to me?* she wondered in the dark recesses of her mind.

The bell rang, jarring her to attention. She took one last glance into the mirror and shuddered before hurrying back to class to get her backpack and head out to lunch.

She spotted Miles sitting with some of his friends. Brianna Heatherton, one of the cheerleaders who was really popular with the guys, was next to him, laughing and giving him a playful shove. As soon as he saw Madison, he stood up, said something to the group, which evoked another round of laughs, and then walked over to where she was standing.

Leaning down, he kissed her. "Hey," he said with a smile.

"Hey," she replied, once again forcing herself to look happy, like everything was fine.

"Wanna go sit and eat behind the gym?" he asked, referring to the spot they sometimes disappeared to together. They had privacy there. Something Miles seemed to be seeking out more and more.

Madison thought about their spot. It was shady and cool there, and suddenly she felt chilled, like sitting in the sunlight was important right now. "Think I'd rather just sit here," she said. "I'm not feeling so good."

"Okay, whatever," he replied, clearly disappointed by her response.

Madison tried to force down a few bites of her lunch, but it seemed to stick in her throat.

"You'd better start eating," he said, as she shoved her lunch bag back into her backpack. "You're starting to look like a skeleton."

The image of her face in the mirror flashed in her mind. Great. Now he was noticing, too. She began to feel a little panicky again. "I need to go to the bathroom," she said, standing up and grabbing her backpack. "I'll be back in a minute."

He nodded, glancing back toward his friends.

"Why don't you just go back over there," she suggested. "It might be more than a minute." By now, she knew she wasn't going to completely lose it, but she didn't feel like hanging out with him either.

He didn't argue. "Okay. See you after school." He stood up, leaned over and kissed her again, and then walked away.

When Madison spotted Miles in the parking lot that afternoon, her anxiety crept in again. All she wanted to do was go home and hide by herself in her bedroom. She felt like she could lose control and do something really strange. Something that would show everyone she really was losing her mind.

Miles was talking with a couple of girls and smiling at whatever they were saying. As Madison approached them, she noticed that one of the girls was Brianna. She whispered something to one of her friends, and they both looked at Madison and laughed. She could feel the heat surge through her face, and she felt like she couldn't get her breath. Turning, she started hurrying away.

Miles caught up with her and grabbed her by the shoulder. "Hey, where are you going?" he asked.

"I don't feel well," she replied under her breath, hoping she could push away the nausea that overtook her with each panic attack.

"Do you still want a ride home?" he asked, his voice laced with impatience.

"No. I'll just take the bus," she said.

Miles stepped in front of her. "What is going on? You aren't pregnant, are you?"

She looked at him dumbfounded. Of course that would be what he would think. "No. I'm not pregnant. I just feel funny," she said, tears blurring her vision.

"Okay," he replied, putting both hands on her shoulders. "Are you sure you don't want a ride?" He glanced away, and she followed his eyes back to the car where Brianna and her friends were still talking.

"Yeah. I'm sure," she said. "See you tomorrow."

He nodded. "Right. Hope you feel better."

Madison could hear the relief in his voice. She forced a smile and replied, "Thanks," before walking away.

Lucy sat beside her on the bus chatting away about her day. "And then he said," she began, but paused. "Are you listening, Maddie? You look like you're daydreaming about something."

"Sorry. I'm just really not feeling well," Madison replied. "Could we talk about it later?"

"Sure." Lucy settled back against the seat and stared out the window for the rest of the ride to Madison's stop. "Call me tonight if you feel better," she said as Maddie walked toward the bus exit.

"I will," Madison promised, taking a breath to calm a wave of claustrophobia as she waited for the people in front of her in the aisle.

When she was inside her house, she fled to the bathroom. Standing and staring at the toilet, she waited to see if she was going to throw up. After a couple of minutes, she began to relax a little, washed her face, and avoided looking into the mirror before she walked out. She stretched out on her bed and tried to pray, but soon dissolved into tears.

"What is *wrong* with me?" she asked after she stopped sobbing. Although she was exhausted, she couldn't fall asleep. Nervous energy propelled her to her feet, and she paced the room for a few minutes before deciding to go for a run. The thought of being away from home by herself was suddenly daunting, but she remembered how good it used to feel to run, so she changed into her workout clothes, laced on her shoes, and headed out the front door, leaving a note behind on the kitchen counter so her mother wouldn't worry.

She ran for thirty minutes, circling a three-block radius so she wouldn't be too far away from home if another attack happened. The fresh air and the feel of her body in motion calmed her anxiety somewhat. As her mind began to clear, she found herself praying again.

Dear God, Please help me. I don't know what is happening to me. Am I going crazy? I don't know what to do. Please show me who to talk to or what will help me feel better. She paused and listened in her heart. Although she believed God had heard her, she wasn't hearing an answer. A thought about God's timing flitted through her mind. Something she'd heard in youth group. About how God's timing is always perfect. But she didn't know how much longer she could hold on.

Before school the next day, Madison walked across the field toward the lunch tables. She thought she saw Miles talking to a girl. He was sitting on one of the tables and the girl was standing facing him. It was Brianna. She put her knee on the bench and leaned toward Miles, placing her hands on his shoulders.

Then Madison saw something that sucked all the air out of her lungs.

Miles placed his hands on Brianna's waist, pulled her close, and kissed her.

Madison turned and quickly walked in another direction. She didn't think he'd seen her, and she needed to get away before he did. A minute later he was by her side.

"Hey, Maddie. Are you feeling better?" he asked innocently.

She glared at him. "I was until I saw you making out with Brianna."

He looked away. "It wasn't what you think it was."

"Really?" she asked, not trying to hold back the sarcasm in her voice.

"Look, if you don't trust me, just say so."

"How am I supposed to trust you when I see you kissing someone else?" she asked, her voice shaking with anger and hurt.

"I'm telling you it doesn't mean anything. Bri and I are just friends. She was upset about something, so we were talking. And then she kissed me. Like a friend."

Madison shook her head. "Is that what we are, too? Friends?"

"You know that's not true," he replied, his voice now carrying an edge.

"What? We're not friends?" she asked flippantly.

170

"Of course we're friends, Madison. But we're more than friends. You should know that after everything that's happened."

She nodded. "Right."

"So are we okay?" he asked, clearly wanting to dismiss the whole incident.

"Would you be okay if you saw me kissing some guy?" she asked pointedly, amazed at the sudden clarity in her mind. Where was the anxiety right now in the midst of this anger?

"If you told me it didn't mean anything, I'd believe you," he said, but she knew he was lying.

"Okay, I'll remember that," she replied.

"What's that supposed to mean?"

"It means just what I said. I'll remember that you don't care if I kiss other guys as long as it 'doesn't mean anything' to me."

"Whatever," he said, turning and walking away.

When history class rolled around, Madison could not face him. She decided to ditch for the first time ever. She went to their hiding place behind the gym, took out the math homework she'd failed to finish the night before, and sat working on it until she heard the bell ring. As she worked her way through the crowded hall to her next class, she saw Miles walking with Brianna, his arm draped over her shoulder.

After school, Miles was waiting for her in the hallway outside of her last class. "Sorry about this morning," he said. "What happened to you during history?"

"I cut," she replied, pushing past him and beginning to walk to the bus pick-up area.

"Did you hear me say I'm sorry?" he asked.

She just nodded.

"So is everything okay?" he pressed, as he hurried to walk beside her.

She ignored the question.

Draping his arm over her shoulder, he tried to draw her close. The once welcome feel of his touch now suddenly made her cringe. Rather than leaning into him the way she usually did, she pulled away.

Miles stopped in his tracks. "Madison," he said. "Look at me, would you?"

She stopped and looked into his eyes. Her heart began to melt as she saw what appeared to be genuine regret.

"Let's go to your house and make up," he said hopefully, a twinkle in his eye.

So that was it. He wanted to push the whole thing aside and get back to the passion they'd shared when their bodies came together. Like that would make everything okay.

"I can't, Miles. I need time."

"Time for what?" Again the edge crept into his voice.

"Time to think and to figure things out."

"What's to figure out? We love each other, right?" he asked.

"I thought we did," she replied. "But now I'm not so sure."

He leaned down and kissed her, and her resolve began to melt. Then, out of the corner of her eye, she saw Brianna walking past them with a triumphant smile on her face. Madison pushed away from Miles. "I can't do this. Not right now." She walked away, hoping her boyfriend wouldn't turn and chase after the girl he'd kissed that morning.

A few miles away at Shoreline Manor, Joan and her handful of prayer warriors were meeting for tea and intercession. Joan's hand trembled a bit as she carefully poured the vanilla brew into her cup after the other ladies helped themselves. Margie had brought her blueberry scones, still warm from the oven, and their aroma filled the tiny apartment.

"Shall we pray?" Clara asked, holding out her hands, which prompted an unbroken chain of solidarity around the tiny kitchen table. With heads bowed, she asked a blessing over their treats and meeting. "Our dear heavenly Father, we are so very thankful for each other and for the blessing of bringing our concerns to this table. Would You please help us intercede for our loved ones? And we want to thank You for these treats. Please bless the hands that prepared them. In the name of our Lord and Savior, Jesus Christ, amen."

"Amen" they all echoed as they gave each other's hand a squeeze of friendship.

The scones were delicious, and Margie beamed as compliments flowed from the circle of friends. As the last crumbs disappeared, and the teacups were refilled, Joan suggested they begin exchanging requests. She retrieved her prayer journal from the teacart and waited while the other ladies pulled theirs out of purses.

Soon the tabletop was ringed with open books ready for the task at hand. Joan licked the point of her pencil, a habit from further back than she could remember, and wrote today's date at the top of the next clean page. As the Silver Sisters went around the circle and shared updates on previous requests as well as new ones to add to their journals, Joan tried to focus and keep up. But her mind kept straying to Madison. And her spirit was troubled.

"Isn't that the truth!" Beverly exclaimed in response to a comment by Clara. "Right, Joan?"

Joan felt her cheeks redden. "I'm so sorry. I missed that."

"Are you alright, dear?" Margie asked, leaning over and putting a hand on Joan's arm.

Tears welled up in her eyes, surprising even Joan herself. "It's Madison," was all she could choke out.

Her friends all shifted in their chairs and began reaching out, taking Joan's hands in theirs or resting a hand on her shoulder. "Tell us," Clara said. "What is it?"

Joan's heart swelled with love for her friends. Here they were coming alongside just as Phil would have done. It bolstered her courage and resolve. The enemy would not have victory if the Silver Sisters had any say in it! Pouring out her concerns, she shared with her prayer group about how concerned she felt in her spirit about Madison. "I don't have any details to give you ladies, but something is very wrong. I can feel it here," she said, pointing to her heart.

Margie cleared her throat and sat up straight and tall. "Madison is going to the top of our list, Sisters!" She turned to Joan and said, "We don't need to know any details. God sees it all. We'll just let Him know we are standing in solidarity on her behalf."

"Amen!" Beverly chimed in, squeezing Joan's hand. Turning to Clara, the one who loved to give voice to their prayers, Bev asked, "Would you lead us in this one?"

Clara rose to her feet, and the other ladies joined her. Once again linking hands, they all bowed their heads, all except Clara, who raised her face heavenward as she interceded for her friend's great granddaughter.

When they took their seats again a few moments later, Joan's heart felt lighter and her pencil was ready to go to work.

"Madison, we need to talk," Michelle said later that night. "I got a call from school today," she added as she sat down on the couch beside Maddie. "What's the deal with cutting history class?"

"I didn't feel well," Madison replied, crossing her arms and looking away.

"That's why they have a school nurse. When you don't feel well, you go there. You don't just cut class."

"I didn't feel like going to the nurse, Mom," Madison said, feeling cornered. "I'm not some little kid who goes running to the nurse's office to call my mommy."

"No one said you were a little girl," Michelle replied curtly. Then her voice softened a little. "Tell me what's going on."

"You wouldn't understand," Madison said, wishing she could just disappear.

"Try me. You might be surprised."

"I can't explain it, Mom," Madison began. "I just don't feel like myself. Something's wrong."

Michelle paused and took a deep breath before asking, "You're not pregnant, are you?"

"Why does everyone keep asking me that?" Madison said as she stood and started walking out of the room. She had to get away. She couldn't breathe.

"Everyone as in whom?" Michelle demanded.

"You, Lucy, Miles."

"Miles asked if you were pregnant?"

Madison's heart stopped. The room closed in on her as the realization of her admission sunk in. Spinning, she faced her mother. "I'm not the perfect daughter you always thought I was. And I'm NOT pregnant," she added, grabbing the car keys from the hook by the door and racing outside.

"Madison, wait!" her mother called.

But she bolted to the car, climbed in and locked the door, and then drove off into the night.

CHAPTER FIFTEEN

Sheila and Rick were snuggled up together on the couch watching an old movie when they heard a knock on the front door. "Who could that be?" Sheila asked as she sat up.

"I'll go," Rick replied, standing to his feet and pushing the pause button on the remote control. Sheila followed closely behind him suddenly feeling a wave of concern for her mother. Was this Michelle coming over to deliver bad news?

Neither of them was prepared for what they saw when Rick opened the door. Standing on their doorstep was Madison, tears spilling down her cheeks as she hugged herself tightly.

Rick immediately moved aside, giving Sheila access to her granddaughter.

"Maddie? What's wrong?" Sheila asked and then added, "Come inside."

Madison rubbed her nose with the back of her hand and sniffed away her tears as she entered the house. Sheila wrapped her arms around her and tried to comfort her, a myriad of questions rushing through her mind. *Was everyone okay? What would bring her granddaughter here alone this late?* As Madison began to relax in her embrace, Sheila gently pulled back and wiped her granddaughter's tears away.

"What's wrong, sweetheart?" she asked, studying Madison's face for answers.

Madison took a shaky breath and said, "Everything, Grandma."

"There, there," Sheila murmured softly, remembering some of Michelle's teenage woes. Hopefully this was nothing more serious than a break up with that boyfriend. "Come and sit down, and let's talk," she said to Maddie as she glanced over and made eye contact with Rick, hoping to send a silent message.

He took her lead. "I'll be in the kitchen if you need me," he said as he walked out of the room.

Sheila led Madison over to the couch, and they sat down side-by-side. Her granddaughter looked so distraught and lost. Sheila knew Michelle had been concerned about Maddie, but as she looked at Madison's face, concern was rapidly replaced with alarm. She'd never seen her granddaughter so pale and gaunt. It was as if a big part of her was missing, leaving behind a nearly empty shell.

"Do you want to tell me what's going on?" Sheila asked softly, reaching over and taking Madison's hand in her own.

Maddie sank back into the soft cushions of the couch and let out a ragged sigh. "I've ruined everything," she said as she stared off across the room. "My life is completely messed up. And I'm scared, Grandma. Something's really wrong with me. I think I'm going crazy." Once again her eyes filled with tears as her voice shook.

"Madison, you are not going crazy," Sheila said, hoping she sounded convincing and calm. "I think you'd better start at the beginning and explain to me what is going on. But first, does your mother know where you are?" she asked, suddenly picturing Michelle worrying frantically.

Madison shook her head.

"Then I need to call her and let her know you are okay."

"I can't go home, Grandma. Can I please just stay here tonight?" she pleaded.

Sheila nodded as she patted her hand. "Of course you can. You just sit here and gather your thoughts, and I'll go call your mom and get us some hot cocoa. Then we can talk."

"Okay. Thanks," she replied, offering a weak smile, while her eyes remained solemn.

Rick looked up from the kitchen table as Sheila entered. "Everything okay?" he asked.

"I honestly don't know. Right now, I'm going to call Michelle and let her know Madison's here. Would you get the cocoa from the pantry? I'm going to make us some hot chocolate, and then try to get her to tell me what's the matter."

"Sure," he replied, retrieving the cocoa while Sheila dialed Michelle.

As she waited for someone to answer at the other end, Sheila glanced over and saw him set it on the counter and get the milk out of the fridge.

"Mom?" Michelle's voice spoke through the receiver.

"Yes, it's me, hon," Sheila replied. "I'm calling to let you know Maddie is over here."

"Oh, thank God," her daughter said, the relief traveling across the wires. "Can I talk to her?"

"Let me have a little time with her first, okay? She seems pretty distraught. Rick's fixing some hot cocoa for us, and then I'm going to let her vent about whatever is bothering her. Did you two have a fight or something?"

"She cut class today. I was talking to her about what was going on, and she got really upset and stormed out the door."

Sheila paused for a second. "Madison cutting class? That doesn't sound like her."

"That's what I said," Michelle replied. "She's not acting like herself, Mom. Something is really troubling her." She paused and then added, "I can come over, if you want."

"No, it's okay. I told her she could stay here tonight. Is that alright with you?"

"Hold on a second, Mom."

Sheila could hear muffled voices. It sounded like Michelle was talking with Steve.

A few moments later, she was back on the line. "Okay, that's fine. But I'll need my car in the morning for school. I think I'll have Steve bring me over to pick it up. We won't come to the door or anything."

"What about the keys? Do you want me to set them out on the porch?" Sheila asked.

"No. Steve's got a set for the van. I'll use his," she replied. "Let me know how it goes, okay? Call me after you two have talked. If it ends up being pretty late, I guess Madison can miss the first couple of classes in the morning, but she'll need a note and a ride to school at some point."

"We can take her, honey. Don't worry about that," Sheila said. "Rick's got an appointment at work at ten. He can drop her off on his way."

"Okay. If I don't hear from you later tonight, I'll call during my conference period around eleven," Michelle promised. "And Mom?"

"Yeah?"

"Thanks."

"Of course, dear."

"I'll be praying for you to have the right words for Madison," her daughter added before hanging up.

Sheila said a silent prayer of her own as she retrieved the two cups of hot cocoa Rick had made and headed back into the living room. *Please help me, Lord. You know what is going on with Madison. Help me understand and know what to say to her.*

180

Madison was slouched back into the cushions of the sofa, biting her nail as Sheila entered the living room with their cocoa. Sheila couldn't remember seeing her granddaughter displaying that nervous habit, one Sheila's son Tim had struggled with all his life. Sitting down beside her, she set the cocoa on the coffee table and put her hand on Madison's shoulder. "Feel like talking?" she asked. "Or do you just want to sit and sip for a while?" she added, gesturing to the steaming mugs.

Her granddaughter glanced over at her and then to the cocoa. She leaned forward and picked up one of the mugs, cupping it in her hand and staring down into the creamy chocolate. "Smells good," she said softly.

"Rick makes a mean cup of cocoa," Sheila replied with a smile as she reached for her own mug.

They sat for a few minutes, sipping the sweetness as Madison skirted the issue at hand. "So how do you like being married again, Grandma?"

Sheila looked into her eyes and replied, "It's better than I could have imagined, honey. After your grandfather died, I thought this stage of my life was over. Being a wife, I mean. Then, when Rick came along, I was skeptical at first." She paused. "You know he was your mother's professor a while back, right?"

"Yeah. She told me the whole story."

"So you can guess why I was reluctant to get involved with him."

Madison nodded.

"But, you know, the truth is that people sometimes change. With God's help, that is. And Rick is one of them." She took another sip of cocoa and then added, "He's not perfect, Maddie. No one is. And we've had to adjust to each other's ways. But overall, I feel very blessed to have found him."

"You *are* blessed, Grandma," Madison replied, her voice dropping as she set her half empty cup down. "You're a good person. You deserve a good husband."

Sheila was a bit taken aback by her granddaughter's tone of voice. She sounded so much older than her years. Older. Wiser. And yet somehow more vulnerable than ever. She reached over and patted Madison on the knee. "What's going on, sweetheart?"

Madison looked away and took a deep breath. After letting it out, she replied, "There's something wrong with me, Grandma."

Sheila studied her face. All traces of her usual smiles were gone, replaced by a furrowed brow and invisible dark clouds threatening to unleash a storm of sorrow. *What could be troubling her so much?* Sheila asked herself. Searching for words of reassurance, she tentatively said, "Sometimes things look worse than they really are. Why don't you tell me what you think is wrong?" she suggested.

Madison looked into her eyes for a moment and then glanced away again, focusing on the window across the room as she began to open up. "Freaky things are happening to me. I keep getting these panicky feelings, like I can't breathe, like I have to get away, but there's nothing to get away from." She hesitated, and Sheila could see tears beginning to pool in her eyes. When Madison turned back to face her, she noticed one escape and make a trail down her granddaughter's cheek. It was quickly brushed away before Madison said, "I think I'm going crazy, Grandma."

And then the storm broke loose. An onslaught of tears led to uncontrollable sobbing, as Sheila watched her shatter into shards of sorrow and fear. Drawing her close, Sheila held tightly, rocking her granddaughter in her arms the way she did when Maddie was a little baby. "It's okay. Let it all out," she said gently.

They remained locked together for several minutes, rocking through tears. Two generations apart, and yet hearts so closely woven together.

Finally Madison pulled back. Her face was red and her makeup was streaked from the tears. She sniffed and wiped the sleeve of her sweatshirt across her eyes as Sheila reached for a tissue on the end table and handed it to her.

After Madison had calmed down a bit, Sheila spoke again. "I don't know everything about what's going on with you, sweetheart, but I know you're not crazy. It sounds like you are having some anxiety attacks, and they can be pretty scary. I've had a few myself."

"Really?" her granddaughter asked, her face showing a sliver of relief.

"Really." Sheila reached over and took Madison's hand. "Mine happened when life started rushing too fast, and I couldn't seem to catch up."

Madison nodded.

"Do you want to tell me what's going on in your life right now? Maybe we can figure this out together."

Madison's eyes met hers. She seemed to be seriously considering the question. Finally she slouched back against the cushions again, looked down into her lap, and said softly, "I've ruined everything."

"What's 'everything'?" Sheila asked.

"My life. My future. Everything."

Sheila thought for a moment. How should she respond? *Help me, Lord. How I wish Dad were here. He'd know exactly what to say,* she thought. "What exactly happened, Maddie? Is this about your boyfriend?"

Madison shot her a quick look and then averted her eyes again. "I guess you could say that. Although I'm not sure he's my boyfriend anymore."

Oh, Lord, is this about a teenage break up? Would that have her this upset? Sheila tried to remember back to her high school years. The crushes, the dates, the hopes for the future.

Before she could ask another question, Madison blurted out, "I gave myself to him, Grandma. I didn't mean to, but it happened. We were just kissing and stuff, and then…we…we went too far."

Oh, no. Please don't let her be pregnant, she prayed.

As if reading her thoughts, Madison said, "I'm not pregnant or anything." She paused and then added, "But now Miles is different. He's flirting with other girls, and he's getting pretty impatient with me about…about…you know, the panicky feelings and stuff. It seems like all he thinks about is being together, that way. Like our whole relationship is about that, now." She took a shaky breath, looked into Sheila's eyes and said, "Look at me, Grandma. I'm a mess. Now no one will ever love me. Not the way Grandpa loved you."

And suddenly Sheila realized this was a divine appointment. An opportunity for her to share some things about her past and her marriage to Maddie's grandfather, John, that would help her see and better understand the redeeming grace of God's love.

She turned to her granddaughter. "Madison, there are some things about your grandfather and me that you don't know. And I think it's high time you did."

Maddie looked surprised. "What are you talking about, Grandma?"

"I'm talking about when I was a young girl, just a little older than you are right now. And the choices I made. Choices I would make very differently today. But those choices are the reason your mother and your uncle Tim are here. And they're why you are here too, sweetheart. So even though I regret some of the things I did back then, God was able to turn them around for good, just like He can do for you."

Her granddaughter was very focused now, eager to hear what Sheila was about to tell her.

"When I was nineteen, I met your Grandpa John. He was five years older than me, and such a handsome man. We met at the restaurant where I was waiting tables."

"You were a waitress, Grandma?"

Sheila nodded. "I sure was. It was the summer after my first year at community college. I was earning some money to help with books for the following year, not to mention some spending money for clothes and other things I wanted."

"So Grandpa just walked into the restaurant?"

"Something like that. I remember seeing him sitting with a girl who looked a little older than me. They were talking about something pretty serious. Later, I found out he was breaking up with her."

"You were their waitress?"

"I was. I took their order, but by the time I got back with the food, the girl was gone. I offered to take her food off the bill, but he insisted on paying for it. 'Why don't you join me?' he asked, gesturing toward her empty seat. It was nearly my break time, and the restaurant was pretty slow that night, so I decided to take him up on the offer. I sat down, and we ate together as we started talking about our lives."

"Wow, that sounds like a movie or something," Madison said, a real, albeit tentative, smile visiting her face for the first time that evening. "So then you guys just started dating after that?"

"Not exactly. He asked for my number, and I gave it to him. But he didn't call for a few weeks, so I figured he wasn't really interested." She paused and gazed across the room for a moment, remembering how she'd waited by the phone hoping to hear from John.

"So what happened?"

"Well, about a month later, he showed up at the restaurant again. He was all smiles and full of charm. Said he'd been busy with a project at his new job, but now it was over and he'd have some time. So we started seeing each other. In fact, we were together almost every day."

"What did your parents think of him?" Madison asked.

Sheila looked her in the eye. "My mother didn't like him. And my father was concerned."

"But you dated him anyway."

"I did. We didn't spend time at my house because I didn't want my parents saying anything that might rock the boat. But we went on lots of dates and had a great time. Your grandfather was a pretty daring guy, and he took me places and showed me things I'd never experienced before."

"Sounds romantic," Madison remarked.

"I guess it was," she agreed. "Then one day, he asked me if I'd marry him."

"Really? Just like that?"

"Yep. Just like that."

"But you were only nineteen still right?"

"I was. But I thought I was very grown up."

"What did you say?"

"I said yes, but that he needed to talk to my parents, too. By that time, I was convinced he was the man for me. And I just knew my parents would see that, too."

Madison shook her head in amazement. "My parents would totally freak out if I was thinking about getting married that young."

Sheila smiled. "Believe me, my parents freaked out, too. They started asking John all kinds of questions about God and what he believed. All the church stuff I'd been raised on. I knew he wasn't a Christian, but I figured after we got married, I'd just ask him to go to church with me and he'd go. He seemed pretty willing to do whatever I wanted at the time."

"So did your parents say you couldn't get married?"

Sheila nodded. "In so many words, yes. They said they could not bless the engagement."

"What did you do?"

"I left with John, and I moved into his apartment."

"Seriously?"

"Seriously. I told my parents that if they couldn't bless our marriage, I'd just live with John instead."

"Grandma! I can't believe that!" Madison exclaimed, her eyes big as saucers.

"I wish it wasn't true, honey. But that's what I did."

"So what made you guys decide to get married?"

"One month, about a year after I'd moved in, I thought I was pregnant. I went and told my mom, and we both talked to my dad. They agreed that I should marry John and give the baby a father and a stable home."

"So that was Mom?"

"Actually, it turned out I wasn't pregnant after all. But by the time I figured that out, the wedding had been planned, and we decided to go forward with it, especially now that my parents seemed to accept the idea. I actually moved back home for a few months before the wedding. It was tough, but my father thought it was important to step back and make sure this was what I wanted to do with my life."

"That must have been weird. Being back with your parents again."

"It was a little weird, yes. But it showed me how much I loved your grandfather and wanted to spend my life with him."

"So you got married."

"We did. And eventually your mother came along. Then your uncle."

"Did grandpa start going to church with you like you hoped he would?" Madison asked.

"No. He refused to go. I went for a while by myself, and even took your mother and her brother for special holidays like Christmas and Easter. But basically, I turned my back on how my parents had raised me. John seemed so intelligent and so worldly wise. He was very persuasive in his arguments against my faith, and over time I began to think maybe he was right."

"Wow. Your parents must have been pretty upset, your dad being a pastor and all," her granddaughter said.

"I'm sure they were, Maddie. But they didn't voice their opinions. They just kept praying for us and for our kids, that we would find our way to Jesus."

"So how *did* you, Grandma? How did you and Grandpa finally come to the Lord?" By now Madison's countenance had completely changed. Sheila could see her relaxing and really listening with open ears and an open heart.

"Your mother told you about your grandfather's accident, right?" Sheila still couldn't bring herself to say attempted suicide when she referred to John's desperate act.

Madison nodded. "Yes."

"Well, that was the beginning of a big change in our lives."

"But that was, like thirty years after you got married," Madison said, incredulously.

"Twenty-five, actually. Yes, it was a long time. Many years of living without God." She paused and took Madison's hand in hers. "During those years, honey, I had my share of anxiety attacks. Times when I thought I was going crazy, too."

"What did you do?" she asked.

"I tried to ignore it most of the time. Sometimes I'd go talk to my dad, and he would pray for me. That seemed to help. And I just kept telling myself, 'You'll be fine,' until I'd finally believe it."

Madison reached out and embraced her. As she felt her granddaughter's arms around the back of her neck, Sheila flashed back to Maddie's chubby little arms as a toddler, and how special it felt when those arms were in the same place they were in right now.

"I love you, Grandma," Maddie said softly.

"I love you, too, sweetheart," Sheila replied, her heart soaring as she realized that God was using her testimony to bring hope to her granddaughter's life.

CHAPTER SIXTEEN

Madison lay in bed in her grandmother's guest room feeling exhausted. Her talk with her grandmother had helped her feel a little more normal. Maybe she wasn't going crazy after all. Grandma Sheila seemed to have gone through some of the same fears and anxieties that she'd been experiencing herself. But her life turned out okay.

Madison was just closing her eyes and surrendering to sleep when her cell phone rang. It was Miles. She couldn't face talking to him. Not tonight. So she hit the silence button and turned away from the phone. She'd figure out what to do about him in the morning when she wasn't so tired.

As she drifted off, she found herself suddenly back at school, out near the gym. She heard Miles' voice coming from the distance. Glancing over, she saw him talking to a girl who was sitting on his lap on a bench. The girl's arms were wrapped around Miles' neck in an intimate embrace. Then Madison saw them kiss. A long, passionate kiss like the ones she and Miles had shared in her bedroom.

Walking closer to them, she heard talking again. It was Brianna. "Want to come over to my house?" she asked. "We can be alone there."

"Yeah. Sounds good," he replied, pulling her close and nestling into her chest.

Madison was devastated. She turned and began to run away. As she ran, she heard another voice calling her. It was Luke. "Madison?

Where are you?" he called from across the field. She tried to call back to him but no words would come. Turning, she fled in his direction, but by the time she got there, he was gone.

"Luke? I'm here!" she called out as she frantically searched for him.

"Who's Luke?" a voice behind her asked.

Spinning, she found herself looking into Miles' face. He was alone now.

"Where's your girlfriend?" she asked in an accusatory tone.

"What are you talking about? You're my girlfriend," he replied, trying to pull her into an embrace. She resisted at first and then surrendered to his arms.

"Let's go to your house," he said as he began walking her toward the parking lot.

Soon they were back in her bedroom doing the things she knew she shouldn't do. Her phone buzzed, the vibrator audible even though the ring was silenced. Groping for it, she answered. It was her grandmother. "What are you doing, Maddie?" she asked cheerfully.

Pushing away from Miles, Madison sat up. Her heart was pounding and she was having trouble swallowing.

"Maddie? Are you okay?" her grandmother's voice asked again.

Madison struggled to find her voice. Then she felt a hand on her shoulder. She tried to shake off Miles touch.

Her grandmother's voice seemed closer now. "Wake up, honey."

Opening her eyes, she saw Sheila standing beside the bed. "You've been talking in your sleep, sweetheart. You sounded upset. Were you having a bad dream?"

Madison nodded. "Yeah. But I'm okay now," she said.

Her grandmother sat down on the edge of the bed. "Do you want me to stay in here for a few minutes?"

"No, it's okay. Thanks, though."

After leaning over and kissing her forehead, her grandma said, "Alright, honey. I'll see you in the morning."

Madison forced a smile. "Yeah. Thanks again for letting me stay here, Grandma."

Sheila rose and walked out of the room, giving her one last smile before gently closing the door.

Madison wandered into the kitchen the following morning, her hair in disarray and her eyes still fighting daylight. It was nearly eighty-thirty, Rick was immersed in emails on his laptop, and Sheila was having a second cup of coffee. "Good morning, sweetheart," she said to her granddaughter.

"Good morning, Grandma. I think I overslept a little. School started forty-five minutes ago." She sank down into a chair at the table and rested her elbows on the checkered tablecloth, propping her head in her hands.

Sheila reached over and rubbed Madison's arm. "Rick will take you to school on his way to campus in about an hour. Your mother said it was fine for you to miss a couple of classes this morning."

Madison nodded. "Okay. Thanks."

"How about some breakfast? I could scramble you some eggs or whip up some pancakes."

"I don't want you go to go any trouble, Grandma. I can just have some toast or cereal if you have any," she replied.

"Nonsense. It's no trouble at all. If I remember correctly, you used to be pretty fond of my blueberry pancakes. And I just happen to have some fresh blueberries on hand," Sheila said.

"Really?"

"Really. Why don't you go get dressed, and I'll have them ready in a jiff. Your mother dropped off some clothes on her way to work this morning. They're in a bag by the front door."

Madison stood up and hugged her. "Thanks, Grandma. I'll be back in a few minutes."

By the time she returned, Sheila had three pancakes waiting for her on the table. "Eat up," she said with a smile.

Madison ate about half and then began pushing the rest around on her plate. "Grandma?" she asked.

"Yes?"

"Do you think I could stay here for a few days?" Her voice sounded casual but her face was telling a different story.

"I'd need to talk to your mother about that," Sheila replied, glancing over at Rick who was looking at her over the top of his computer screen. "I'll try to reach her during her break today. How's that? And then we can talk after school."

"Okay," Madison agreed. "Thanks for the pancakes," she added, taking another bite before taking her plate to the counter. "They're really good. I just don't have a huge appetite these days."

"No problem, honey. I'm glad you liked them."

As soon as Madison had left the room to finish getting ready for school, Sheila turned to Rick. "What do you think?"

"About?"

"About Maddie staying here for a few days."

"It's up to you, Sheila. Whatever you think is best is fine with me. She seems to be responding to you pretty well. Maybe you'll be able to talk to her more easily than her mother can right now."

Sheila nodded. "That's what I was thinking. She might see me as a little more objective."

Rick grinned. "I wouldn't say that, exactly, 'Grandma,' but I think she feels safe with you."

"Yeah. You're right. That's a better word for it." She walked over to where he was sitting and stood beside him, resting her hand on his shoulder. "I love you, Dr. Chambers," she said.

"Really?" he asked with a teasing air of surprise.

She swatted his arm softly before leaning down to kiss him.

Sheila sat with her Bible after Rick and Madison left. Her hand resting on its leather cover, she thought about how comforting her faith had become to her. It remained such a personal thing. One that she shared with Rick, but not yet to the depths of her parents' spiritual bond.

There was something about being alone with God that peeled off layers she didn't even realize she was wearing. Layers of false confidence, of protection from vulnerability, of hiding past hurts and doubts. One by one, they seemed to fall away as she sat with her heavenly Father and poured out her heart.

Resting her head against the back of the rocker, she closed her eyes and began to pray. *Thank you, Father, for bringing Madison here last night and for giving me the courage to share my story with her. Please help her through the day at school, guard her from darkness, and help her know how precious she is to You. I pray for Michelle and Steve to have wisdom and to know how to help their daughter through this season of life. Please give all of them a broader perspective and the assurance to trust You to work it all out. And may Your will be done regarding whether or not Madison would benefit from staying here for a while.*

Opening her eyes again, she found the spot in her Bible where her favorite verse waited for her each day. Psalm 46:10, a verse that had been her default guide whenever she was confused. The words caressed her heart and eased her mind.

Be still and know that I am God.

In the margin beside it, she'd written 'Isaiah 41:10.' She flipped there next.

Fear not, for I am with you; be not dismayed, for I am your God; I will strengthen you, I will help you, I will uphold you with my righteous right hand.

Closing her eyes, she recited both verses in her mind. She was just about to pick up her devotional book, when the phone rang. Her daughter's name appeared on the caller ID screen.

"Michelle? Are you on break already?" she asked.

"Hi Mom. Yeah. We are on assembly schedule today, so my break is earlier than usual. I've only got about twenty minutes. How did it go with Madison this morning? And what did she say last night?"

"We talked about her boyfriend and some things that were worrying her. She is really down on herself, Michelle. And she dropped a pretty big bomb when she opened up to me. You two need to talk." Sheila thought for a moment and then added, "She's such a beautiful girl, and you and Steve have done a great job letting her know how special she is to you. To all of us. But it seems like nothing matters right now except this boy and her peers."

"I know," Michelle agreed. "I see this all the time with my eighth graders. They are so focused on peer approval and being in relationships, that they often lose sight of themselves. Were you able to help her see the bigger picture?"

"I hope so, honey. I actually shared some pretty personal things about my own life, including my relationship with your father before we were married. She seemed to really plug into that."

"Did you tell her you lived with Dad before you got married?"

"I did. And I shared with her how difficult it is to be married to someone who doesn't share your faith or the faith of your family."

"How did she respond to that?" Michelle asked.

196

"She nodded and seemed to be listening," Sheila replied. "But who knows what was going on in her mind. She's pretty hooked on that Miles kid."

After a pause, Michelle asked, "What was the bomb she dropped?"

"I want to give her a chance to tell you herself. But she needs a little time. She asked if she could stay here for a while."

"Really? What do you think of that idea? I'd hate to have her intruding on you and Rick. I mean you two are newlyweds and all."

Sheila laughed. "I guess you could say that, honey, but it's not quite the same as the first time around. We enjoy being together and treasure our alone time, but we both agree that she's welcome to stay if you and Steve approve. As Rick said this morning, Maddie seems to feel safe with me. Maybe God could use that to give me a chance to share some things she might not be able to receive from you two right now."

She could hear Michelle take a deep breath on the other end.

"Okay. Let me talk to Steve and get back to you. How was Madison planning on getting home today? Did she tell you?"

"Rick offered to pick her up. He's only teaching a couple of classes today, and then he has a short meeting in his office. He said he could time his departure to be waiting at the school when she got out."

"That husband of yours is pretty special," Michelle said. "You know that, right? I mean the way he's taken over for Dad in a grandpa role with Caleb has meant the world to him."

"It's meant the world to Rick, too, Mimi. He never thought he'd have a chance to be a grandfather, so he loves that the kids call him Grandpa and that Caleb likes to spend time with him doing guy stuff. Your father adored your kids, but he was so limited in what he could do with them after his accident. It's a gift that Rick could step into this role."

"Yeah. We're really thankful for that," Michelle replied. "Well, I'd better get off the phone. I'll try to reach Steve, and I'll call you back later today."

After they'd hung up, Sheila picked up her book and flipped to the next devotional message. She couldn't help but smile when she saw the scripture at the top of the page. Galatians 6:9.

Let us not become weary in doing good, for at the proper time we will reap a harvest if we do not give up.

She hoped that meant God might use her and her life to bring perspective and renewal to her granddaughter. Although she'd never been part of a formal ministry, as she read the message under the verse, she realized that being a grandma could be a ministry in itself.

Ten minutes later, Michelle called again and told her that they'd decided Madison could stay there for a while. "But only under one condition," her daughter said.

"What's that?" Sheila asked.

"You've got to tell us if it gets to be too much for you, Mom. Or if it starts to interfere with you and Rick. Promise?"

"I promise," she replied. "When she gets back here from school, I'll run her over to your house to get clothes and whatever else she needs."

"Okay. Thanks, Mom. I mean it. Really. She can stay for a few days. Maybe a week if you are up to it. But call me anytime."

"I will. And I'll keep you posted on what's going on over here with her. I want Maddie to feel safe with me. But she needs to know that I'll be in communication with you, too."

"Great. I think this will be really good for her." There was a brief pause, and then Michelle added, "I've gotta run, Mom. My next class is waiting outside the door."

After saying goodbye to her daughter, Sheila stood up and headed for the guest room. "I'd better make sure there are a few empty drawers in the dresser and some room for hanging clothes in the closet," she said aloud to herself, as she pictured all the items she and Rick had stored in that room after they got married.

Madison missed history class that morning and purposely hid in the library during lunch to avoid seeing Miles. But after school, as she walked out to meet Rick, she heard him calling out her name. "Hey, Madison! Wait up!"

Looking over her shoulder, she could see him weaving through the masses exiting campus. A moment later, he was by her side, his arm draped over her shoulder. "Where were you this morning?" he asked.

"I slept in."

"Nice," he replied approvingly. "Want a ride home?" He pulled her close and kissed the top of her head.

"I'm not going home. I'm staying with my grandmother for a while."

"Really? Are your parents out of town? Maybe we could go there first, and then I could drop you at your grandma's house."

She felt herself bristle, knowing full well why he wanted to go to her house first. "I can't. Rick's picking me up."

"Rick?" he asked, with what sounded like a possible twinge of jealousy.

Madison hesitated for a moment before answering, enjoying the fact that he might finally realize he didn't own her. "Yeah. Rick." She looked up at him and smiled. "He's my grandmother's new husband."

Relief written across his face, Miles replied, "Oh. Okay. No problem."

Madison thought about her dream and about what Grandma Sheila had shared about the difficulty of being married to someone outside of her faith. "Miles?" she began.

"Yeah?"

"I think I'm going to get more involved in the youth group at church again. Do you think you'd want to come with me Thursday for their pizza and game night?"

Miles' arm dropped from her shoulder. "I thought we already talked about all this. I'm not into the church thing, remember?"

"Yeah. I remember. I just wondered if you might reconsider. I mean now that we've gotten so serious and everything. It's really important to me," she explained.

He shook his head in what looked like frustration. "You do whatever you want, Madison. But honestly, I'm not into that. Don't expect me to suddenly become some holy roller and start going to church with you all the time. Okay?"

"Okay. Got it. No church for you."

"Well, I guess I'll head home," he said. "See you in the morning."

"Right."

Miles leaned down to kiss her, but she pulled away. "Bye," she said, as she turned and walked toward Rick's car, waiting at the curb.

Madison looked pretty upset when she got into the car. "Everything okay?" Rick asked.

"Why do guys have to be so impossible?" she replied.

"Well…I'm not quite sure how to answer that one. Maybe it would help if I knew what 'impossible' thing we're talking about." *Give me wisdom here, God,* he prayed silently, feeling very inadequate to the task of addressing her issues with her boyfriend.

"Miles. He can be such a jerk sometimes." Her words were harsh but her voice betrayed her hurt.

Rick glanced over and could see that she was on the verge of crying. *Should I say something or just wait for her to say more?* He was accustomed to the college students he taught, but high school girls were out of his comfort zone completely.

"Grandpa?" Madison said, her voice silencing his thoughts, as the term 'grandpa' melted his heart.

"Yes?"

"Don't you teach about ancient civilizations?"

"I do."

"What do you think about all the old laws in the Bible? I mean like how they are so strict about sex only in marriage. Aren't they kind of outdated? Like, I mean, we don't stone people for adultery anymore, and we don't follow all the old dietary restrictions. It seems like we've sort of evolved from those old rules." She glanced over at him and then continued. "Don't you ever find it difficult to reconcile your new faith with what the Bible says on stuff like that? My mom told me about how much you've changed since when she was in your class. But did you change your mind on all of that?"

"By all of that, you mean?"

"I mean like all the rules in the Bible about sex and stuff."

Whoa. How do I answer that one? he thought, as he quickly shot up another prayer for wisdom. And then, almost as if he could hear God speaking to his heart, clearer than ever before, the thought penetrated to his core—*I have prepared you for this from the beginning.* And as the professor in him

201

merged with the new man of faith, he was suddenly able to speak to her question with confidence.

"Okay, Madison, here goes." He looked over at her to be sure she was listening. "I've been studying human societies and cultures for years. You're right. That's what my job is as a professor of cultural anthropology."

"Yeah."

"So to answer your question, there was a time when I had disdain for the Bible and what you call its 'rules' about so many things. But now...now that I've spent the past few years digging deeply into scripture and coming to understand the heart of God, I see the absolute beauty and perfection of what I once dismissed as outdated. And when I look back and reexamine the societies of the past that perished, I see how applying God's wisdom to their culture could have saved them the decay that triggered their demise."

"Oh," she replied, not sounding convinced.

Pulling the car into the driveway and turning off the motor, he turned to her and said, "Let me see if I can explain how I understand it."

"Okay," she replied.

"God's Law has three parts," He held up three fingers and tapped each one as he stated, "moral laws, ceremonial laws, and civil laws. Since most of the laws we, as Christians, no longer follow are in the Old Testament, I'll give you Old Testament examples first."

Madison nodded, now clearly intrigued.

"Moral laws are God's standards for moral living, as in the Ten Commandments. They bridge both the Old and New Testament and are addressed in both. The moral laws in the Bible are still in effect for us today. They are God's *moral* standards for *all* individuals and *remain the same* yesterday, today, and forever. Those laws encompass the boundaries for relationships, including marriage.

"Ceremonial laws relate to the manner of worshipping God through sacrifices, burnt offerings, and ceremonies. Ceremonial laws were required for animal sacrifices. Those foreshadowed the perfect sacrifice of God's Son." He paused and she nodded. Then he continued. "Certain dietary restrictions in the Old Testament were also under the category of ceremonial law because they helped the Israelites distinguish between 'clean' and 'unclean' animals. Those ceremonial laws are no longer required because of Jesus' death on the cross. His death was the perfect sacrifice, which once and for all completely satisfied God's demand for righteousness. That's why animal sacrifices are no longer required to satisfy God's judgment and wrath against our sin. And God made that clear when He instructed Peter, in the New Testament, to eat all types of animals." He looked over to see her tracking along.

"So here's the key, these ceremonial laws, *unlike moral laws*, are *not* reinforced in the New Testament since Christ's death fulfilled them. We don't need them now because we have access to God through Jesus' sacrifice, which is why we don't perform animal sacrifices anymore."

Madison nodded again. "Right. That makes sense." She paused and then added, "Keep going."

"Okay, lastly, we have civil laws, which relate to the administration of justice. Civil laws can and do change, as they are relative to the civilization existing at a specific time. The civil laws in the Old Testament were the laws given by God specifically for the children of Israel. Civil laws vary from country to country with different forms of government. So, for example, in the United States we are not under the same civil laws as individuals living in Cuba."

"Right," she replied.

I think she's getting this, he thought, feeling relieved. "You know, Madison, in Hebrew culture a person could sell himself into slavery as a means to repay a debt, but we would never do that in our culture. That's another example of how civil laws evolve."

"Wow, I never knew all this," she admitted. "And I've been going to church all my life."

Rick smiled. "Trust me, Madison, there's a lifetime worth of concepts and truths to learn in scripture."

"Yeah. For sure," she agreed. "But wait a second. Isn't marriage a civil law thing? I mean like how the Supreme Court just changed the laws about marriage so now same-sex marriages are legal?"

He paused a moment. *Help me out here, Lord.* "It's become a civil law issue for our secular society, yes, because of concerns about rights and justice for all. But from what I've studied in scripture, Maddie, God was the One who invented sex and marriage. He had a plan for them to go together from the very beginning, as a sacred bond. The goal was to provide intimacy between one man and one woman in the boundaries of a lifelong relationship that would foster individual growth, spiritual partnership, and a balanced male-female structure to procreation and childrearing."

"So what do *you* think about the same-sex marriage law?" she asked.

Grasping for the right words, he replied, "Here's *my* perspective on why marriage was commanded by God to be between a man and a woman. In addition to the obvious matter of procreation, I believe God is in a continuous process of growing and stretching us beyond our comfort levels. It's not easy for two very different genders to build lasting companionship, understanding, and intimacy. But that was part of the reason for His plan.

"I believe He foreordained the relationship to be between a male and a female, who are built with very different shapes, needs, and strengths, to come together and be one for life. In the process the two sides of God— His strength and power, and His perfect love and boundless grace, are joined in marriage and families to bring a glimpse of divinity." He looked over at her and smiled. "To be honest, Maddie, women tend to civilize us men. We like strength and power. They are better at expressing love and grace."

Rick studied her reaction and could see a light go on in Madison. It reminded him of his students when they'd grasp a new concept during a discussion or lecture.

"Oh, *yeah*. I never thought of it that way," she said "but it makes sense." She paused and then asked, "But what about the idea of a guy and girl needing to be *married* to have a moral intimate relationship? Can't they still experience that without a piece of paper to make it legal and morally okay?"

He smiled. *Ah, yes, the age-old argument of young men trying to skirt commitment.* "It's not the piece of paper that makes the difference, Maddie. It's what that paper represents—a lifelong commitment. That's how God laid it out."

When he glanced over, she seemed deep in thought.

"I'd imagine it's a pretty tough time to be a teenager," he said.

She looked out the window and replied under her breath, "Sure is." She paused and then added, "Did you know that my grandma lived with my other grandpa before they got married?"

"Yes."

She seemed surprised. "Did you ever live with someone?" she asked.

Kids sure are bold these days, he thought before replying. "I did. When I was much younger."

"What happened?"

"You mean why did we break up?"

"Yeah."

"It was because of one of her friends' parents."

Madison glanced over at him, and he could see the question mark on her face.

205

He cleared his throat and launched into the story. "Her parents were pretty upset about our living situation, and they confronted her one time when she was home to pick up some things. Her father started calling me names—some pretty strong language, from what I recall her saying."

He paused to look over and see her furrowed brow.

"So what did she do? Break up with you?" she asked.

"Not at first. She stormed out of the house, told her parents she never wanted to see them again, and then fled to a friend's house for consolation."

Madison nodded.

"But her friend wasn't home. In fact, no one was there except the friend's father."

"What did she do?"

"Believe it or not, she actually told him the whole story. She was so distraught about the fight with her parents and their parting words, that she couldn't contain her emotions another minute."

"Wow. What did he say?" Madison was clearly soaking in every word.

"After he heard the whole thing, he said, 'Let me ask you something.' She said 'Okay.' And he asked her this unexpected question—'If something happened to Rick, like he fell off the roof and broke his neck, and he was paralyzed from the neck down, would you be willing to quit college and work full-time to support him and take care of him for the rest of your life?'" He paused to let the challenge soak in for a moment.

Madison's eyebrows lifted. "What did she say?"

"She said she didn't know." Rick looked over and smiled. "Then this dad said, 'Until you can answer that question, you are just playing house. You need to move out, and decide what you want in life. If you really love Rick and want to be with him forever, then get married and make that commitment permanent.' I guess it suddenly made sense to her because she came back to our place, packed up her stuff, and moved back home."

"Really?"

"Yep. She said we could get married or call it quits. And I wasn't ready for marriage, so that took care of that."

Madison sat silently for a couple of minutes. Then she said, "Thanks, Grandpa."

He looked over and saw something he hadn't expected. Relief. Her face glowing with relief.

CHAPTER SEVENTEEN

As Sheila was driving Madison over to the house to pick up some clothes, Madison's phone rang. Glancing down at her granddaughter's phone screen, she saw a picture of Miles. Maddie hit the silence button and tossed the phone back into her purse.

"Something wrong?" Sheila asked.

"I wish he would just leave me alone," her granddaughter replied.

"That was Miles?"

"Yeah."

They rode on in silence for a few minutes. Then Madison asked, "Did you ever think about breaking up with Grandpa John before you got married?"

Sheila's mind tumbled back in time to the many doubts she'd had before marrying Madison's grandfather. Would she lose her relationship with her parents? What would life be like in a home without God at the center? And how would she feel if John wanted to teach their children his philosophy of self-sufficiency instead of faith?

"You know, Madison, there were several times I almost left."

"Why didn't you?" Maddie asked.

"I was in love. He intrigued me with his rugged individualism, his confidence in his own ability to rise to every challenge life might throw his way. It was so different from what I'd seen in my own father, who relied completely on God for his strength and guidance." She paused and pictured the young John in her mind. But then the hardships of their marriage rushed back to her. The many years she'd felt insignificant, while he'd immersed himself in the world of success.

"The truth is, Maddie, I was fooled. What I saw as strength in John and weakness in my own father was actually really the opposite. My father had the strength of God dwelling within him. But John was relying on the mere strength of himself." She sighed and patted Madison's hand. "He did finally realize his need for God in his later years, after his accident. But we had a difficult marriage up to that point. And there were lots of challenges after he became an invalid."

Madison nodded. "I guess sometimes things don't turn out the way we thought."

"You're right. So, how about you? Are you thinking about breaking up with Miles?" Sheila asked, trying to sound only mildly curious while at the same time frantically praying that God would give Madison the courage to do just that.

"Yeah. I do love him. Or at least I think I do. But I love God, too, and Miles is totally against church. He says he doesn't care if I go, but he'll never go with me."

Sheila pulled the car into the driveway and turned off the engine. She looked over at her granddaughter and saw the same confusion and heartache she'd known as a young girl herself. It was only by God's grace that she'd gotten a second chance at love with a man who was seeking to grow in faith himself and share that experience with her.

With every fiber of her being, she wanted that for Madison, too. God had been patient with Sheila through her wrong choices and the years she'd turned her back on Him. But there'd been consequences along the way. If it was possible for her to help her granddaughter avoid that path, she wanted nothing more than to do so.

Reaching over, she squeezed Madison's hand. "Of all the things I've learned in my life, Maddie, the most important one is to put God first. You've probably heard that many times from many people. But it's absolutely true. I remember my father, your great grandpa Phil, used to start each day by praying, 'Lord, I want to know You more and love You deeper today.'"

"Grandpa Phil was one of my favorite people," Madison said, her voice filled with affection.

"Mine, too," Sheila replied with a smile. "And if he were here today, I think he'd advise you to be very careful about who you choose to be your lifelong mate. The world is pulling further and further away from God. We need those closest to us to be beacons of light, not a strong current to pull us away. Does that make sense?"

Madison studied her face. "You remind me of him," she said.

"Who?"

"Grandpa Phil."

Sheila's heart soared and the surge of emotion caught her off guard. After so many years of spiritual wandering, she'd never imagined that anyone would compare her words with the godly wisdom of her father. Fighting back tears, she once again smiled at her granddaughter. "That's the nicest thing anyone's ever said to me."

Madison leaned over and hugged her. "I love you, Grandma. And I think I know what I need to do now."

That night, as Madison was getting ready for bed, Miles called again. This time she answered.

"Finally!" he said. "I tried calling you twice this afternoon."

"I know," she replied.

Silence.

"We need to talk, Madison," Miles said, sounding very much in charge.

"You're right. We do," she agreed.

"You know I love you, right?" he asked.

"I know you said you do," she replied, sinking down onto her bed and praying silently, *God give me strength.*

"So that means I do."

"Okay."

"So are we fine now? I mean is everything back to normal with us?" he asked.

"If you mean are we going to keep making out at my house, the answer is no."

There was a pause at the other end, and then Miles said, "What's going on with you? We have a good thing going. Is this about your church? Are they making you feel guilty or something? Because if they are, they're just stuck in the dark ages. We love each other. Who are they to judge us?"

Madison could hear the desperation in his voice. And the anger.

"Look, Miles. I never should have let things get this far. And it isn't the church. It's my own beliefs about what is right and wrong. What we were doing is wrong."

"Says who?"

"Says me. Says the Bible," she replied.

"Like I said, it's that church of yours. They refuse to recognize that everyone our age is doing this. It just means we love each other." His voice broke as he continued, "I need you, Madison. And I do love you."

For a fleeting moment, Madison remembered how it felt to be in his arms as he murmured words of affirmation into her ear. Without warning, she began to cry. It was so hard to put a stop to something that made her feel loved. Her voice shaking, she said, "I can't be with you, Miles. I can't be with someone who doesn't love God first." Her heart ached as the words tumbled out. And then an unexpected peace fell upon her.

After a moment of silence, Miles said, "Goodbye, Madison. I hope you don't regret this." And then the phone went dead.

When her anxiety threatened to surface again, Madison fell to her knees in prayer. And the peace returned.

The next morning was Saturday. Sheila was in the kitchen about to call Michelle, when Madison walked into the room. "I did it, Grandma," she said. "I broke up with Miles on the phone last night."

Sheila breathed a prayer of gratitude and relief. It would be a little easier talking to Michelle now. "I'm so proud of you, honey. I know that must have been really tough," she said.

Madison's face revealed a gamut of emotions. "I hope someday, someone else can love me the way Grandpa Rick loves you," she said, her voice breaking.

Sheila stood and drew her close, holding her in a firm embrace. "God has someone special for you, Maddie. I just know it."

As Madison dissolved into tears, Sheila found herself feeling a strength and inner confidence that could only come from above. It was as if God were using her as His arms around Maddie. 'Jesus with skin on' is what her father used to call it. It was a sacred moment she'd never forget.

"You know, he helped me make my decision," Madison said, wiping her tears with her sleeve.

"Who?"

"Rick."

Sheila's heart leapt. "He did?" She thought back to their discussion in bed the night before when her husband had shared about his conversation with Maddie.

"Yeah. We talked on the way home from school yesterday. He's really wise."

Sheila smiled. "I'll tell him you think so. That will mean a lot to him." Cupping her granddaughter's chin in her hands, she brushed Maddie's hair off her face. "I love you, sweetheart. Everything's going to be okay. I promise."

Madison gave her a half smile. "Thanks, Grandma."

"You sit down here," Sheila said, guiding her to the table and pulling out a chair, "and I'll fix you some of my blueberry pancakes."

"I'll help you," Maddie replied, ignoring the chair.

Sheila smiled. "You're on. You can wash these blueberries, and I'll start the batter."

"Where's Rick?" Maddie asked as she pulled out a strainer and began her task.

"He went to campus to get a file he forgot to bring home," Sheila replied. "He's got a lot of work to do this weekend."

"What are you doing today?" her granddaughter asked as Sheila added the berries to the batter.

"I'm going to see your great grandmother. Want to come along?"

Madison nodded. "Sure." She looked relieved to have something to do with her day. "I'll go get ready," she added, giving Sheila a hug and then leaving the room.

As soon as Sheila was alone, she picked up the phone and called Michelle. They made a plan to go out for dessert that evening.

By the time they got over to Joan's apartment complex, it was nearly eleven. As they walked through the grounds, they passed a group of seniors with easels as an instructor was teaching them how to paint with watercolors. The view of the ocean, with the flowers that skirted the complex in the foreground, was their subject. Madison stopped walking for a moment to watch them work.

"That looks fun," she said to Sheila. "Maybe I'll take an art class for my elective next semester."

"You know, I've actually been thinking of taking one at the college," Sheila said. "They have community non-credit classes that Rick was telling me about, and I saw one for painting. Would you want to give it a go with me?"

Madison's mood brightened. "Okay. Let's do it, Grandma. When does it meet?"

"It's late in the afternoon, I think. Around four o'clock."

"Perfect!" Maddie replied, thankful for something to help fill the afternoons she'd been spending with Miles.

"It's a deal, then. We'll try our hand at this together," Sheila said, draping her arm over Madison's shoulder and giving her a squeeze.

Rounding a bend in the path, they found Joan watering some potted plants on her front porch. She welcomed them into her tiny apartment and offered them some cookies. "Michelle brought these over yesterday," she said.

The three of them sat in the living room and visited for a while. Then Sheila asked, "Do you have a list for the store, Mom?"

"Right here," she replied, reaching over and picking up a piece of paper from the end table.

"I can go if you want," Madison offered.

Sheila smiled. "Thanks, honey, but why don't you stay here and visit? I won't be gone long, and I'll bring back something from the deli for lunch, too."

"That would be nice, Sheila," Joan agreed. Turning to Madison, she added, "We could go check on my vegetables in the garden."

Madison had loved the vegetable garden as a child, and she still hoped that one day when she had a home of her own, it would include a spot for growing her own food. "Good idea, Grams," she said. "And did you know about the watercolor class here? It looks like a lot of fun. Maybe you should try it."

"Let's go have a look-see at that class," Joan replied. "My neighbor is in it, and she's been wanting me to join."

The three of them headed out, Sheila with the grocery list in hand, and Joan and Madison along the path toward the class. Not wanting to disturb the instruction, they observed from a distance. Shortly after they got there, Joan's friend looked over and waved, and then returned her focus to her easel.

"Doesn't it look fun, Grandma?" Madison asked.

Joan nodded, but she looked a little skeptical. "I'm not much of an artist," she said. "And these old hands are getting kind of shaky. But it's fun to watch them work," she agreed.

When they got to the vegetable garden, there was one other woman just leaving. She had a basket full of fresh-picked tomatoes and broccoli.

"You've got a good harvest there, Olivia," Joan said as she eyed the vegetables. Then she gestured to Madison. "You remember my great granddaughter, Madison, don't you?"

Olivia smiled. "Hi Madison. It's good to see you again."

Returning the greeting, Maddie held the gate open for Joan. They walked over to her corner of the garden. Raised beds made it easier for the residents to plant and tend their vegetables. She noticed a few stray weeds were threatening Joan's tiny crop. "I'll get those," Madison said as she pointed to them. After that was accomplished, Joan gave her instructions about which vegetables to harvest. They walked away with a bunch of carrots and some cucumbers.

As they headed back to the apartment, Joan asked, "How's that youth group of yours these days?"

"I haven't been attending lately," Madison admitted.

Joan nodded. "I looked for you when they came last weekend to paint the fences." She paused and then added, "Life must be pretty busy for a young lady like you."

Madison cringed inwardly. Images of her and Miles together flashed through her mind. "I guess you could say that," she replied evasively. "If I would have known the youth group was going to be doing a workday here, I would have tried to come, though." A part of her wanted to believe that was so.

When they got back to Joan's apartment, they found Sheila inside unloading the groceries. As Madison helped put things away, a scripture on the refrigerator caught her eye.

The steadfast love of the Lord never ceases; His mercies never come to an end;
They are new every morning; Great is Your faithfulness.
Lamentations 3:22-23

"That was one of your great grandfather's favorite passages," Joan said, pointing a bent finger at the paper.

"I really like it," Madison replied. She went to her purse and retrieved her cell phone then came back and took a picture of it. "I want to mark it in my Bible," she added, noticing both her grandmother and great grandmother smiling at each other.

Joan put her hand on Madison's back. "There are many wonderful promises in God's word, dear. Come sit with me," she said. "I want to show you something."

Madison followed her into the living room and over to the chairs by the front window. A basket between them held Joan's worn Bible and a journal. They sat down and Joan leaned over, retrieving the burgundy leather volume of scriptures. She pulled it open to a ragged bookmark in the first chapter of the Old Testament book of Joshua.

217

The pages were marked with a multitude of underlines and words scrawled in the margins. Beside one verse, she'd drawn a heart. Pointing to it, she said, "Listen to this, Maddie. When God took the Israelites through the wilderness and into the Promised Land, He told them, 'I will give you every place where you set your foot, as I promised.' Did you catch that? They had to walk throughout the land and stand on the very soil in order to possess it."

Madison nodded.

"Do you see what that means, sweetheart?"

Studying her great grandmother's face, she tried to understand the significance of what she was saying.

"It means that we have to actually know and personally stand on God's promises in order to possess them for ourselves."

"So how do you do that, Grams?" Maddie asked, realizing she'd never heard anything like that before.

"You find a promise in here," Joan said, patting her Bible, "that applies to a need you have. You take that scripture to heart and you stand on it just like the Israelites had to set their feet on the Promised Land to possess it."

Sheila piped in, "For me, that means I memorize the scripture, and I keep saying it to myself until it becomes real in my life and my situation. That way it moves from the pages of the Bible, into my mind, and finally into my heart. That's how I stand on it."

A light went on for Madison. "Oh, now I get it," she said. "I've heard people say they stand on God's word, and I always thought they meant they believe it. But now I see what you mean about the promises in scripture. There might be lots of promises we don't even know about. They aren't really ours until we find them, learn them, and let them sink in to who we are."

"Well said, young lady," Joan replied. "You just might have a future as a Bible teacher someday."

Madison shook her head thinking about how her life and choices would certainly disqualify her from that possibility. "I don't think so, Grams."

"You never know," Sheila replied knowingly. "God is full of surprises."

"You didn't tell Grams about me and Miles, did you?" Madison asked her grandmother on the drive home.

"Not about the things you shared in confidence," Sheila replied.

"Thanks for covering for me when she talked about me becoming a Bible teacher. I know I've blown any work I could do for God. He's probably pretty much over me by now."

Grandma Sheila looked shocked. "Madison, don't ever think that about God. He is in the business of restoration. There's nothing you've done that He won't forgive. He's able to take the fractured parts of our lives and bring beauty out of the brokenness."

Madison stared out the car window, trying to imagine God using her life for something good.

"You know, Maddie, you are a sweet person with a beautiful, gentle countenance. God's given you a sensitive heart and a love for others. I know for certain He has a good plan for your future. You need to spend some time alone with Him, and let Him show you all that He has for you."

"How do I do that, Grandma? Every time I start to pray, I think about how I let Him down and compromised on things I knew I shouldn't."

Her grandmother glanced over at her with compassion. "Oh honey. We all make mistakes."

"Yeah, but mine are pretty bad. I'm not sure how to even begin to make this right."

"Here's what I do when I need to really have a good talk with God," Sheila said. "I go down to the beach alone and just sit and watch the waves for a while. Then I start telling Him everything that's on my heart and mind. I tell Him how badly I feel about the mistakes I've made, I ask Him to forgive me, and I usually end up shedding a few tears in the process."

"Really?" Madison was surprised to hear that.

"Yes, really. And those tears end up helping to wash away my pain, as God reaches down and forgives me."

Madison tried to imagine her grandmother crying with God that way.

"You want to give it a try?" Sheila asked.

"You mean go to the beach and talk to God?"

"Yes," Sheila nodded. "You can take my car if you want."

Madison thought for a moment. The idea of just sitting and watching the waves sounded really soothing. She wasn't sure she'd be able to talk to God the way Grandma Sheila did, but maybe it would help her sort through her thoughts and make some decisions. "Okay. Yeah, I'd like to do that," she replied.

Before she headed out the door, Grandma Sheila stopped her. "Hold on. Let me get something for you."

She returned a moment later with an old flannel shirt in her hand. "This belonged to your great grandpa Phil. It was his favorite bum-around-the-yard shirt. After he died, I asked my mom if I could keep it. Now, whenever I'm wrestling with something or just plain missing him, I pull it on, and it's almost like he's with me again. Take it with you," she said.

"Thanks, Grandma," Maddie replied, her heart touched by the intimacy of the gesture. Pulling on the soft, warm flannel, memories rushed back of a very special man, and she hugged it to her chest as she walked out to the car, feeling like a part of him was going with her.

Parking her grandmother's car on a road that led to the beach, Madison carefully locked it and walked down onto the sand. The sky was a little gray but didn't look like rain. Not yet, at least. The cool air nipped at her cheeks, and she drew her great grandpa Phil's flannel shirt close over her thin frame as she made her way toward the surf.

Standing at the crest of the slope leading down to the water, she gazed out over the sea, thankful the beach itself was empty. She could see a boat far out in the distance, but otherwise she was completely alone. She wandered over to an old picnic table perched in the tall grass, and climbed onto it, taking a seat on the rough wood top.

Memories began washing over her like the salty foam on the shoreline. Memories of Luke and their playful times at the beach growing up, her crush on him in junior high, and how their relationship had evolved into something much more to her than just friends. Memories of Miles, his eye-catching smile and the electricity that he had sparked in her heart and body when they were together.

And heaviness settled over her, crushing her hope for the future. Worthlessness played in her mind as she thought about the mistakes she'd made. Who did she think she was to believe that she and Luke would ever end up together? He was destined for great service to God. She could see that. But there was no way she'd ever fit into that life. Especially now. She'd made sure of that by giving herself away to Miles.

Well, it didn't matter. She was sure the Lord had a godly girl for Luke. Someone who'd saved herself for him and for God. Someone who could minister right alongside him and be a light to the lost.

Someone worthy.

And that was not her. Not now.

He was coming home in a few days for Christmas break. She'd really looked forward to that when he left. Now she cringed at the idea of facing him. How could she even be his friend now?

She thought about what her grandmother had said about talking to God. But what would she say? He obviously knew how she'd blown it. And she knew it was wrong—what she and Miles had done. But she'd gone along with it anyway. It had just felt so good to have someone love her. Or so she thought. Now she knew he'd just been using her. And it was her own fault. Maybe if she'd said no and set up boundaries in the first place, things would have ended differently between them.

Then she remembered their conversation about God and church. No way was he going to change in that regard.

I'm such a loser, she thought, as tears swam in front of her. *I'll never be good enough.*

That's right, Madison, a voice of condemnation spoke into her mind. *You're going to be alone forever. Even God doesn't want you now.*

Draping her arms over her knees, she buried her face in them. The tears turned to sobs as she mentally beat herself with her words. She levied heavy charges against herself—her looks, her actions, and her decisions—all of them disastrous in her eyes. How *could* God ever love her when she loathed herself?

Rocking back and forth, she thought about all the ways she'd let Him down. Surely He was finished with her now.

I'm sorry. I'm so sorry, Lord, she repeated over and over as she hugged her great grandfather's shirt to her chest and rocked, eyes closed to the world and her surroundings. Diving into the darkest places in her soul, a world of hurt rushed out, a raging river of regret. As she sobbed, the violent release of her pain drowned out the sound of the waves lapping the shore.

Finally spent, she sat silently, a hollowness replacing the fiery grenade of emotions. The gentle waves continued their endless cadence. One after another, she watched them roll in. And as she gazed out toward the horizon, a still small voice spoke into her spirit.

I am with you.

An unexpected peace descended upon her heart. What was happening? She sat very still and listened intently.

And then a rush of scriptures from her younger days came flooding back. *I have loved you with an everlasting love; therefore with loving kindness I have drawn you... I will never leave you nor forsake you... Whoever touches you, touches the apple of My eye... Do not fear for I am with you, do not anxiously look about you for I am your God, surely I will help you, surely I will up hold you with My righteous right hand... There is therefore now no condemnation for those who are in Christ Jesus.*

One after another, faster and faster they came. And with them came an unexpected assurance of God's perfect love.

Her emotions swelled again. This time with a joy she could not remember ever experiencing before. He was here. Right here with her. And He still loved her.

She looked up at the sky. There in the distance she saw the sun break through the clouds sending a beam of light down onto the calm sea, creating a circle of glittering iridescence on the water's surface. Smiling through her tears, her spirit soared heavenward in silent praise as she soaked in His grace, mercy, and love.

Then, climbing off the table and stretching out on her back on the sand, she watched the clouds dancing overhead, as the caressing melody of the waves became her friend, easing her into a state of complete peace. Closing her eyes, she prayed without words, allowing the fullness of her heart to be her song to God.

And then, she heard the sound of sand crunching under her. And she realized she was no longer alone.

CHAPTER EIGHTEEN

"Madison, are you okay?" a familiar voice asked as she sat upright and glanced over her shoulder.

"Luke?" She was on her feet in an instant.

He held out open arms. "Yep. It's me."

They moved toward each other and embraced briefly. "What are you doing here?" she asked.

"I was able to get a ride home from a friend at school whose folks live in Portland. So I thought I'd surprise everyone."

"Do your parents know you're here?"

"Yeah. I went by there first. Then I decided to drop by your place, but your mom told me you're living with your grandmother for a while. So I went over there, and that's how I found out you were here." He paused and looked into her eyes. "Is everything okay?"

Madison smiled, thinking of how different her answer would have been just an hour earlier. "It is now," she said.

His surprised expression made her realize that he thought she meant it was because of him. Not wanting to hurt his feelings, she just gave him a playful shove and said, "Don't let it go to your head."

He laughed. "Wanna go for coffee?"

"Okay," she replied, happy for the chance to spend time with him. Maybe she'd even share some of what just happened to her. Or maybe this was just a good time to find out more about what was happening in *his* life.

They walked toward the street side-by-side, not touching each other. In the past, Madison would have yearned to have him take her hand or put his arm over her shoulder. But now... now God's love so filled her heart that she didn't crave that anymore.

"You seem different," Luke said as they sat across from each other at the Coffee Stop.

"Different? How?"

"I don't know. Older I guess."

She wondered if he sensed the changes in her since her relationship with Miles. Or was it what had just happened at the beach. Either way, she sensed a shift in their relationship to one of peers in his eyes.

"You seem different, too," she replied. "So tell me about college."

"Okay, but first what's up with moving to your grandmother's place?" he asked, looking concerned.

"It's a long story. I just needed to get away for a while and sort some things out."

He studied her face.

"What?" she asked.

"So are you doing that?" he asked.

"What, sorting things out?" she replied. "Yeah. It was time to make some changes," she added. "I think I'm getting myself on the right track now."

Nodding, he said, "That's good. I'm glad to hear that."

"So how do you like college?" she asked before sipping her coffee.

"It's good," he replied. "I miss everyone here, of course, but I love the school and I'm really learning a lot. I'm even taking an art class, if you can imagine that. Me with my stick figures. The professor is teaching us that drawing is a matter of learning how to really look at something. It's cool because it's not only helping me draw better, it's helping me with life stuff—you know, learning to really look carefully before acting."

226

She soaked in his words. "Yeah, that's cool." Smiling, she added, "Grandma and I are starting a watercolor class at the university. Maybe we'll all be artists."

"Pretty sure I won't," he said. "But I think you'll like your class. Art's a good way to get a glimpse into the heart of God, you know."

"Really? How?"

"Well, like His creative side and how He's made everything so complex and yet so beautiful in a simple way, too."

"Now you sound like Rick," she said.

"How's he doing these days? I'll bet the students are having the surprise of a lifetime when they find out he's become a Christian."

"Yeah. It's kind of taken over some of the discussions in his classes. I know he's spent time with your dad discussing how to answer the questions and challenges presented to him."

"What a flip from the days he used to make it a point to discredit the believers who were in his class."

Madison nodded. She thought back to the stories Rick had told her about how her mother handed him a sealed envelope on the last day of her class with a letter inside that shared her journey to faith. "Mom says she wishes she'd had him now instead of back then. But considering she got him thinking about God, it seems like it was maybe God's plan from the beginning."

"Pretty amazing, huh?" Luke asked. He finished the last of his coffee, and then added, "I'd better get going. Mom made me promise not to be gone long. They want to take me to the Cliffhanger for dinner."

"Wow. Upscale," she replied with a teasing grin.

"Want to come along? I'm sure they wouldn't mind."

"Really? Don't you think they'd want this to just be a family time?" she asked.

"You *are* family," he replied. "Besides, Lucy said she hardly ever gets to talk to you anymore."

Madison hesitated for a moment. It sounded like fun. "If you're sure they won't mind," she said.

"They'll have to deal with me if they do," he said. "Come on. Let's get going. You can go back to your grandmother's and change, and I'll borrow Dad's car to pick you up. They made a reservation for seven-thirty. I'll come by at seven-fifteen."

"Okay," she replied, standing and following him to the door.

That night was wonderful. Sitting and talking and laughing with Luke's family pushed Madison's recent life issues away, and she felt normal and loved again. Lucy didn't mention Miles, and Madison was thankful for that.

As she sat next to Luke and listened to his college tales and his ever-increasing love for God, she wondered how she could have ever been attracted to a loser like Miles. Yeah, he was cute. And there was lots of chemistry between them, but it was all so physical. Luke, on the other hand, had a heart for people and for the Lord that put him heads above Miles.

After dinner, Luke pushed back from the table a little and draped his arm over the back of Madison's chair. "Ready to head out?" he asked.

"Yeah, I guess," she replied, looking longingly around the table and wishing she could just stay there forever.

"You should come to youth group tomorrow night," Lucy said to her.

Madison turned to Luke. "Are you going?" she asked.

"Yeah. I'm meeting with the college and career group because they're planning a short-term mission trip for the summer," he said. "I'm thinking of going along on that trip," he added.

"You *are* going," Lucy interjected. "You promised."

"Okay, so I didn't really promise, but I'm pretty sure I'm going."

"Whatever," Lucy replied, rolling her eyes but still smiling. "Come to the meeting, Maddie. Maybe you'll decide to go, too."

Smiling at Lucy's challenge, Madison replied, "Okay, you've convinced me, Luce."

With that, Luke stood and pushed in his chair. "I'll see you in a while," he said to everyone, as Madison joined him on her feet, retrieving her purse, which was hanging on her chair.

"Thanks for dinner," she said to Ben and Kelly. "I really enjoyed it."

"Yeah, thanks, Dad," Luke added.

"My pleasure," Ben replied.

"Come by the house anytime," Kelly said to Madison, adding, "I know you'll want to see Luke while he's home."

Luke shot his mom a warning look. Then he turned to Madison. "Moms," he murmured under his breath as he took her elbow and guided her toward the door.

Madison caught herself reaching for Luke's hand as they headed up the walkway to her grandmother's front door. She'd gotten so used to continuous physical contact when she was with Miles, that she had to remind herself Luke was not her boyfriend. Not by a long shot.

As she unlocked the front door and pushed it open, Sheila called from somewhere inside the house, "Is that you, Maddie?"

"Yeah, Grandma. It's just Luke and me," she called back.

A moment later, Sheila appeared from the kitchen. "Luke! It's so good to see you again."

"You, too, Mrs. Chambers," he replied politely.

"Come on in and have a seat," she said, gesturing to the couch. "I want to hear all about college."

Before Luke could begin to talk, Rick came in from the den, prompting Luke to jump back to his feet, offering a handshake and a "Hello, Dr. Chambers."

"Son," Rick said, nodding and then shaking his hand.

Wow, Madison thought. *Miles wouldn't have done that.*

Sitting stiffly at the other end of the couch, she watched as Luke carried on an adult conversation with her grandmother and step-grandfather. He seemed so at ease but respectful at the same time. Miles had always tried to avoid the grownups in Madison's life, preferring to spend time alone with her instead.

As they all settled in and Luke described his college experiences, Madison could tell that Rick was really interested. "It must be refreshing to have professors who share your faith," he observed.

Luke nodded. "With all the social issues these days, I'm glad there are still schools like mine where students can hear a Christian worldview in their classes."

"Rick's been trying to interject some of that into his classes at the university, haven't you, dear?" Sheila said, turning to Rick.

"Yes, but I have to be more cautious about when and how I do that. All you have to do to get a visual for the broad road leading to destruction that's mentioned in scripture is to look at the mainstream professors today. What used to be considered radical is now the norm. If anything, me being a Christian professor makes me the radical these days. Unfortunately, that is supported like the antiestablishment mindsets of yesterday were."

"It must be difficult for you," Luke observed.

Rick agreed. "But your father's been a big help."

Luke looked at Madison and smiled. "Yeah. I heard."

A lull in the conversation led Rick to his feet. Turning to Sheila, he said, "Maybe we should leave these two alone to catch up."

Sheila glanced over at Madison and smiled. "You're right, honey." She stood up. "I hope we get to see you again before you head back to school."

Luke nodded. "Me, too."

After her grandparents had left the room, Madison shifted nervously, drawing her knee up onto the seat beside her as she turned her body to face him. "I could tell Rick was a little envious of your professors and their freedom to be open about their faith."

"It must be really hard for him to be surrounded by people who look at the world so differently."

"Yeah, especially after the one-eighty he's done in his own life," she agreed. "Now he can see even more clearly how messed up they are."

There was another lull, and then they both started talking at once.

"So you," Madison blurted.

"Are you," Luke began.

They both laughed. "You go first," she said.

"I was just going to ask if you're going tomorrow night—to youth group," he said.

"Uh, yeah, sure," she replied, suddenly looking forward to going for the first time in a long while.

Luke leaned over and put his hand on her knee. "How long are you going to stay here, Maddie? Your family must really miss you."

She looked away, her stomach suddenly clenching. "I don't know. We didn't part on the best of terms."

"What happened?" he asked.

231

Madison took a deep breath. "It's kind of a long story," she hedged.

Pulling his hand away, he said, "I'm sorry. Well, it's really not my business." He stood up and added, "I'd better get going."

She walked him to the door. "Thanks again for the fun night," she said, wishing she had the nerve to talk to him about everything that had happened. But if he knew, he probably wouldn't want to be her friend anyway.

"See you tomorrow," he replied with a smile as he walked out the front door.

"Yeah. See ya," she answered.

Before he got into his car, he turned and looked at her again, tipping his head to the side and giving one last smile as he waved goodbye.

Madison lifted her hand in reply, her heart wishing desperately that their relationship were something much more. But that could never be. She'd ruined that for sure. At least she now knew that God still loved her. But a guy like Luke? She could never deceive him, and if he knew the truth, well that would take care of any future they would have had. Even God couldn't fix that.

When Madison came back into the house, her grandmother was alone in the living room. "Come sit by me," she said, patting the cushion beside her on the couch. "How was your evening?"

Plunking herself down, Madison looked over and replied, "It was good. How was yours?"

Her grandmother patted her on the knee. "I had a good talk with your mother."

Madison's heart stopped. "Did you tell her about me and Miles?"

"I didn't, honey. But you need to. She's your mother, and she needs to know."

"Do you think she'll hate me?" Madison asked, trying to imagine her mother's reaction.

Grandma Sheila looked surprised. "Of course not, sweetheart. Your mom loves you very much. Nothing could ever change that. If anything, she may even partly blame herself."

"Herself? Why?"

"Because parents feel responsible when things like that happen. But I can also tell you that she will be very relieved and proud of you when she hears that you broke it off with him."

Madison nodded. "Yeah." She paused and then said, "Grandma?"

"Yes?"

"I love you," she said softly, leaning into the open arms of her grandmother.

CHAPTER NINETEEN

Madison hurried toward the church building, already running late for the meeting about the mission trip. She'd spent over an hour in front of the mirror trying to decide what to wear and how to do her makeup. She hadn't been spending much time at youth group and the clothes she'd been wearing lately were not exactly what she'd consider church outfits. She'd finally settled on a pair of jeans and a sweatshirt. Although the neckline was cut to fall off the shoulder, it didn't look too bad with a tee shirt underneath. And she'd really downplayed her eye makeup, so she looked a little more like her old self.

Who am I kidding? She thought to herself as she headed for the high school room where the meeting was being held. *I don't fit in here anymore. And it's crazy to think they'd want me on the mission trip. Me? Really? What a great example of God's holiness.* She considered turning around and going back to her grandmother's house.

"Madison!" a voice called. "We've been looking for you."

Glancing over, she saw Lucy waving from the front of the church office.

"Here goes," Madison said softly to herself as she returned the wave and changed directions to join Lucy.

"I'm glad you made it," Lucy said with a smile. "My dad had to change the meeting place. They just waxed the floors in the classrooms, so we're meeting in the fellowship hall instead."

Madison nodded. "Is Luke here?"

"Yeah. He's helping Dad set up the stuff for the slideshow."

As they walked into the big fellowship hall, Madison spotted Luke in one of the alcoves plugging in some equipment. Chairs had been pulled over to form a semicircle that faced the screen on the wall, and a huddle of kids from the youth group were talking and horsing around nearby.

Pastor Ben was focused on his laptop that rested on a stand. "Okay, I've got it pulled up," he said to Luke. An image appeared on the screen showing a cluster of children with smiling faces. Across the bottom were the words: Summer Youth Mission.

Ben stood and cleared his throat. Walking over to the group, he said, "We're going to get started, so take a seat."

After everyone was settled, Ben asked Luke to come up and lead them in prayer. Madison bowed her head but peered up to see Luke's earnest face as he stood beside his dad and prayed. He looked so much older and more mature, and she suddenly noticed the uncanny resemblance between the two of them. *Luke's going to be just like his father. A good man who serves God and helps others.* Her first response was admiration. Then she felt the familiar weight of condemnation.

You'll never be good enough, the voice of darkness reminded her.

Her heart pounding, she felt the grip of anxiety surging once again. If only she could sneak out of the meeting unnoticed. But there was no way that was going to happen. She'd just have to make it through the next hour, and then she'd figure out some reason why she couldn't go on the trip. That would get her out of the rest of this charade.

Ben's voice interrupted her thoughts. "We're going to start this meeting with a slideshow to give you an idea of where we are going and what we will be doing. As most of you know, our high school pastor and his wife are expecting their second child any day now. So they are not going to be involved in this trip. Luke and I will be leading it, and Kelly may come along as well. As you watch the slideshow, think about where you feel God might best be able to use you. And consider any questions you may have about the mission."

Luke flipped off the lights and the slideshow began. Images of teens and adults sanding and painting playground equipment, repairing furniture, and building an outdoor shed were mingled with photos of playing with the children, reading stories to them, and putting on skits. One slide caught Madison's attention. It was a girl about her age doing an art project with a small group of kids. She thought about her art class and how much she enjoyed it. It would be fun to do art with the kids. *If* she were going, that is.

The dark cloud returned. *Forget it, Madison. Let the good kids go.*

After the final slide of smiling faces waving at the camera, Luke flipped on the lights and stood in front of them with his dad. "So any questions?" Ben asked.

A few kids raised their hands and asked about their accommodations while on the trip and about the fundraising.

"The girls will have one room to sleep in and the boys another," Ben explained. "They provide cots, but we will be bringing our own sleeping bags. You'll be packing light because there isn't much room for luggage in the sleeping quarters, so a duffle bag with your sleeping bag and clothes in it is the best way to go. For fundraising, we'll be sending out support letters that we'll write at our next meeting, and then we'll have a series of car washes, bake sales, and parents' night out babysitting events."

Ben turned to his son. "Luke has been communicating with the orphanage and has a pretty good idea of what they need from us while we are there."

Luke nodded. "So I've been emailing with the director, and she'd like us to conduct a VBS in the mornings. Afternoons we'll be painting the dining hall, repairing bookshelves in the classrooms, and building a retaining wall for their new vegetable garden. If there's time, we'll help the kids do some planting."

It sounded like a lot of work for one week. Madison tried to imagine this group of her peers accomplishing all of that in only seven days. The VBS part sounded fun and she loved helping her grandmother in the vegetable garden at Shoreline Manor.

"Any thoughts about what you might want to help with?" Luke asked the group. "We're thinking guys for the retaining wall, but the rest is pretty open to whomever wants to jump in."

Lucy piped up, "Madison and I will organize the VBS stuff if you want."

Madison winced inwardly. Really? Lucy was already volunteering her? She turned to her friend and gave her a questioning look. Lucy just smiled and leaned over to whisper, "This will be really fun. You'll see."

The guys began talking about the retaining wall, asking about the materials and what they'd need to bring. "I'd recommend some good work gloves," Ben replied. "Otherwise you may get some pretty bad blisters."

"The rest of the materials will be provided," Luke added. "They just need our manual labor to complete the project."

"So all the paint for the dining hall and the materials for the bookshelves will already be there?" a girl asked.

"Yep," Luke replied.

A few more questions were raised and addressed, and then Ben said, "Even though all of you know each other, this trip is going to bring you closer than you've ever been before. You'll be relying on each other in ways you won't understand until you get there. So it's really important that you trust one another."

Heads nodded as kids from the group looked at one another, a few of the boys elbowing or playfully shoving each other.

Ben cleared his throat to get their attention again. "Before we leave tonight, we're going to do the first of a few trust exercises to help build that important quality in the group. So if everyone would stand up and follow me." He glanced over to Luke and, gesturing to a sack on the floor, said, "Would you grab that bag, please?"

Nodding, Luke retrieved it and walked beside his father as they exited the building.

Once outside, Ben opened the bag and pulled out a handful of bandanas. "Pair off in twos," he said.

Madison turned to Lucy, who had already been grabbed by another girl. She turned to look around the group and saw that Luke was the only one without a partner.

"Hey, Maddie," he said. "Guess it's you and me."

She forced a smile and nodded, hoping she looked relaxed and normal despite her uneasiness.

Ben began walking through the group, handing one bandana to each pair. Then he gave his directions. "Okay, so one of you is going to be blindfolded first. The other is going to lead the blindfolded one around the grounds here. Leaders, be sure you warn your partner about any steps up or down. Changes in terrain are also good to note because walking on grass is different than on pavement. And don't walk too fast. Remember, treat your partner the way you want him or her to treat you when it's your turn. In ten minutes, I'll blow the whistle and you'll switch leaders."

Luke held the blindfold out to Madison to wear. "I think not," she said with a nervous laugh. "You first."

"Okay," he replied with mock resignation. He pulled the bandana over his eyes and tied it in back. Then he stood with his arms hanging limp at his sides.

Madison flashed back to junior high and their brief stage of almost dating. It had gotten pretty comfortable holding hands back then, but now the thought made her really nervous. Miles was one thing, but Luke? He was so far above her in so many ways.

"Are we going to just stand here?" he asked playfully.

Taking a deep breath, she reached out and took his hand. It was warm and larger than Miles'. "Okay," she said tentatively. "So here we go." Glancing around, she saw the other pairs had dispersed in a variety of directions. She decided to take him around past the church office and into the grassy area out front. That should be pretty easy. No steps except the curb along the edge of the parking lot.

As she guided him, she noticed how tall he was getting. It seemed like he'd grown a couple of inches since summer. He followed her with relative ease except for one raised lip in the pavement she hadn't noticed until it was too late. He tripped a bit, but regained his footing. "I'll have to remember that when it's my turn," he teased.

"Sorry," she replied, warning him about the upcoming curb. "You're stepping down in just a second."

He shuffled his feet a little to feel for the edge.

"Okay, now," she said.

After safely navigating the curb step down, they crossed the parking lot with Madison steering him clear of the few cars in the lot. "Now we're going on grass," she warned as she led him onto the lawn. He looked a little funny as he walked, and she started giggling a little.

"What?"

"You," she replied.

"What about me?"

"You're walking funny."

"Oh, you just wait," he replied. "Your turn's next."

As if on cue, the whistle blew. As he took off his blindfold, Madison noticed they were the only ones on the front lawn. Maybe this was a good time to tell him she wouldn't be going on the trip.

"So, Luke?" she began.

"Yeah?"

"I've been thinking."

"About?"

"About the trip and everything."

"And?"

"Well, I'm thinking maybe I shouldn't go," she blurted.

He paused and studied her face. It made her feel like he could see right through her and see all the bad she was trying to hide. Then a smile spread over his face. "Oh, I get it."

"You do?"

"Yeah. You don't want to take *your* turn," he replied, handing her the bandana. "Nice try, Maddie."

His smile was so sincere and his voice, even in its teasing tone, touched a part of her heart that Miles had never reached. She took the bandana from him. "Fine. But you'd better not trip me. It really was an accident. I promise," she said as she blindfolded herself.

"Mu wah hah hah," he laughed in a mock evil tone. "Now you are at my mercy."

Madison couldn't help but laugh in return. And she noticed that for just a second she felt happier than she'd felt in a very long time.

As she walked back into Grandma Sheila's house later that evening, she heard her grandmother say, "Oh, she just got back. Hold on a second." Turning to her, Sheila said, "Your mom's on the phone. She'd like to talk to you."

Madison took the receiver and said hello. Out of the corner of her eye, she saw her grandmother gesturing to Rick, and they both disappeared into the kitchen. Sinking down into the chair, Madison asked her mother what she wanted to talk about.

"Can we go somewhere and talk face-to-face?" Michelle asked.

"I guess," Madison replied.

"How about if I swing by and pick you up, and we can go to the Coffee Stop?"

"Sounds good."

After hanging up, she went to tell her grandmother. "Mom and I are going for coffee."

"That's nice, dear," Sheila replied with a warm smile.

Rick looked up from his laptop. "How was your meeting?" he asked.

"It was okay. I'm not a hundred percent sure I'm going on the trip, though."

"Really? Why?" he asked.

"Lots of reasons. Just some stuff I need to think about first."

Her grandmother gave her a serious look, and Madison could tell she was onto her. "Don't pass up something you'll regret later," she told Madison. "The past is in the past."

Madison just shrugged. "Yeah, okay. Well, I'm still thinking about it. I signed up for now. But they don't order the airline tickets for a few more months."

Sheila started to say something else, but Rick put his hand on his wife's and said, "I'm sure you'll make the right decision, Madison."

A moment later, the toot of a horn out front signaled Michelle's arrival. "Gotta run," Madison said. "See ya later."

As she climbed into her mother's van, Michelle reached over and gave her a hug. "It's so good to see you, sweetheart. We really miss you."

"I miss you, too," she said automatically, and then realized she really did. A yearning washed over her, but she quickly squelched it. If her mother knew the truth, she wouldn't be so eager to have Madison back home. She'd raised her to know better, and Madison had chosen to live a lie and compromise on things that her mom had clearly taught her would lead to regret. At least her grandmother knew everything and still loved her.

"Grandma said you were at church," Michelle said.

"Yeah. The high school mission trip meeting," she replied. "But I'm probably not going," she added hastily.

Her mother glanced over for a moment, revealing a hurt expression. "I see."

Why do I have to be such a jerk to her, Madison thought. *I'm the one who messed up, not her.*

Once again attempting conversation, her mother asked, "So have you had a chance to spend any time with Luke?"

Just the mention of his name brought a longing to Madison's heart. "A little. I had dinner with his family the night he got home."

If Michelle already knew about that, her face didn't give it away. "That's great. I know Kelly and Ben are so happy to have him here for the holidays."

"Yeah," Madison agreed. "Lucy and the rest of the kids, too."

Her mother nodded and maneuvered the car into the lot in front of the Coffee Stop. After parking and getting their coffees, they settled into a booth in back. "So what are your plans for Christmas?" Michelle asked.

Madison looked up and saw the pain in her mother's eyes. Shrugging, she replied, "I don't know. What do you want me to do?"

Immediately her mother put her hand over Madison's. With tears in her eyes, she said, "I really want you to come home. We all do. We're a family, and we belong together."

"You might not feel that way after you find out everything," Madison replied. "I'm not the perfect girl you raised me to be, Mom."

Her mother's face looked stunned. "Honey, *none* of us are perfect. Me especially. There's nothing you could ever do that would make me not want you. Nothing." She held Madison's gaze unwaveringly.

Suddenly Madison was the one with the tears. Her mom came around to her side of the booth and slid in, wrapping her arms around her and holding her close while the dam broke open and all of Madison's heartache and regret poured out. "Oh, Mom. I'm so ashamed," she said between sobs. Bit by bit, the truth tumbled out until all the secrets lay bare before her mother. Not once did Michelle look appalled. It was only sorrow Madison saw in her mother's eyes.

"I'm so sorry," Michelle said, rocking Madison in her arms. "Oh, my sweet, sweet girl. I'm so very sorry."

Madison was taken aback by her mother's words. Pulling back, she looked up at Michelle's face and saw tears streaming down her cheeks. "Mom? Are you okay?"

Her mother shook her head. "I feel responsible, Madison. Your father and I had concerns about Miles from the very beginning. We tried to protect you, but clearly, we needed to do more."

Hardly believing her ears, Madison said, "Mom, this is *not* yours and Dad's fault. I made my own choices. And no matter what you would have said or done, Miles and I would have found a way to be alone together. So don't ever think that way."

Michelle gave her a sad smile as she carefully guided Madison's hair off of her face. "Oh, Maddie," she paused and then added, "you're becoming a very wise young woman, you know that?"

"Took me long enough," Maddie replied with a half grin. The tremendous weight of her secret had been lifted, and the relief was almost euphoric.

The next day, Madison moved back home, just in time to help her family select their Christmas tree.

CHAPTER TWENTY

Four generations of women sat together around the little table in Joan's apartment. She'd been looking forward to her annual Christmas tea party for months. The table was draped in a festive holly print tablecloth with a decorative teapot serving as a vase for some white roses surrounded by tiny glass votive candles. The teacart that had been the first piece of real furniture she'd bought after marrying Phil those many years ago held the steaming teapot of vanilla cinnamon tea and a tray of assorted tea sandwiches and scones. Finally, a small crystal bowl cradled the sweet whipped cream to garnish the pastries.

"Everything looks so yummy," Madison said, as she took her seat between her mother and grandmother. Under the table, she tugged at her short skirt, bringing it as close to her knees as it would go.

"You've outdone yourself again, Grandma," Michelle added, giving Joan a hug before joining her daughter at the table.

Sheila popped up and disappeared into the kitchen, returning with a box of matches. She proceeded to light the votives, adding a flickering glow to the atmosphere. "There," she said. "Now we are really ready to begin." Then helping her mother into her seat, Sheila sat down, too.

Joan looked around the circle and smiled. *What a treasure these girls are to me,* she thought. And suddenly she felt as if she might begin to cry. *No time for tears, you silly old woman,* she chided herself. Then, reaching toward her daughter and granddaughter, she said, "Shall we pray?"

The four women joined hands as Joan asked the blessing. "Dear Heavenly Father, it is with full hearts that we thank You for this time together." She paused to clear her throat and the emotion in her voice. "At this most special time of year, when we get ready to celebrate the birth of Your Son, we treasure our family so very much." Thoughts of her dear Phil, who was celebrating yet another Christmas face-to-face with God, rushed into her mind. Then she rallied herself and finished her prayer with, "Please bless this food to the nourishment of our bodies and this fellowship to the encouragement of our souls. In Jesus' name, amen."

Sheila was immediately on her feet again, taking the teapot around the table and serving all of them. Next, she served the sandwiches and scones, followed by the sweet cream. Then, taking her seat again, they all began enjoying the delicious tea and treats.

"I'm so glad you do this every year, Grandma," Michelle said. "It helps me get refocused after the final hectic week at school before the break."

Madison agreed. "It's like this is the kick off to Christmas," she said with a grin.

"I'm just glad you girls have time for it," Joan said, her heart warmed by their comments. "Remember when we used to do this with the neighborhood moms and their daughters?" she asked Sheila.

"Of course I do, Mom. It was the big hit of the season." She took a bite of her scone and added, "especially these. Christmas tea was the only time you made the cranberry scones, and everyone loved them so much." She glanced over to Michelle and Madison. "Tea parties were your Grandma Joan's specialty. We had one about every two to three months to celebrate some occasion. She'd make blueberry scones or cinnamon scones, but the cranberry ones were always for Christmas."

Joan smiled as she thought back to birthday parties, end of the school year gatherings, and lazy summer afternoon teas with her friends and their daughters. Life had been good to them, and her heart was full of the blessing of sweet memories.

As they enjoyed their party, she reflected on how each of them had changed and grown over the years. Sheila was now well into her sixties, yet she had the fresh glow of love from her recent marriage to Rick. Michelle was a seasoned teacher, and her daughter was becoming a young woman. *I must be very old,* she thought to herself. *But inside, I don't feel all that different. I can still remember clearly the rush of new love, the joy of becoming a mother, and the ministry of being a pastor's wife.*

"Mom?" Sheila's voice interrupted her thoughts.

"Yes?"

"You look like you're deep in thought."

All eyes were on her. Joan smiled and sighed. "I'm just thinking about how blessed my life has been." She reached over and patted her daughter's hand, noticing a shadow in Madison's countenance. "I heard your friend Luke is home from college," she said to Maddie with a smile.

Madison nodded, but her face did not light up the way Joan had expected. *I guess we will be spending some more time together over that sweet one tonight, Lord,* she thought silently.

Although her vision was fading, and she'd had to give up her volunteering at the elementary school, God had replaced it with a vibrant prayer ministry. What a blessing to know that she still had a purpose, even as she stepped into her nineties. Prayer was something she'd always be able to do.

So many of her family members were busy with work or school or other life demands. But she could faithfully carry their needs and concerns to the throne of grace on a daily basis. The only thing that would be better would be to have Phil there by her side, leading them both in their intercessions. But, even though she could not see him, she suspected he was actually doing just that from the other side of the veil. And it gave her great peace and joy each time she went to prayer.

After the tea party was over, Sheila offered to give Madison a ride home, since Michelle had some Christmas errands to run. The three of them helped Joan clear the table and do the dishes, and Sheila made sure the candles were out before they left. It was likely Joan would take her afternoon nap once they were gone, and she'd forgotten about lit candles in the past.

On the way home, Sheila asked, "So how are things going with Luke?"

"What do you mean?" Madison replied.

"I mean between the two of you. You do like him, right?" She hoped she wasn't overstepping her bounds, but she and Michelle were both concerned and wondering where Madison stood with him now.

"It doesn't matter how I feel," Madison replied.

"Why would you say that? He seems like he really cares about you, honey."

"He might care about me, but not the way you think, Grandma. And even if he did, I could never go there. Not now."

Sheila glanced over at her. Regret—it was so toxic. She hated to see her granddaughter drowning in it. "You know, Maddie, none of us are perfect. Even Luke."

Madison nodded. "Yeah. But I'm not talking about being perfect. I'm talking about the kind of girl Luke deserves, and it's not me."

"But shouldn't you let Luke decide that?" Sheila asked.

"Could we just drop this, please, Grandma? I know you mean well, but there's no way it could ever work between Luke and me. Okay?"

An arrow pierced Sheila's heart as she realized the victory darkness had won in Madison's heart and mind. *Oh please, Lord. Help her find her way out of this sea of self-condemnation and worthlessness.*

They rode in silence for the last few minutes. Then Madison reached over and gave her a hug before getting out of the car. "I love you, Grandma. I'm sorry if I was short with you. It's just hard for me to talk about Luke right now. Maybe it'll be easier after he goes back to school."

Sheila nodded. "I understand, honey. Just don't short sell yourself. God still loves you as much as He ever did, and so do I."

"I know," she replied, "and I'm really thankful for that." But her voice did not sound convinced.

That night over dinner, Rick could see that Sheila wasn't herself. "Are you feeling alright, sweetheart?" he asked.

Sheila looked up at him and replied, "Yeah. I'm fine. I'm just worried about Maddie." She paused and then added, "She's so down on herself."

He put his hand over hers. "She's young. Give her time. I think eventually she'll snap out of it." He hoped his words sounded reassuring. There was a fine art to this husband thing, and he was still trying to find his way.

"I was really hoping Luke's homecoming for Christmas might do the trick," Sheila continued, "But she's totally closed off to the possibility of anything ever developing between them."

Oh. I see where this is going, he reflected silently. "So you were hoping they'd become a couple, right?"

"Don't you remember how cute they were together when Madison was in junior high?" she asked, her voice sounding almost defensive.

What do I say now? "Of course I do. But things change. They're both older now, especially Luke. Going off to college is a big step in maturity. A high school girl may seem pretty young to him at this point."

"If that was all it was about, I'd be fine. But this is about Madison thinking she's not worthy of a guy like Luke." She looked him in the eye and added, "She drowning in regret, honey."

He nodded. Rubbing his hand over his face he thought about the situation. "You tried to talk to her about it, right?"

"Yes. But she cut off the conversation."

"Is there anything I can do?"

His wife took his hand. "Just help me pray for her. There's something in me that just says those two belong together. I don't know exactly why. But I can't shake it."

"Prayer I can do," he replied, relieved to have a direction to take.

They joined their hearts in a prayer of intercession for Sheila's granddaughter, Rick hoping his words would match the fervency he could see his wife was feeling about Madison's troubles. And then Sheila reached over and placed her hand on his cheek. "I love you, Rick," she said in a voice that told him he'd met her need.

"And I love you, my beautiful wife," he replied, standing and pulling her up and into his arms. They kissed and Rick felt his body responding to hers. "Shall we turn in early tonight?" he asked.

She smiled and replied, "I just need to clear off these dishes and then I'm ready."

"How about if I do the dishes in the morning?" he asked with a wink.

"Promise?"

"I promise," he replied as he took her hand and led her to their room.

Joan was about to climb into bed when she remembered she'd wanted to say a special prayer for her great granddaughter. Knowing that she'd likely drift off into dreamland if she prayed after she got under the covers, she sat down on the edge of the mattress and gazed at a photo of Phil on the nightstand as she began to pray. Her heart filled with love, she felt the power of God surge through her veins as she began to intercede for Madison.

Oh Father, You know my concerns already. And I believe You are doing a mighty work in our precious Maddie.

She glanced at the photo again and remembered how Phil had been able to make their great grandkids laugh. Although he was gone, his love lived on in all of them.

Returning to her purpose, she continued to pray silently. *Even though you are already at work, I know You want Your people to pray. So here I am. And tonight I especially want to intercede for Madison's future. She seems so defeated. The enemy is after her, Father. And she doesn't yet recognize that You have secured her victory.*

Oh that wretched devil. He wants to convince her she's not worthy of love, especially the love of a good young man like that Luke fellow. Would You please open her eyes, Lord? Help her to really understand the cross and the cleansing power of Jesus' blood? It's all she needs. It's all any of us need.

She paused and waited for what to pray next.

And Father, if You do have a plan for Madison and Luke to be together, would You give that young man the confidence to reach out to Maddie? Would You help him have wisdom beyond his years to grasp the wonder of grace and his possible role of communicating that to her?

Joan waited again in the silent stillness of her room. And then it happened. A peace filled her heart, and she knew her prayer was finished. With a quick *Thank you, Lord,* she pulled back the covers and climbed into bed. It was only eight-thirty, but she was soon in a deep sleep.

Madison was in her bedroom reading a few emails when her cell phone rang. The screen showed Luke's picture, one she'd taken shortly before he left for Missouri that summer. Her heart danced in her chest as she hit the answer button.

"Hi, Luke," she said, trying to sound relaxed and casual in her tone.

"Hi there. What are you up to?" he asked.

"Not much. How about you?"

"I was thinking of going to the show. Wanna come along?"

She hesitated for a moment. Was he asking her out?

Before she could reply, he piped up, "It's that new sci-fi film playing at the Town Cinema, *Inclusion.* Have you heard of it?"

"About the guy who discovers a secret language transmitted from space with some kind of hidden warning?"

"Yeah. That's it," he said. "Kind of a guy movie, I guess. But I just thought I'd see if you were interested."

Normally it wasn't a movie she'd choose to see, but something about Luke's voice sounded different. Almost lonely. And she knew he wasn't expecting anything more than friendship from her. She could do that. Right?

"Okay, yeah." she replied. Glancing at the clock she noticed it was already after eight. "What time does it start?"

"Eight-fifty. I'd need to pick you up in about twenty minutes. Is that too soon?"

She stood and glanced into the mirror. Finger combing her hair into place, she replied, "No, that should be fine." Then she thought about it for a moment. She was just getting settled back into living at home. "Let me run it by my parents, and I'll call you back in a few."

"Sounds good," he replied.

Madison found her dad sitting in his recliner watching the news while her mom was finishing addressing Christmas cards. She cleared her throat to get their attention and her dad hit the mute button on the remote. "Something up?" he asked.

"Luke just called. He wants to know if I can go to the show with him."

Her mother's eyebrows arched. "Really?"

"Yeah. It's that new movie, *Inclusion*."

"Are we talking about tonight?" Steve asked.

"Yeah. Is that okay? It starts at eight-fifty."

He glanced down at his watch and then over at Michelle, who gave him a nod. "Okay, so you'll be home before midnight?"

"For sure," Madison promised.

"If this were anyone else, I'd probably hesitate," her father warned. "But I trust Luke, so go ahead and have a good time."

"Thanks, Dad. And don't worry about staying up for me. I'll take a key."

Her parents exchanged glances again. She could tell they were trying to find the right balance between setting boundaries and trusting her. "I want you to come into our room and let me know when you get home," her mother said. "I'll be setting my alarm clock for twelve-fifteen. Just tell me you're home, and shut off the alarm before you go to bed."

Madison smiled and nodded. That had been their policy in the past. Before Miles. If she happened to be going somewhere that involved a late night return, her mother always set an alarm to wake up fifteen minutes after Madison was due back. That way she'd wake up and know if her daughter hadn't made it home yet.

"And be sure Luke walks you to the door," her father added.

"Dad, you know Luke," she replied. "There's no way he'd drop me off at the curb." She gave him a kiss and thanked him, then headed upstairs to call Luke and quickly get ready.

Fifteen minutes later, she heard the doorbell and then her parents' voices mingled with Luke's. Grabbing her purse and tossing her phone into it, she made one last check in the mirror and then went to greet him.

"We told Madison to be home by twelve," her father was saying as she approached.

"No problem. We should be back by eleven-thirty," Luke replied. "The movie's only an hour and twenty-five minutes long."

As they walked out to the car, Madison again felt the awkwardness and stiffness she now felt with Luke. It was so different to be with a guy who wasn't draping his arm over her shoulder and copping a feel from time to time. For just a brief moment, she imagined what it would look like if the two of them really were a couple. She flashed on an image of them holding hands—a memory from her junior high days.

Luke clicked the car fob to unlock the doors and then opened hers for her, waiting for her to be seated before closing it. Then he jogged around the front to the driver's door and climbed in. "I'm glad you could make it," he said with a warm smile.

"Me, too," she replied.

As they took their seats in the theater, she noticed him turning off the volume on his cell phone and followed suit. Soon the theater was dark and they were immersed in the drama of this suspenseful tale. At one point, a hand reached out and touched the shoulder of the main character as he was intently decoding a cryptic message of doom on his computer screen. It jolted not only the character, but many in the theater as well, including Madison, who instinctively reached out and grabbed hold of Luke's arm as she gasped for air.

He turned and smiled at her, putting his other hand over hers and giving it a squeeze before releasing it.

She could feel her cheeks flushing hot and red and was thankful for the darkness surrounding them. A little while later, another tense scene found her clutching her purse and covering her eyes with it. A moment later, she felt Luke's hand guiding the purse back to her lap.

"It's safe now," he assured her with a little laugh.

She glanced over and could see the humor in his eyes. Flinging her purse his way, she bopped him on the arm in retaliation.

Then he began leaning toward her during the more suspenseful parts and whispering funny things to put her at ease. She flashed him a smile of gratitude, and a moment later felt his arm over the back of her seat. She glanced at him questioningly, and he said, "In case the alien shows up here."

By the end of the movie, she was in adrenaline fatigue. "That was exhausting," she said, as they stood to leave the crowded theater.

Luke reached back and took her hand as they wove through the people toward the front exit. Madison knew it was only a practical measure to keep them together, but his hand sure did feel good in hers. As soon as they were in the parking lot, he released his hold. "So other than being exhausted, what did you think?" he asked.

"I actually liked it," she admitted. "I'm usually not that into sci-fi, but the idea behind the movie was pretty cool, and I liked the way it ended, leaving something dangling but still solving the main problem."

"Yeah. You can tell they're planning a sequel," he agreed. Pulling out his cell phone, he flipped the volume back on and checked the time. "So it's only eleven-twenty. Want to stop for a coffee and chocolate chip cookie at the Coffee Stop? They've got these huge new cookies for the holidays."

"Sure. Sounds good," she replied. "But I've got to be home by midnight for sure if I ever want to go anywhere at night again," she added.

"Got it," he said. "We'll get you home before the stroke of midnight. I promise."

She laughed at his dramatic tone. "Even if we encounter an alien with an end-of-the-world message?"

"Depends on whether or not the end will be coming before midnight," he said with a grin.

As they entered the Coffee Stop, the aroma of coffee bathed their senses. "Smells good in here," Madison observed. She really wasn't much of a coffee fan, but the smell of fresh roasted beans was one of her favorites. They ordered their drinks and bought a cookie to share, then sat down at a table.

"You know, a year ago I wouldn't have even thought of coming here," Luke replied, looking around the restaurant. "But I'm definitely into coffee now after doing some of my work hours at the campus coffee shop. And this stuff's gotten me through some long nights of studying," he added as he stirred the creamer into his cup.

Madison nodded. "I'll bet," she said. After a moment of silence she added, "College must be really fun."

He nodded. "It is. I like it more than I thought I would. But I'm also missing home more than I expected I would." His eyes seemed to linger on her for a moment.

"Well, I'm sure I'd get a little homesick, too," she agreed. "It's like I'm looking forward to it in so many ways, but I can't imagine living that far from my parents and everyone."

"You should think about my school," he said. "Then at least you'd have me bugging you from time to time." Smiling at her, he winked.

And her heart was awakened again. Trying to appear unaffected, she laughed nervously and changed the subject. "We'd better get going pretty soon."

He checked the time on his phone. "Yeah. I'll get lids for our cups."

When they pulled up in front of her house, Luke turned off the motor and turned to her. "Madison?"

"Yeah?"

"I had fun tonight," he replied, suddenly looking a little nervous himself.

"Me, too," she said.

"I was thinking," he began, and then paused. "Well, I was wondering if…" his voice trailed off.

Madison's stomach started doing somersaults. She looked at him and waited, trying to figure out where he was going with his thoughts.

"What I'm trying to say is…do you think you'd maybe want to kind of go out with me while I'm home?"

"You mean like tonight?" she asked.

He looked a little frustrated. "I mean, like on real dates."

She didn't know quite what to say. Her heart screamed yes, but her mind told her to run as fast as she could before she got hurt again. There was no way in the world Luke would ever want to date her if he knew everything.

259

Luke must have read her hesitation as a *no* because he said, "Hey, no worries. I hope I didn't make you feel uncomfortable just now."

"No, it's okay," she stammered. "I just…I just wasn't expecting you to say that. I mean, I had such a huge crush on you in junior high," she admitted.

"Junior high, huh?" He flinched like he'd been wounded. "Hey, like I said, no worries."

She wanted to turn the whole conversation around and say, 'YES. Yes, I want to go out with you!' But a voice warned her to let it go.

Just then, her phone beeped, giving her a warning it was almost midnight. "I'd better get going," she said. "But, Luke?"

"Yeah?"

"I had a really good time. Really. Thanks for asking me." She unbuckled her seat belt and opened her door before he could get around to do it for her.

They walked up to the front door with a couple of feet between them. No chance of any physical contact.

Then she quickly opened the door and slipped inside, whispering another thanks for the evening.

CHAPTER TWENTY-ONE

"How'd it go with Maddie last night?" Lucy asked.

Luke looked up from his cereal and forced a smile. "Fine. The movie was good."

"I'm not talking about the movie, dummy. How did it *go* with Maddie?" she repeated.

Leaning back into his chair, Luke looked his sister in the eye. "How would you expect it to go?"

Lucy leaned in and smiled. "Personally, I think she has a thing for you. She always has."

"And what about her boyfriend, Miles? Seems like she was pretty into him this year," he said, wondering just how deeply Madison was involved with him.

"Miles is a loser," Lucy blurted out. "I mean, he's cute and everything, but he's nowhere with the Lord. I think he was just a distraction for her since you were gone."

Luke pushed away from the table and carried his empty bowl to the sink. "I think you've misread Madison's interest in me, Luce. She made it pretty clear last night that she just wants to be friends." The look on his sister's face revealed complete puzzlement.

"Are you sure?" she asked.

"Yep. Just friends."

As he walked out of the kitchen, he heard her mumble under her breath, "We'll see about that."

Fifteen minutes later, Lucy was on the phone to Madison. After the usual small talk, she cut to the chase. "So how was your date last night with my brother?"

Madison was silent for a moment and then replied, "It wasn't a date, Luce."

"Whatever. Did you have fun?"

"Yeah. The movie was pretty good," she replied, a hedge to her voice.

Lucy smiled. "That's what Luke said."

"You guys already talked about it?" Maddie asked.

"Yeah. He said he had a good time," Lucy paused then decided to dive right in. "He likes you, you know."

"What are you talking about?"

"Luke. He likes you."

"How do you know?" Madison asked.

"Because I can tell. He acts all nervous whenever I bring you up."

"Maybe that's because he feels like you are pushing me on him," Maddie replied.

"I don't think so. He doesn't act annoyed. He acts like he's trying to hide his feelings or something," Lucy confided. Then she added, "He thinks you don't like him, though."

"What? Why do you say that?"

"He as much as told me so. He said you're not interested in him. What's the deal? I thought you kind of had a crush on him all these years."

Madison cleared her throat and the tone of her voice changed. "Things are different now than in junior high, Luce. Your brother's a great guy and all, but he deserves someone better than me."

Lucy was stunned. What was she talking about? "Okay, so I don't know where you're getting that idea, but there's nothing wrong with you, Mad. You should give him a chance."

After a pause, Madison replied, "Just let it go, Lucy. And don't tell Luke you talked to me, okay?"

She hesitated and then answered, "If that's what you really want. But I think you're making a mistake."

"It's what I want, and trust me, it's not a mistake."

After they hung up, Lucy sat and stewed for a few minutes. Then she thought, *I didn't actually promise not to say anything to Luke.* Tossing her phone on the bed, she headed downstairs to find him.

After cornering her brother as he was about to go for a run, she said, "So I just talked to Madison. There's something that's eating at her. She thinks she's not good enough for you."

He gave her a serious look. "What are you doing, Lucy?"

"I'm just trying to help two people I love figure out that they are meant to be together. Is there something wrong with that?" she asked, feeling defensive and hurt by his tone. "Madison told me you deserve someone better than her. I thought you should know that." Spinning around, she left him alone on the porch before he could reply.

A moment later, their mother stepped out the front door. "What was that about?" she asked, tipping her head toward the door Lucy had just disappeared through.

Luke raked his fingers through his hair. "Nothing."

"Really? It didn't look like nothing." She reached out and put her hand on his shoulder. "Something's really bothering you. Want to talk about it?"

"Maybe later. I need some time to think," he replied, leaning over and giving her a kiss on the cheek. "I'll be back in a little while," he added as he descended the porch steps.

"Have a good run," Kelly called out to him, and he turned and waved.

As Luke ran, the rhythm of his steps calmed his mind, and he was able to think through his evening with Madison. She'd seemed like she was having a good time until he brought up seeing her. Then she'd frozen and made it clear she wasn't interested. Or was Lucy right? Was it something different that put the brakes on their dating? Maybe the timing just wasn't right. She was still in high school and had another year after this one before she'd graduate. Did she have her eye on someone else at school? Someone who could take her to football games, dances, and the prom?

Or maybe she was still hung up on that Miles guy. Although Luke hoped not. Especially since the guy had no spiritual roots at all. He was surprised Madison had even gone out with someone like that.

And what was the deal with her saying he deserved someone better than her? Probably just the 'let him down easy' line that lots of girls used so they wouldn't hurt a guy's feelings.

As he ran and tried to sort through all of it, he began to pray. *Jesus, I know You know exactly what's going on with Maddie. Wish I did, but I'm trusting You to help me figure out my part here. Do I back off, go with the 'just friends' scenario, or what? I just want to do whatever You want me to. You know how I feel about her. I guess I always have. But the last thing I want to do is give her any grief.*

Tap, tap, tap, tap. The sounds of his feet on the pavement were all he heard. And then a verse from Ecclesiastes popped into his mind. *He has made everything beautiful in His time.*

Timing.

He needed to talk to her one more time.

Luke stood at Maddie's front door and rehearsed one more time in his mind exactly what he wanted to say. Rubbing his sweaty palms on his jeans, he cleared his throat and rang the doorbell.

"Luke!" Michelle greeted him with a smile. "I didn't know you were coming over. Come on in." As he entered, she gave him a quick hug. "Is Maddie expecting you?" she asked.

"Uh, no. I just decided to drop by," he replied. "Is she here?"

"Yeah. Let me go get her. I heard the shower go off about fifteen minutes ago." Michelle disappeared upstairs, and he stood nervously waiting.

Finally, Madison appeared at the top of the stairs. Her hair was wet but brushed and she didn't have on any makeup. Luke liked her best without it. "Did I miss a call from you?" she asked as she came down to where he was standing.

"No. I thought I'd just come over and talk to you in person. I was hoping you'd be here."

"Oh. Okay, well, what's up?" she asked.

He glanced around the room. "Could we go outside? Like maybe on the porch or something?"

She nodded. "Sure." Opening the front door, she gestured for him to go first.

Luke fought the urge to take her hand and lead her to the steps. Instead he just walked over there himself and sat down. She followed suit and joined him on the top step, sitting a couple of feet away.

"Sorry about this," she said, lifting and then dropping her wet hair. "You caught me before I got my makeup on or anything."

"I think you look great," he replied with a smile.

She rolled her eyes. "Right."

"I mean it, Maddie. You always look good to me."

She sighed and looked away.

Luke shot up a quick prayer, and then, once again rubbing his hands over his jeans to wipe off the nervous sweat, he began. "So, I wanted to apologize for last night."

Madison looked puzzled. "Why?"

"You know, the thing in the car when we got back here. I didn't mean to put you in an awkward spot," he explained. "It's just so...so good to see you again. I guess I didn't realize how much I'd missed you. And I kind of let myself blurt out some things that...that obviously made you uneasy." He looked over but she was still gazing out over the front yard. "Maddie?"

She turned and looked at him, and he saw something he hadn't expected. Tears. Her eyes were filled with tears.

"Oh, man," he said. "I really messed up, didn't I?" He felt so helpless and lost.

Shaking her head, Madison brushed her cheeks with the backs of her hands. "You're not the one who messed up. I am," she said softly.

Luke didn't know what to say. Lucy's words rang in his ears. *She thinks she's not good enough for you.* He wanted to take her in his arms and hold her tight, to somehow let her know his true feelings, and that everything was going to be okay.

Then she said something that landed like a punch to his gut. "I'm not a virgin, Luke. Okay? I messed up big time with Miles." She looked away and started crying as the words came tumbling out. "I was a fool. I thought he loved me." She paused to catch her breath. "He made me feel so...attractive. Like he really thought I was beautiful or something."

As she turned and looked him in the eye, Luke could see such pain that his own heart was overwhelmed with aching. She was only seventeen. How could this happen? And what was he supposed to say now?

Madison didn't give him time to consider that. She stood up, brushed off the back of her jeans, and headed for the door. "You deserve a really special girl, Luke. It's not me." With that, she left him alone on the porch.

CHAPTER TWENTY-TWO

As Luke drove home, his emotions rocketed in several directions at once. His first response was devastation and sorrow, for Madison and for himself, as he finally admitted his love for her. Then anger raised its ugly head as he thought about Miles and how he'd taken advantage of Madison's vulnerability. *What a jerk!*

Instinctively, Luke wanted to go find the guy and make him pay for hurting Maddie and fracturing her future like that. Then thoughts of God rushed at him. Where *was* God when this happened? Why hadn't He somehow put the brakes on it? Surely He could have.

And finally, resignation. He knew a piece of his heart would always belong to Maddie. But things would never be the same now. She didn't want him anymore. And his feelings for her? He pounded his fist into the steering wheel, and then surrendered to tears himself.

He'd never once considered that Madison, two years younger than him, would be at risk for this type of fall. He tried to imagine them dating and maybe even courting. But something had shifted inside. Although he felt terribly sorry for her, he knew his pity was not what she would want or need. And he wasn't sure he could offer her anything more than friendship at this point. Somehow friendship seemed so hollow after what he'd felt for her last night and even this morning when he'd driven over to see her.

He changed his mind about going home, and drove down to the beach for a walk. As he skirted the water's edge, a cool wind picked up and the winter clouds darkened above him like the storm that brewed within. He tried to pray, but the words were lost before they were even spoken. Only moans made it out of his mouth, only to be swallowed by the sounds of the surf. Funny how now that he knew this, he realized even more how much he'd hoped for a future with Maddie.

Flashing back to the past, he remembered their closeness when they were both in middle school. A spark had begun that long ago. When he moved on to high school, she started to seem like a child to him in comparison with his peers. He could remember one day when he'd told her about a girl he liked in his class, and how her face had dropped momentarily before she perked up and said how happy she was for him.

Could he have said or done something before he went off to college that would have made a difference? If he'd said to her then what he tried to say last night, would she have been spared the pain her relationship with Miles brought into her life? And how would he handle the next couple of weeks before he left again? Should he avoid her completely? That shouldn't be too hard with all the family festivities of Christmas. Church would be the only time he'd probably run into her. And there'd be lots of other people around then anyway.

Church. He suddenly remembered the mission team. She'd signed up for that, too. How would it go to be on the trip together after all this?

Rain began to fall, and he made a dash for the car, heading home with all his questions still swirling in his mind.

270

His mother was baking bread in the kitchen when he got home. The fragrance drew him to her side, as she pulled a fresh loaf out of the oven. "This weather always gets me in the mood to bake," she said after glancing to see who was there.

"Looks good, Mom," Luke replied, trying to sound upbeat.

She turned and looked at him. "Are you okay?" He looked different—like he'd just lost his best friend.

"I don't know. I guess," he replied, sinking down into a chair at the table.

Something's up, Lord, Kelly prayed. *Please give me wisdom here.* "So Lucy said you went to see Maddie again," she began.

"Yeah."

Kelly hesitated. He wasn't volunteering any information. Should she just back off? It was always hard to know with Luke. Since he was their oldest, they had to figure out each new stage of parenting on him. Then it was easier with the other five kids. Luke was nineteen now and he'd been living on his own at college for several months. Was she supposed to treat him as an adult now? Or did he still need a mom sometimes?

"Want a slice of the bread?" she asked.

"Uh, sure. Thanks, Mom."

She smiled. *The way to a man's heart...*she thought to herself. Carefully running the serrated knife through the warm loaf, she cut off a thick piece and set it on a plate. Then she retrieved the butter from the fridge and placed both in front of him. "Want some milk, too?"

He nodded without looking at her. "Yeah. Sounds good."

After she placed his full glass on the table, she sat down across from him. "You look like you've got a lot on your mind," she said.

271

For the first time, he made eye contact with her. She saw such pain in his eyes, that she almost looked away. "What is it? What's going on?" she asked.

He sighed. "It's Madison."

"Is she okay?"

He shook his head. "Not really."

"What? What's wrong?" Kelly could feel her pulse quicken. Madison was like another daughter to her. Their friendship with Steve and Michelle during their early years in Sandy Cove had cemented the two families together in an inseparable bond.

"I don't think I should tell you, Mom," he said, his voice thick with emotion. "But I'm worried about her."

"You two have always had such a special connection," Kelly said. "I'm sure your friendship is a help to her now, whatever the situation is."

Luke shrugged. "I don't know about that."

As silence filled the room, Kelly debated about something that had been on her mind for a long time. Finally, she decided to speak up. "You know, Luke, I've felt for a long time like God's been telling me that you and Madison are meant to be together. I know that sounds pretty presumptuous, and I don't even really know what your feelings are for her. But deep in my heart, I feel certain God has a plan for your relationship, and I just can't shake it."

Luke leaned forward and buried his face in his hands. Then Kelly saw his shoulders begin to shake. Was he crying? She reached out and touched him gently. "Luke?"

He didn't look up. Shaking his head in warning, she pulled back. *I need to get Ben,* she thought. Rising to her feet, she walked out of the kitchen and caught her husband as he was walking in the front door. She'd promised him freshly baked bread for lunch, and he was taking a break in his sermon preparation to feast on it.

"It's starting to really come down out there," he said as he greeted her with a kiss. "I can smell that bread from here."

"Ben," she said, grabbing a hold of his arm. "Something's wrong with Madison."

He stopped in his tracks. "What's wrong?"

"I don't know, but Luke went to see her this morning, and now he's a mess. He's in the kitchen, and he won't tell me what's going on. Maybe he'll talk to you."

Ben nodded. "I'll see if I can get him to open up."

Walking into the kitchen, Ben saw his son slumped over the table, resting his head face down on his folded arms. "What's up, bud?" he asked as he put his hand on Luke's shoulder.

Luke lifted his head and gazed up at him, eyes red-rimmed but dry. "Hi, Dad."

"I see you've already gotten a start on Mom's bread," Ben said, pointing to the crumbs on the plate in front of his son.

"Yeah. It's probably still warm if you want some." He sat up and rested back in his chair.

Ben helped himself to a slice and heated up a cup of coffee before joining him at the table. "So how's your morning going?"

Luke laughed cryptically. "Not so great."

"Your mom said you went to see Maddie today," Ben probed gently.

"Yeah."

"So why the long face?"

"It's complicated, Dad."

"Life usually is. But sometimes talking about it helps," Ben suggested.

Luke nodded. "I could really use your advice. But this kind of involves Madison's reputation, too. And it's pretty personal stuff. Stuff she probably doesn't want anyone knowing."

"But she told you."

"Only because I kind of backed her into a corner."

Ben thought for a moment. "I don't want you to reveal anything she shared with you in confidence, son, but from what your sister's told me, I have a feeling this has something to do with that boy, Miles, that Maddie was seeing."

Before he could stop himself, the words tumbled out. "He took advantage of her, Dad. Now she is really down on herself. She thinks she's not worthy of a relationship with me."

"And what do *you* think?" Ben asked, praying for God to give his son wisdom.

"I think I could kill the guy," Luke confessed.

Ben sat back in his seat and nodded. "I can understand that." He hesitated as he prayed for the right words. Then he said, "You know, Luke, I *was* that guy."

Luke's expression changed from anger to shock. "What are you talking about? You're nothing like him."

Ben smiled. "Not anymore, thanks to God. But trust me when I say that I was just like Miles in high school."

"With Mom?" Luke asked, on the edge of his chair.

"No. Thankfully not with your mother. God got hold of me before I met her."

"Does she know? About your past, I mean?" Luke asked.

Nodding, Ben replied, "She does. She did before we started dating. We met through some friends who had been mentoring me in my faith. Your mom, well, for some reason, she took a liking to me. But she was so innocent and pure. I didn't want her to get mixed up with someone who'd been such a jerk."

"So what did you do?"

"I tried to convince her she deserved better than me."

"That's exactly what Madison said," Luke replied, shaking his head. "So how did you and Mom end up together?"

"She finally wore me down," Ben said with a smile.

Luke laughed. "She's pretty good at that. Like Lucy."

"Yeah. The apple doesn't fall far from the tree," Ben agreed with a grin as he thought about Lucy's tenacity when she set her mind to something. "It wasn't just your mom's persistence, though, Luke. My buddy, the one who set us up, challenged me on the idea that I wasn't good enough for her."

"How did he do that?"

"He took me to the cross and asked me if I'd like a ladder."

"A ladder?"

"Yeah, so I could climb up and tell Jesus face-to-face that His sacrifice wasn't good enough for me and my past."

"Whoa." Luke slumped into his chair and stared at him.

"He said that if I was going to live in the shadow of my past, I'd never experience the real power of God in my life." Ben looked into Luke's eyes. "Do you love her, Luke?"

"I do."

"Then maybe you're the one to take that sweet girl to the cross and offer her a ladder, too. But with Madison, I'd say the ladder isn't to challenge her to tell Jesus His sacrifice isn't enough. It's so she can get close enough to gaze into His eyes and see the depth of His love for her. A love that couldn't be satisfied by anything less than the cross."

Relief washed over Luke's face. "Wow, Dad. You should be a pastor," he teased.

Ben reached out and ruffled Luke's hair like he used to do when Luke was a young boy. "Sometimes you can be a real smart aleck," he said with a wink.

Luke tried to call Madison after his father went back to work, but she wasn't picking up. He texted and asked if he could please talk to her one more time, but she replied that she wasn't feeling very well and was going to take a nap.

By morning, the storm had passed and the sun actually peeked out for an hour or so. Luke did his morning run, and while he was running, he prayed for Madison. With Christmas only a week away, he wished he had something really special to give her. Something that might help her realize how much he cared. And how much God cared, too. Maybe some kind of jewelry? Like a cross necklace or something? That would be okay even if they were just going to be friends, right?

After taking a quick shower and getting dressed, he took off for the jewelry store beside the library. It was small, but surely it would have something that would be good.

His spirits soared as he embarked on his shopping venture. The gloom that had taken root in his heart after his talk with Madison was replaced by an excitement over the idea of finding the perfect gift. His love for Madison was different now. Not just a human love, but a filling of supernatural love from above. And he wanted more than anything for Madison to experience it.

It didn't matter whether or not they ever had a romantic relationship down the road. All that mattered now was for her to grasp the lavish love of God and to know in her heart that He'd never stopped loving her unconditionally.

The store was crowded with last minute Christmas shoppers, so Luke just worked his way around the displays. His eye landed on a glass-encased tray of silver charms. There were three crosses he liked. Then he spotted something else. A tiny ladder with a heart at the top. His heart leapt. He'd give her both on a silver necklace. Weaving through the customers, he found a girl about his age, who was wearing a name badge for the store. Crystal. He smiled at the appropriateness of her name in a shop that glittered with jewels.

Flashing a white-toothed smile, she asked, "Can I help you with something?"

Luke nodded and led her over to the charm case. "I'd like to look at the middle cross and the ladder."

She used her key to unlock the display and carefully lifted out the two charms, placing them on a velvet cushion she'd also taken from the case. "That ladder's pretty cute, isn't it?" she asked. "I think it's inspired by that country song, *A Ladder to Your Heart*. Have you heard it?"

He glanced up at her. "No. I don't listen to country much."

"Oh. Well, it's kind of a love song about a guy who says he'd climb the highest ladder to get to her heart."

"Nice," he replied, still amazed at the symbolism in the tiny charm. "So, I want both of these. But I'll need a chain to go with them."

She pulled a small fabric pouch out of a drawer under the case and slipped the two charms into it. "I'll show you the silver chains," she said, turning and leading him to the far wall. "For charms this small, I'd recommend something light and pretty short." She pointed to one of them, secured to the wall by a straight pin. It sparkled as she lifted the bottom of it and let it rest in her hand.

"I like it," Luke replied.

Crystal unfastened the necklace from the wall and carried it to the register with the charms. After ringing them up, she offered to gift-wrap his package.

"That would be great. Thanks," Luke agreed.

Soon he was in his car and heading for Madison's house. The sun was no longer out, but the overcast sky was white rather than dark. Maybe he and Maddie could take a walk or something.

Michelle answered the door. "You looking for Maddie?" she asked.

"Yeah. Is she here?"

"No. Sorry. She's at the beach. She said she wanted to get a run in between storms. Should I tell her you dropped by?"

Luke shook his head. "I think I'll go look for her down there." He had an idea where he might find her.

Sure enough, she was sitting on the old, worn-out picnic table where they used to have lunch when their families would go down there for the day. She was gazing out over the ocean, and he cleared his throat as he approached so as not to startle her.

"Luke? What are you doing down here?" she asked, scooting off the table and standing.

"Your mom told me you were here. I brought you something."

She looked hesitant.

"It's an early Christmas gift," he added.

"Luke..." She sighed. "I don't have anything for you." She held up her empty hands.

"Perfect. I didn't want to set this up as some big gift exchange between us. I just had something to say and something I want to give you." He took a seat on the table and patted the place beside him. "Come on. Sit down." He tried to give her his most casual smile, even though every fiber of his being was on high alert. He wanted this to go perfectly. For both of their sakes.

She sighed again, and then joined him, sitting down on the table next to him.

Luke placed the package on her lap. "Before you open this, let me explain."

"Okay."

278

"So, I wanted to get you a ladder." He glanced over and saw the confused look on her face.

"A ladder?"

"Yeah. But I wasn't sure how tall I needed it."

She studied his face, and he flashed her another smile, this time winking, too. Her cheeks blushed, and she playfully pushed him. "What are you getting at?" she asked.

"I wasn't sure how tall because I don't know how high the cross was."

Now her face fell, and she looked away. This was not going right. Luke knew he'd better get to the point. "Madison, I'm fumbling a little here. But there are two things you need to know. First, I love you."

She glanced at him and gave him a warning look.

"I'm not just talking about romantic love. I mean I really love you. You—my friend. And yes, I admit I may love you in another way, too. But that's beside the point. The point is that I can't stand to see you down on yourself. I know you think you've really blown it. But who on this earth hasn't?"

She shrugged.

"And that brings me to the second point. Whether you believe this or not, Jesus loves you, too. And that's the reason for the ladder. If there was any way I could help you climb up a ladder beside the cross and look into His eyes, I know you'd see a love you're not letting yourself receive. I'm not a pastor or a theologian, but I know this much— that cross is about a love that never ends."

She looked into his eyes, and he saw a glimmer of hope.

"Anyway, I want you to have this." He lifted the package and placed it in her hand. "Open it."

"Now?"

"Yeah. Now."

He noticed her hands shaking a little as she unwrapped the box and lifted the lid. She lifted the dainty necklace, and a sweet smile spread across her face. "A ladder. And a cross."

He nodded.

"It's beautiful," she whispered. Opening the clasp, she tried to fasten it behind her neck.

"Here. Let me help," he offered, carefully taking the two ends from her hands and linking them together. "There."

She fingered the charms for a moment and then turned and hugged him. "Thanks. I love it."

Luke smiled. "Good. So here's the deal. We'll stay just friends for a while. But I'm asking you to pray about our relationship this next semester while I'm gone. And I'll do the same. Then we'll talk more when I come back next summer. Okay?"

"But..."

"No buts. There's no harm in praying, right?"

"I guess," she replied, sounding skeptical.

"You're still going on the mission trip, right?"

"Yeah, I guess," she said again.

"So we'll pray until then and see what God has for each of us. Agreed?"

She took a deep breath and let it out again. Nodding, she replied, "Agreed."

This time it was Luke who reached out and hugged her.

EPILOGUE

Madison glanced across the room to find the source of the laughter. Luke was on the floor wrestling with a passel of boys from the preschool wing of the orphanage. As he feigned distress, they laughed uproariously and continued to pounce on him.

Finally, an assistant worker came to his rescue, peeling the boys away with a promise of lunch. As she led them out of the room to wash up and head over to the cafeteria, Luke stood up, brushed himself off and flashed Madison a smile. "I notice you didn't come to my rescue," he said.

"Who, me?" she asked innocently.

He strolled over and took a look at the box she was unpacking. Vacation Bible School materials, including props and games, awaited sorting and preparing for their use. "This will be fun," he said, pulling out a pack of brightly colored batons for the relays.

"Are you two coming?" a familiar voice asked from the doorway.

Luke looked over at his dad and nodded. "Come on. Let's go get some eats," he said to Madison.

After lunch, the children had a quiet time. The older ones read books, and the younger ones took siestas. It gave the team time to finish unpacking the supplies for VBS and go over their roles. Because of the summer heat, the events would be held in the evening after an early dinner. Beginning with songs of worship, they would then move into a Bible story told by Ben, followed by games, crafts, and special snacks.

The evening went well. No major glitches other than some initial problems with the sound system that were quickly corrected. The kids were so excited and seemed to have a great time. She noticed their willingness to help each other out at every station, even if it meant lending a hand to a friend on another team in the relays. They were tight— friends who had learned to stick together and be there for each other. Orphans who had made each other family.

Madison was impressed, and she could not believe how excited she was to be experiencing all of this firsthand. Here she was, in a foreign country, on a mission trip. Who would have thought, especially after all that had happened over the past year? And to be ministering beside Luke? That was even more unbelievable.

It will be really hard when he goes back to school, she realized. But all good things must come to an end.

"Time to take your group to snack," Lucy said, nudging her.

"Oh! Sorry. I got lost there for a minute," Madison replied, blushing. She rallied her troops and headed over to the snack station. From there, it was on to crafts and relays. Her team won the first prize, much to Lucy's chagrin.

As they were putting things away later that evening, Madison noticed Luke and Ben talking. Whatever it was about, they looked pretty serious.

"Guess that's it for tonight," Lucy said as she closed the final box of supplies. "Want to take a walk before we go inside?"

Madison thought for a moment. "Thanks, but I think I'll go take a shower and get ready for bed."

"Okay. See you in there," her friend replied, as she headed off to join a group of girls across the lawn.

Madison's mood shifted as she gathered up her things and went to take a shower. A sense of sadness and unexplainable loneliness filled her heart. The pit of unworthiness she'd been fighting to crawl out of all year seemed to swallow her once again.

"What's wrong with me?" she asked herself as she went through the motions of showering and getting into bed. Exhaustion, coupled with despair, took hold of her. *I need to pray,* she thought, but the words wouldn't come.

Ever since Christmas, she'd been praying, just as she and Luke had agreed to do. But from the time he'd returned home for summer, he'd treated her just like a friend, nothing more. Deep in her heart, she'd known that was the way it had to be. And she'd reminded herself of that after every prayer.

Luke was different. Really special. And God had a plan for him that likely included a very special girl as well. Someone who could come alongside him without any dark past. Someone who could be his "first" just as he could be hers.

Closing her eyes against unwanted tears, she silently begged God to take away the ache in her heart. *Help me stay focused on the kids, Lord, and remember why I'm here. And help me let go of Luke.* She fell asleep feeling completely spent.

The next five days, she tried to limit her contact with Luke. If he was playing with the kids outside, she'd go inside and offer to help prepare the next meal. When he worked on the retaining wall, she volunteered to paint the dining area. At VBS, they sometimes crossed paths in a relay or at the snack table, but she focused her attention squarely on her charges, trying to keep her eyes always on them.

"Are you mad at Luke?" Lucy asked on the second to the last day.

Madison flinched inwardly. Then feigning surprise asked, "Me?"

"Yeah. You. You seem different," Lucy observed.

Shaking her head in denial, Madison replied, "No. Everything's fine. I'm just trying to do whatever needs to be done around here before we leave to go home."

Lucy studied her. "Are you sure?"

"Positive." Madison took a deep breath. "Well, I guess I'll go start packing." Before Lucy could say anything else, she disappeared into the sleeping quarters.

That night, after all the activities were completed and the final VBS prizes were distributed, Luke approached Madison. "Can we talk?" he asked.

Madison knew what was coming. He'd try to let her down gently, so there were no questions to resolve when they got home. After all, he needed to head back to college in another ten days.

"I was thinking you might like to see that retaining wall we've been working on all week," he added with a smile.

"Sure." Steeling her heart against disappointment, she followed him across the grounds and behind the schoolhouse. Dusk was settling in, and a welcome breeze joined them.

"So what do you think?" he asked as he swept his arm across the expanse of air in front of the wall.

"It looks great," she replied, hoping her voice sounded enthusiastic.

"Here, give it a try," he suggested, taking a seat on it and patting the spot next to himself.

Madison felt torn. Should she sit down beside him, or would it be better to just stand her ground?

"What?" he asked, a puzzled look on his face. "Sit."

She forced a smile and complied.

They sat silently for a bit, then he asked, "So what did you think of everything this week?"

A flicker of joy alighted upon her. "I loved it. The kids are amazing. They're so appreciative of everything. The staff, too." She paused and then added, "It's made me realize how much we take for granted back home, and how fun it is to do something for others who have so little." She glanced over at him and saw a warm smile.

"That's exactly how I feel, too," he replied. "And it makes it easier for me to say what I've been waiting to tell you."

Here it comes, she thought, her stomach in her throat as she readied herself for the inevitable. He was silent for a moment, so she looked over and saw something she hadn't expected. Tears. His eyes were filled with tears.

"So, I've been praying," he began, "like we promised each other we would at Christmas."

"Me, too," she said softly.

"And the thing is…"

Before he could go on, Madison interrupted him. "You don't have to say it, Luke. I already know."

"You do?"

"Yeah. And I understand." She couldn't believe her own strength. But she pressed on, "You don't owe me anything. I'm just glad we could be friends."

Luke turned and looked her in the eye. "Whoa. Hold on. No one said anything about owing anyone something."

"I know. You know what I mean," she replied.

"Madison, would you please give me a chance to say what I need to say?" he countered.

She looked over and waited silently.

He gave her a smile, and his voice trembled a little as he said, "The thing is, Maddie, the more I prayed, the more I realized that my heart already has a home."

She froze.

"With you." He reached over and took her hand. "It always has."

Madison tried to swallow. Her heart about leapt out of her chest with its pounding. "What are you saying?" she managed.

"I'm saying I want the chance to move into the future with you. I don't know what that will look like down the road, and we both have a long way to go before we can even begin to talk about things like marriage. But I need to know if you feel the same way about me that I feel about you." His eyes pleaded for understanding and agreement.

Then the voice of darkness cut into her joy. *You are not good enough for him, Madison. He will figure that out soon. Better to let him go now.*

Suddenly she was in tears herself.

"Madison, what is it?" he asked. "Why are you crying?"

She shook her head, unable to speak.

He pulled her close and the dam broke, tears turning to uncontrollable sobs.

What a jerk I am, she thought. *This just proves he shouldn't be with me.* The words Luke had spoken were words she'd never allowed herself to imagine, even in her deepest dreams. The joy she should have been feeling was stolen by the realization that she'd have to turn him down. How else would he ever find a girl who deserved someone as sweet and pure as him?

Finally the tears subsided, and she pushed away from him, standing up to look him in the eye. "It would never work between us, Luke." She turned and started toward the orphanage, but he was instantly by her side.

"Wait," he said. "I need to know why."

Madison hesitated, groping for words. "I think you already do."

"Is this about Miles and you?"

She hadn't thought about her old boyfriend once the entire trip. Now his name brought a bitter taste to her mouth. "Yes, and about what you deserve, Luke. Someone who is better than me. Who hasn't been with someone else, like I have. Someone who can be your first, and you can be hers. Okay, so now I've said it."

He nodded. "I know you think that, Maddie. But you need to know how I see it. Sure, I'd love to have been your first. But what we could have someday—you and me—it would be different. Not like you and Miles. I promise. And because it would be different, it *would be* like a first for you, too."

She studied the earnest expression on his face. He really believed that. "But," she began.

"Madison, stop beating yourself up. The past is over. And you're not the only one who's made mistakes. I knew my feelings for you before I even went off to college in the first place. But I convinced myself you needed to be free to date guys in high school and do all the high school stuff like Friday night football games, the prom, all that stuff. Now I realize that I was wrong. If I would have told you how I felt before I left, maybe you wouldn't have had to go through all of that with Miles."

She didn't know what to say.

"The thing is, Madison, I can't imagine a life without you."

His words touched Madison's heart deeply. She realized how different Luke's love was from the self-centered love she'd received from Miles. Luke's heart overflowed with God's love—unselfish and unconditional.

"Come here," he said softly, opening his arms wide.

As they embraced, she rested her head against his chest, and she could hear his heart pounding just like hers. She looked up into his eyes, and he smiled. "I really want to kiss you," he admitted. "Would you mind?"

He was asking her permission! It touched her heart in ways that moved mountains within. Suddenly she felt special, really special, like maybe she and Luke *could* make it work. Reaching up, she put one hand on his cheek. "I don't mind," she said with a smile.

And when their lips met, she realized God was starting something brand new in her life. The past was over. Luke was her future.

In an apartment a world away, Madison's great grandmother was about to turn in for the night when her phone rang. It was one of her Silver Sisters. "Did I wake you up?" her friend asked.

"No, I'm just getting ready for bed," Joan replied.

"Well, I wanted to call you because I've been praying for that granddaughter of yours," she began, "and I suddenly got this feeling in my spirit that she's going to be just fine."

NOTE FROM THE AUTHOR

Dear Readers,

There are two important themes in *Behind Her Smile*. One is about the importance of every generation and the interactions and relationships between them. We live in a time and culture where family has become so fractured. Many young people are completely disconnected from their grandparents, not to mention their great grandparents, if they are still alive. Even within a nuclear family, siblings and parents rush off in separate directions much of the time, leaving a vacuum that can result in detriment to everyone.

While some cultures respect and even revere the elderly, western cultures tend to see them as necessary burdens to be managed rather than gifts to be treasured. Although productivity in a worldly sense usually declines after a certain age, godliness and wisdom often grow in place of it. With most families struggling to balance two-income households and keep up with a myriad of side activities for both the children and the adults, time with God is often compromised. Even among those who truly love Him and want to follow Him. Prayers are hurried and sometimes forgotten altogether.

Herein lies the hidden gift of age. For, although many elderly saints like Joan are limited in their physical abilities as their bodies break down, their spirits can shine even brighter as their access to the Throne Room becomes nearly unlimited by time demands. And so, a sense of purpose can actually grow in the spiritual realm for these who have persevered in their faith. Now they can intercede and move mountains on behalf of family and friends, increasing eternal rewards and productivity exponentially. For even a bedridden saint, this can become a season of great investment and reward.

I hope the Silver Sisters of the Sword have inspired you to see aging through a new light.

A second and profound theme pierces into the depths of hearts and minds. Regardless of surface appearances of confidence and self-assurance, secret doubts invade many of us on an occasional or even ongoing basis.

If you've ever heard these words of condemnation, — 'Not Good Enough'—playing in your mind, you are not alone. In the realm of good versus evil, the forces of darkness are masterful with lies. And because each lie is part truth with an added twist, we can easily be duped into believing this particular lie from the pit.

Madison wrestled it and desperately sought to find affirmation through a thinner body, a new style of clothing and makeup, and a wrong relationship with an attractive young man. In the end, it was emptiness, and she felt even more worthless than before.

At every age and every stage of life, a sensitive spirit is vulnerable to the label, "Not Good Enough." Godly wives and mothers like Michelle still find themselves wrestling with how they measure up in their multi-faceted roles. When people age and become grandparents and even great grandparents, their worldly accomplishments begin to wane as the younger generations assume the productive years of work and parenting. And so, the aging population can also feel "Not Good Enough" to be of measureable value.

The staggering truth is that none of us are 'good enough' to stand before a Holy God without the miraculous cleansing and transformation provided through the cross of Christ.

But another most amazing truth is that God valued and loved us before our first breath, and He will continue to do so until our very last. Then, those of us in Christ will find ourselves standing in His very presence, clothed in majesty and welcomed into a mansion He prepared just for us.

I hope *Behind Her Smile* communicated how pervasive the feelings of "Not Good Enough" live in the hearts and minds of even those who love and follow hard after Jesus. As new challenges arise, we often question our own ability or worthiness to undertake them with success. As much as Steve loved Madison and tried to make her feel like his princess, he still felt inadequate to the task of rescuing his daughter from her own self-abasement. And Michelle blamed herself when she realized how far Madison's journey to finding love had taken her down the enemy's rabbit hole.

Meanwhile, Joan struggled to overcome her own feelings of declining value and purpose as her memory faltered and her body broke down. If it weren't for the love of her family and the Silver Sisters of the Sword, she could have easily succumbed to the depression so common in elderly people in our culture, who no longer feel good enough.

It was clear from Rick's thoughts and inner feelings that he, too, was grappling with his new role as a husband and grandfather. He'd waited a long time for this, and he didn't want to blow it. When Madison showed up on their doorstep, both he and Sheila wondered how to handle the crisis in young Madison's life.

Amidst all of these self-doubts and inner questions of whether or not they were or could ever be "good enough," God was moving forward with His plan of redemption. Like a beautiful tapestry, He wove each person's backgrounds, strengths and weaknesses, and their love for each other and Him into a masterful picture of His provision and grace that is available to us all.

Looking back on my own life, I recall a time when I was going through one of my many seasons of questioning whether or not I was "good enough." I awoke in the middle of the night filled with thoughts of self-condemnation, replaying every mistake I'd made and all my failings as a wife, mother, daughter, and friend. As I sat praying and crying, God made His presence known. And the words He spoke to my spirit startled me. "When are you going to stop beating up My little girl?" He asked.

Whoa. I never thought of it that way. But that was exactly what I was doing.

When we come to Him in all our brokenness, He welcomes us into His family, and we become His children—children He loved from the beginning of time, who have finally recognized our need for Him. From that moment forth, we are completely His. While we may still stumble and fall, His unconditional love never wavers, and He never calls us "Not Good Enough." Never.

In His grace and mercy, He takes even our failings and shortcomings, and miraculously uses them for good. I'm sure you've witnessed that from time to time in your life. I know I have.

Although it breaks His heart when we sin, He is able and willing to cast away the darkness and heal and restore us, using those wrong choices to teach us important life lessons and to use them to someday minister to someone else in a similar struggle, just as Sheila was able to do with her granddaughter, and Madison will likely do herself someday down the road.

It always thrills me when I see how God is able to bring our background to bear on His messages of truth. For me, that involved my years of tampering with New Age beliefs and practices that became the first novel in this series, *Out of a Dream*, a book revealing the deception of that false religion. For Sheila's husband, Rick, God took the years he'd spent as an anthropology teacher to prepare him for a very special divine appointment with Madison, at a time when she was questioning what she'd learned about God and marriage. Although that was a fictional scene, the reality is that God stages miraculous encounters like this every day. We just need to be open to His prompting and be willing to share honestly from our hearts when He calls us to do so.

If you have ever wrestled with the label "Not Good Enough," know that I am right there with you. As a wife, mother, and grandmother, I get caught up in questioning myself and chastising myself on a regular basis. But God is teaching me some important lessons on this. And I believe He is preparing a Bible study for me to share with you—a study that helps us understand how *He* looks at us and why that is what really matters. Interested? Or know someone who might be? If yes, drop me an email, and I will be sure to add you to my notification list if/when that study is completed and ready to share.

If this is your first Sandy Cove book, and you enjoy traveling in time, you might want to go back to the beginning of the series and read the back-stories of these characters, who have become dear to so many. The stories flow seamlessly in chronological order from Book 1- Book 6. The first book, *Out of a Dream* is permanently free in eBook form and is also available as an audio book through Amazon or Audible.

For those of you who have journeyed through all the ups and downs of Michelle and her family, please join me in prayer about what God might have next for the series. Something is brewing in the back of my mind, but I'd love to get your input as well.

Thanks again for walking through these tough times with Madison. I hope her journey and the loved ones who traveled it with her have inspired you to see God's love from a new perspective and to begin questioning the whispers of "Not Good Enough" when they seek to invade your heart and mind.

In Christ,

Rosemary Hines

www.rosemaryhines.com

https://www.facebook.com/RosemaryHinesAuthorPage

www.rosemaryhines/amazon.com

P.S. If you enjoyed this story, please take a moment to post a review. Here is the Amazon link for its page ~
http://amazon.com/dp/B014JOW1RM

ACKNOWLEDGMENTS

Every time God enables me to complete the process of writing a book, I am reminded of the many people who have come alongside to help me. From the encouragement of readers and friends sharing the ways God has used the characters and themes of the novels in the Sandy Cove Series to guide, bless, or inspire them, to their pleas to keep writing, I have found the courage to tackle a brand new writing ministry here.

In addition, the Lord has blessed me with two wonderful, dedicated friends, who diligently and carefully read through each manuscript, giving me feedback on the stories themselves as well as the technical editing needed to purge the manuscripts of a multitude of typos and errors. These women, Nancy Tumbas (editor) and Bonnie Vander Plate (proofreader), bring needed refinement and polish to what ends up being a completed novel.

For doctrinal issues that arise in the story, I rely on the trusted counsel of our pastor and friend, Terry Walker. His biblical knowledge, love for people, and passion for God make him the perfect person to review and advise me on the spiritual content of the storylines.

A special part of the journey from manuscript to publication is the design and refinement of a cover. Benjamin Hines always comes through with just the right combination of setting and artistic layout to draw readers into the pages of the books. Once again, he created a beautiful, thought-provoking cover for this new installment in the series.

Finally, my expert formatter, Daniel Mawhinney at 40 Day Publishing, takes over and transforms each document into an ebook and a paperback.

Big thanks go to all of these contributors. Without them, I would be floundering!

But most of all, my heart swells with gratitude and love for my God, who pulled me out of a miry pit thirty years ago and set my feet on the solid rock of Christ. He is my everything. He is my life and breath and the inspiration behind each tale I craft. To Him be the glory, forever and ever, amen.

BOOKS BY ROSEMARY HINES

Sandy Cove Series Book 1

Out of a Dream

Sandy Cove Series Book 2

Through the Tears

Sandy Cove Series Book 3

Into Magnolia

Sandy Cove Series Book 4

Around the Bend

Sandy Cove Series Book 5

From the Heart

Sandy Cove Series Book 6

Behind Her Smile

Made in the USA
Lexington, KY
22 October 2016